Wendy Brandmark

The Stray American

Holland Park Press London

Published by Holland Park Press 2014

Copyright © Wendy Brandmark 2014

First Edition

A CIP catalogue record for this book is available from The British Library.

ISBN 978-1-907320-46-0

Cover designed by Reactive Graphics

Printed and bound by
CPI Group (UK) Ltd, Croydon CR0 4YY

www.hollandparkpress.co.uk

The Stray American beautifully captures the sense of rootlessness and search for identity. Set in 2003, Larry Greenberg escapes from his corporate law job in Boston to teach in a seedy American college near London's Waterloo Station.

He lives alone in Wimbledon, and his British lovers want him out of their beds before the morning. Then he meets Carla who lets him stay the night, but who has to face her own demons. His search for companionship takes him to the Un-Americans, a tiny group of disaffected expatriate Americans. Though repelled by these eccentrics, he stays for Devorah, a dancer whose radical politics he tries to ignore.

He has always been rootless, unwilling to commit himself to a job or woman or cause. If he grows up, must he shed his wings? Is he condemned to forever consider himself to be an outsider?

Follow Larry, a flawed but engaging character, on his journey in search of a soul mate and a sense of purpose.

For Peter and Rosa

*The people stared at us everywhere, and we stared at them.
We generally made them feel rather small, too, before we
got done with them, because we bore down on them with
America's greatness until we crushed them. And yet we took
kindly to the manners and customs and especially to the
fashions of the various people we visited.*

Mark Twain, *The Innocents Abroad,* 1869

*It was in the cab with Jim that impressions really crowded on
Strether, giving him the strangest sense of length of absence
from people among whom he had lived for years. Having them
thus come out to him was as if he had returned to find them;
and the droll promptitude of Jim's mental reaction threw his
own initiation far back into the past.*

Henry James, *The Ambassadors,* 1903

He was out on the street again at two in the morning, adrift in Camden Town. A carless American.

She said just up the road, turn left, turn and turn again and you come to the tube station where the taxis rove. But the streets twisted left into right till he forgot where he came in.

She'd fallen back on to the bed after her moment of grandeur and when she opened her eyes, he saw that she, like all the others, had been taken over. After all her cries and saliva on the pillow, after the scratches and bites, she propped up her head on a feather pillow and asked if he wanted a cup of tea or something before he went, because she had a hard day coming up and couldn't sleep well with a strange man in her bed.

For the first time he missed Talia, their one-bedroom apartment in Boston whose very walls seem to vibrate from her shouting. After years of sitting in semi-circles bad-mouthing men, Talia had wanted marriage.

'Don't sit on the pot if you're not gonna shit.'

'Well, I don't know,' he had said.

'When are you going to know? In this life?'

'You see, how can I tell how I'll feel twenty years from now? How can you tell? I mean to make such a commitment when you don't know is irresponsible.'

His mildness brought out her fury. 'You're just a wimp. You're a prevaricator.'

'Don't holler. Couldn't we just talk about this like grown-ups?'

'You just want your cake. You're like any man. You're not special.'

But she told him how like a bird he was, so light and quick on top of her. She, a big-boned woman with heavy brown hair, felt she was crushing him when she rode to her fierce end.

'I just want to be a fairy,' he once said. A little boy with gossamer wings drinking dew from the moving buttercups. I didn't ask to be a man. And yet he chose the large handsome women who shouted and stamped their feet when they could not bend him. Not that he was stubborn. He did not even fight back.

'You're not there for me,' Talia was fond of saying.

'You mean I'm just a figment of someone else's imagination? Talia, this has serious implications.'

'You know what I mean. Stop this lawyer bullshit.'

'You got the gift,' his father always said. How could she resist him, his black curls and sly smile, his firm thighs? She called him her Jewish princeling.

When he told her he was going to London she said, 'Now you're running away.'

'Who from?' he asked with what he hoped was gay abandon. She was wrong to think he was running from her.

'From your father. Who else?'

In the early evenings his father had come through the door clicking his fingers. 'Can't you hear him?' he wanted to ask his mother, but she seemed not to care about her dead husband. Even while he argued with Talia he heard him moving through the rooms, shaking his head at their words. One day when he was all alone eating tuna fish still in its can shape he felt his father's hand on his shoulder. 'Go from here,' he said.

Where was he anyway? Larry turned, walked back the way he had come, then turned again. If the streets were in argument with him, obfuscating then growing silent, there was no point in going back.

He walked, head lowered, half-talking to himself, letting the streets pull him along, and now he was descending past a playground into a warren of little paths, the dark buildings ringed with walkways rising around him. A great rush of air and an empty supermarket cart flew at him like a skeleton. A door slammed somewhere. If he followed one of these paths he would never be seen again.

He saw a figure in the distance, and began to walk towards him. He was a heavy-looking guy who moved slowly like he was in no hurry to help Larry. Then he seemed to recede. Larry walked faster, willing himself not to run. 'Tell me the way,' he whispered, 'just the way back.' The guy stopped or maybe he had never moved. Then he saw the man's face in the lamplight, the chubby smile, the curly hair red like it had been when Larry was a kid. He felt as if someone had doused him with electricity. He opened his mouth to cry, 'Dad. Dad, I'm over here.' But the guy turned down some path and all that was left of him were footsteps.

CHAPTER 2

The boy with the forelock was sleeping. Surly Joel. Larry raised his voice. He was talking about his beloved: the Bill of Rights. So what if Article III, 'no soldier shall be quartered in any house without the consent of the owner' was archaic, and Article II allowed people to kill each other with hand guns, just reading the words of the founding fathers, so wise, so prescient, sent shivers down his spine.

Joel's eyelashes fluttered. He opened his eyes, looked straight at Larry and then away. He sat with the other Americans in the back rows of Larry's classes. Their milk-fed faces grew languorous, even haggard during their year abroad, but their thick knees could still not fit under the narrow desks. They could not help their clumsiness, the frequency with which they knocked over books and chairs as they navigated their way through the classroom to the back row.

The others, the Nigerians, Egyptians, Koreans sat as close to Larry as possible, copying down every word which dropped from his lips. So assiduous were they that he imagined they copied his thoughts as well and knew, even before the words formed in his brain, just what he would say. At the end of class, when he handed out one of his photocopied lists of references or points to remember, they rushed to his desk, their hands reaching for the precious papers. The Americans at the back waited for him to walk through the rows of empty chairs.

'Another one. You work us hard, Larry.' Only the Americans called him by his first name; to the others he was Mr Greenberg, sometimes even 'Professor'.

The classroom was more like a stage than the courtroom and if no one appreciated his sly digs at the American legal system, at least he could perform unimpeded by judge or prosecutor, with no corporate executive asking him to 'get to the point, why don't you, I don't understand a darn word you're saying.' These kids did not understand his language either. The foreigners weren't even kids; some of them were older than he

14

was and married with babies. He taught to them – the United Nations. The jocks in the last row were like UN observers; neutral, uninvolved, they could go home.

'It was called "taking the Fifth" in the days of the McCarthy trials.' He looked down at wondering faces. 'Article five says "no person shall be compelled in any criminal case to be a witness against himself". So someone who was asked if he was a member of the Communist Party could justifiably say, "I won't answer on the grounds that it will incriminate me".'

The heads of the United Nations were now bent low over their papers: copying, copying. One of them even had shorthand. Or what looked like shorthand. It might be that Chin was writing in his native Korean. The boys at the back lounged, their chairs tilted, phones in their outstretched palms. In their midst, with his head sunk over a Goofy T-shirt, a boy dozed.

'You see. It was a catch-22. Like a legal bagel.'

He noticed Chin writing this down.

'There's no need to write that down,' Larry told him, 'I was just joking. You see. I was just extrapolating.'

But this too went down and Chin asked shyly how to spell 'extrapolating'.

At the back Joel slapped his forehead. 'I don't believe it.' The others laughed. Chin turned around and smiled as if acknowledging what a fool he was.

'Can you help him?' Larry looked to the back now. He knew they could not spell, could not even write a sentence of more than one clause.

They looked at him with the implacable strength of a group of like-minded dolts.

'C'mon Joel. Spell it for him.'

Joel tossed back his flap of golden brown hair. He was always fooling with this hair, which hid one eye and part of one cheek. He was smaller than the others with a narrow tense face. Larry could never get a laugh out of him.

'I'm dyslectic. Like I can't spell,' he said.

15

'He is,' one of the others said. Bob O'Brien, a big good-natured boy who always spoke for the group. 'Really. You should see his notes.'

Larry went back to the Fifth, but he had lost his way. Nobody in that class cared about the beauty of those rights. They were divining rods poking their way through corruption, prejudice and political expediency. In the forest of ifs and buts they would always show you the way. And they were so simple, a child could understand them, a child better than these sated boys at the back, their brains a sludge of beer, cornflakes and milk.

Larry had thought the Americans came to get laid on French beds in hotel rooms their parents would die if they saw. Then he overheard a conversation between two American girl students, so shiny and new, like hatching chicks, that he could not think of them as budding women. They were girls still.

'Like, I wanna grow this year. I wanna change. Like, I wanna come back different. Like you know not too different, but different. You know?'

The girl who listened to her nodded continuously. 'Like you don't want to be the same. But you'll be the same.'

Larry had never heard of the college before he saw the advertisement for an associate professor to teach law in London. Eureka Plains. He had imagined the college rising out of the shimmering land, but it lived in an industrial park outside Gary, Indiana.

Eureka offered students a term abroad, but made its real money from foreigners who were persuaded that three years in its London 'campus' would transform them with its 'bona-fide American degrees' into bona-fide Americans. A real American smiled from the cover of Eureka's brochure, a stocky blond young man neatly dressed, holding his business studies manual against the red, white and blue V-neck of his sweater. His face, as broad and bland as a prairie, bore a look of eager happiness. He seemed to speak to Larry: 'Why can't you be like me?'

He let the class leave early, made a show of looking at some papers on his desk, so they would not stop to ask questions.

16

Only when the class was empty did he raise his eyes, gather his papers, wearily, as if he were some ancient professor, not a boy-man acting the part of teacher. Nobody came to his office hour but he would sit there anyway with the metallic coffee he bought from the machine in the school cafeteria. He'd never bothered to buy an electric kettle, keep mugs and bottles of instant coffee in his office like his English colleagues, because wasn't he just passing through?

Always he had to find the cafeteria, taking one twisted corridor after another from the dim central hall of the ground floor. After all that musty yellowness, the room at the back seemed to shout at Larry with its white walls and floor, its picture windows on the river and red plastic sofas. Beneath rows of giant luminous globes, students gathered in nation states. Larry put a plastic lid on his coffee and was slurping the liquid that had squirted out the top, when Kalifa came up to him.

'You will join us? The boys are just over there.'

The only grown men Larry had ever heard describing themselves as 'boys' were his father's pinochle players. He looked over at the others. He was vague about where they had come from, though he had gone around the class at the beginning. There was something about Arabic countries he could not fathom, what it was that joined Egyptians, Jordanians and Algerians but also made them argue. The other two were so involved in some angry discussion in Arabic that they did not at first notice him. And then they stood up and each shook his hand as if it had been months not minutes since he had seen them.

He would have made up an excuse with almost anyone else. But Kalifa was his favorite, Kalifa, a prince among peasants. A slender, fine-boned man who looked like he had been carved, not born, he had a way of smiling which made Larry feel completely understood, even when he knew the class was baffled.

'It was good. A good class,' Kalifa said.

17

The other two smiled, but seemed too shy to speak. Omar must be at least forty, a balding man with smooth olive skin and a domed forehead who reminded Larry of his Uncle Saul. Omar never spoke in class but his presence was a reassurance, like a shoulder on which Larry could weep his disappointments.

Anwar looked like a playboy, a cross between Omar Sharif and Elvis Presley. He had the long-lashed eyes and full lips of a petulant child. When he did not understand in class, which was often, he giggled. And yet when he and Omar had been speaking their furious Arabic, he had not been so childish-looking.

'The Bill of Rights are very beautiful things. But are they real?' asked Kalifa.

'What do you mean? They're the backbone of American law. They are the law.' He sounded like some cranky Old Testament prophet.

Omar smiled at him, and Larry wished for a moment that he could rest his head against him.

'Such things are written, but...' Kalifa shrugged.

'No, they're real. Of course there are times when people are denied their rights. No system is perfect. But by and large they work.'

Kalifa seemed to wink at the others. Larry thought for a moment that he had brought him over to mock him, but no, not Kalifa, Kalifa was his friend in the class.

Omar said, 'We have trouble. Our understanding is not so good.'

Why did they watch him so, as if he were some performing animal? Larry drank his coffee in silence.

'This is my last year,' Kalifa said. 'I graduate in spring.'

'Good for you.'

'Well. And then I must go back.'

'You've got a job lined up there?'

Kalifa shook his head.

'You've got family there?' Larry tried to remember where Kalifa was from.

'Yes, but is not so simple. Just going back. Not just. Never just.' Kalifa looked at him, his eyes seem to plead. Omar put his

18

arm around Kalifa's shoulders. They were more like his uncles than his uncles.

Larry put the lid back on his coffee cup and stood up. The three men stood up and each shook his hand again. He was reminded of Saturday mornings in his grandparents' synagogue, the men patting each other's shawled shoulders, shaking hands as they exchanged places on the *bimah.*

He climbed the stairs to his office on the top floor. The tiny window which held a corner of the dying light had probably once framed the pale face of a sick man, one of the quarantined kept in the top-floor rooms. The college lived in what was once a Victorian hospital for infectious diseases, a six-storey red-brick building near Waterloo station with the words 'God is our cure' still engraved above the doorway. Eureka had broken down the long wards into classrooms, lowered the high ceilings and covered them with polystyrene tiles, painted the greenish walls a brilliant white and made the long straight corridors garish with rows of fluorescent lights but still Larry could smell the sulphur air.

Since when did he sulk, since when did he peer at this distorted face in the window? How they stared at him, the Arabs, like he was an attractive freak. Or were they trying to butter him up so he would ignore their fractured English? In the whole class there was maybe one who deserved an 'A' and there were many who would have failed if not for the school's policy – a hidden one. The Dean had said to him, 'We have a different system over here, you understand? We see their failure as our failure.' The school would die if students were judged on their merits, and the ghosts of tubercular patients possess it once again.

'Larry, Larry,' he heard his mother, 'don't aggravate yourself so. Give me a dimple. That's better. Now go home.'

'But my bed is always empty Mom, no one to share one night, one night even.'

An hour later when he left his office, the cleaners had switched off the fluorescent lights, leaving only the old yellow lamps. Stepping into the corridor, Larry thought he heard whispering under the sickly pools of light, nurses and doctors bent towards each other. He began to walk more quickly, but the squeaking of carts followed him, carrying covered bodies down to the morgue before morning. What the nights must have been like in those days: the crying, the shrieks, the tiny dark rooms like mouths. He began to run, first towards the back stairs, then turning and heading for the front. But the carts continued to roll behind him.

'I'm not a superstitious man. I'm rational, rational.'

But he was breathless when he reached the great doors of the school with their leaded windows and black wooden portals. He pulled at the huge brass fist, but the door would not open. He pulled and pulled, the darkness swirling around him. He began to pound on the door, but his fists made little impression on the thick wood. Then there was some movement in the shadows. Larry clutched at the brass fist again as if wrestling with it. He had stepped out of himself and could see in his place a cartoon character with sweat flying off his body. The shadow became a young black man with a mop, one of the cleaners, a Nigerian he had spoken to once before. He pressed a button on the latch which Larry had not noticed.

'Sorry. I didn't see.'

The Nigerian looked at him with a serious face. 'You think we will not let you out?' Then he laughed, laughed so loudly that the sound drove out the whispering and crying, rushed through the fetid corridors and with a great 'whoosh' pushed Larry into the colored night.

CHAPTER 3

Jessica lived at the other end of London from him, where the tube broke cover. She said she'd never met anyone from Wimbledon. He noticed that people looked at him funny when he said he lived there, as if it was not a place at all. He was sure that when he went into London for the day, the stage set was taken down and all that was left was a wide plain with a peculiar hill like a bunion.

It was the usual grey Saturday. The dry cleaner gave him his jackets, winked and asked, 'You still here?' He had forgotten to bring carrier bags; at the pushcart where a deaf old man sold fruit and vegetables, he had to pay five pence for them. The bakery had run out of brown bread, and he was forced to buy a white tin loaf. Always he had to tell them he wanted it sliced. On one of his first shopping trips, he had come home with a solid block he had had to saw with a steak knife. Like buying a whole cow.

With two carrier bags in each hand, one plastic-wrapped jacket over each arm, he had to walk like a model, slowly, arms raised, face uplifted so he could see who was coming. He looked with envy at the women who pushed plaid shopping carts down the supermarket aisles and up the steps of buses. Once he had picked a cart from a row in front of a hardware store, and was testing the wheels when the owner came out and gave him a funny look. For the first time since he was a teenager, he blushed. It was as if he had been trying on women's underwear.

Yet here in Wimbledon no one he cared about could see him. He could be as strange as the sallow gangly man who haunted the sidewalk near his flat. During the week, Larry passed him as he walked to the station, a man who spent his days pacing up and down one street, his gaunt face both worried and elated, depressed and filled with unbearable hope. He seemed to age during the year Larry had lived in Wimbledon, his curly brown hair receding, lines of torment deepening in his long face. It did not matter when Larry left the house, whether at eight in the morning or noon or in the early evening, when he turned the corner into the High Street, the man would be striding towards him purposefully. But never on weekends, on weekends the man rested somewhere. Though he showed no recognition and the smile on his face was clearly not for Larry, Larry missed him on his shopping Saturdays and the Sunday mornings when he walked down the desolate streets and escaped into London.

A year in England and he was still not used to living on his own: the Sunday afternoons spent wandering through the deserted squares of Bloomsbury, eating lunch in some hotel carvery where he'd pretend to be the only non-American. He could disappear here and no one would call the police for weeks, maybe never. His body would join the dust of the city, his unclaimed clothes auctioned off by the dry cleaner.

'Back home,' as the boys in his class were fond of saying, 'back home' he had gone from his parents' house to girlfriends' apartments, but in London he could find no one to live with. In interviews at shared flats and houses he had felt too glossy. You had to have a stale, weary look to live in one of these houses, your clothes in shades of washed-out black, your hair erupting from the top of your head. It took Larry a long time to realize that these denizens of Camden Town, Swiss Cottage, Clapham and Lewisham were not the sons and daughters of the poor and downtrodden. They grew up in houses, went to university, held down acceptable jobs in publishing and public relations.

He found no home with the girlfriends who took him to bed on the first night they met. 'Let me stay,' he felt like pleading with the women who wanted him out before morning. 'I won't cause much trouble. Just stroke me. Let me curl up by your radiator.'

In the year that he had lived in England, Larry had never had what they called 'a proper cuddle'. They told him how never before had they had so many orgasms: 'like a volcano. You're brilliant.' He was a tasty delicacy, piquant and tender after those rubbery Englishmen. And just foreign enough. 'You even have hair on your bum,' one of them said, as if he were some lower primate. But they did not love him.

He had hopes for Jessica. He had found her in the lonely hearts of a throw-away Jewish tabloid. 'A Jewish girl will never let you down,' his father murmured.

The last girlfriend had told him he had an unusual smell. What was it? His Jew odor? Jessica of the black locks and earnest smile did not sniff him.

He had thought it a good omen when she had not invited him to her flat after their first date. All through the evening he had watched her shiny lips, waiting for the moment of his end, but she had demurred.

When after three dates she did ask him home for dinner, he felt some movement in his heart, as if a small nervous animal inside him had been shaken from slumber.

There was something odd about her from the beginning of the evening, a smell like freshly killed chicken that he recognized from his life with Talia.

It wasn't until they were lying on the couch that she whispered 'Can't.' He drew back and looked at her. A terrible dread had begun to form.

'You mean—'

She nodded. He was back in his youth when girls talked of going all the way. Perhaps Jewish girls in England didn't.

'I thought maybe I could, but then...'

He gave her his winsome smile. 'You never know. You might change your mind.'

She shook her head. 'I've started.'

Then he understood that she was one of those rare creatures who didn't like to make love when they had their periods.

'Can't,' she repeated.

'Well, we can just have a hug.'

'I'm really sorry.' She sat up now. 'When it starts I don't like to have a man around me. Maybe because I was brought up Orthodox. I guess it feels wrong.'

So she was one of these women who descended into a bath once a month. He remembered the time he was walking with

23

his father past a group of men in black hats arguing outside a synagogue. 'Those are the Jewish Jews,' his father said.

'I mean I'm not, you know, *frum*.'

She stood with her clothes still in disarray as he got on his coat. Beneath her smile he saw relief at his leaving. Maybe it was his smell. His American stench. Pastrami, hot baseball mitts, the BO of a people who adored Ronald Reagan.

He had come by taxi from Golders Green tube, but if he returned the same way it would be as if he had never been. He began walking down the little streets, so quiet and dark he could be in some village. He listened hard; beyond the silence he heard a car backfire and the peculiar vibrating siren of the police which always reminded him of the approach of the Gestapo in war movies. The sounds were tiny crumbs he followed till he was back on Finchley Road.

He made a resolution as he waved his arms at a taxi and saw in the back seat a man alone. He would no longer have English women. They could come from anywhere but England. Not Wales or Scotland either.

He'd gone out with a Scotswoman who left him for some Ghanaian businessman. He did not know why he pursued her. She had thin red hair and freckles so numerous that he grew dizzy just looking at her. She spent her Saturdays demonstrating against what she called 'the American wars', and Sunday afternoons at party meetings, though what party this was he could never remember. She had been friendly, that was it. Never stopped talking. He'd had a pal for three months who was efficient in bed, who made no comments about his smell or hairiness. He thought her a bluff, good-natured Scot till she turned her candor on him.

'Americans are so naïve,' she said. 'They think evil comes dressed up in horns and a black hood.'

Larry just smiled at her. What his father told him to do whenever he couldn't think of the right answer in school: 'Just show your pearls.'

'You don't really believe in evil, do you?' she asked.

'I've never really thought that seriously about it.'

24

'Which perfectly illustrates my point. Americans think the devil could never be them.'

The front of the tube station was a still-life in which a man with a stick held out his hand while an old woman with a lean sunburned face sat at his feet, her legs akimbo. Then they came to life, the man asking in a hoarse voice for money to buy a cup of tea.

'Don't give.' He could hear his mother's shocked voice, for only suckers gave to beggars in America. But he had been broken the first time he saw a woman in a babushka sprawled in the Paris Metro, her baby clawing at her face. He had been broken open and could never stop giving again.

He gave the man with the stick the coins from his jacket pocket, almost as if he were a toll-keeper. Larry felt a tug, the old woman grabbing his leg.

'Got something for me?'

He dug deep into the back pocket of his jeans and emptied the contents into her palm. He was about to move on when he felt another tug at his leg. She returned a paper clip and the wrapper from a condom.

'God bless you luv,' she said.

It was the first endearment he heard that night, maybe in months, maybe in all the time he had been stranded on this island.

He was being childish. There must be a good-hearted woman here. He meant to disarm them with his guilelessness, his American blankness, but maybe they required courtship, the sort of campaign he engaged in as a teenager: approach and hesitate, approach and hesitate, until he was so far inside, they could not let go of him.

No, no. He would lump them all together, north and south. No one born surrounded by these murky waters. Let the hair grow on his palms before he touched the clammy skin of one of them again.

CHAPTER 4

He had been told that they were different once you entered their houses; within their castles, their armour dropped and you could really know them. But Larry had yet to enter a real house. The women he met lived in rented flats and communal houses, their rooms made for one season of their lives, like the booths the runaway Jews built in the desert. The other lecturers at Eureka were Americans or young Brits straight out of university, their homes way stations.

When James Carrington, the new director of Eureka's London campus, invited him to a dinner party he felt both alarmed and flattered. James had a flabby girlish face, long lank hair parted in the middle and an engaging giggle. He seemed a friendly guy for a banker, but Larry could not imagine sitting across a dinner table from him, nodding his head while James let go of himself.

Every few years Eureka had a new director, some British star from the real world of work who would grace them with a few hours of his time and whose name would feature in the brochure, while the Dean, an American who wore checked suits and filled his office with pipe smoke, ran the school. But James Carrington took the job seriously; he was seen strolling down the hallways, even on one occasion in a classroom shaking hands with students.

Larry discovered that he was not special. Gershom Fish, the other American in the law department, had already been to one of the director's dinner parties. All the academics were being invited in groups. Gershom knew this as he knew for certain almost everything that Larry did not. He had been in London for years. He wore T-shirts with his name, telephone number and the words 'Hire Lawyer, Will Sue' in great black capitals. 'It brings in work. You'd be surprised,' he told Larry. Gershom made his real money out of foreigners wanting Green Cards to the States; he called his teaching salary 'peanuts for pea brains'.

After their first meeting Larry tried to avoid Gershom, for he feared he might not be able to control his fingers which wanted to pull his shaggy dog hair, the long grey-brown frizz which reached his shoulders, and his uncut beard. He had never understood how someone could have 'oily eyes' till he met Gershom.

'Great food,' Gershom said. 'Really good grub they give you and a shitload of wine.'

Larry searched for Gershom's mouth in his hairy face, the thick shiny lips which sated themselves at James Carrington's dinner table.

'But boring. Like imagine being stuck in an elevator with the Queen. I was comatose by the end.'

More than anything this annoyed Larry, Gershom's insolent attitude to his adopted country, his total lack of awe for the royal family. Larry knew that should he ever be sequestered with the Queen, he could bring her out of herself.

The invitation had said 'Come at 7:30 for 8'. But what did that mean? That Larry was not to show up at eight sharp ready to tuck his napkin in his collar, that he should expect to meander to dinner? So why not just say 7:30? Or perhaps this was like attending a play. Seven thirty was when the doors opened; those desperadoes who came before would knock in vain. Despite what Gershom said, people were obviously so keen to get into these dinner parties that the hosts had to hold crowds of them back.

Larry put on one of his navy-blue lawyer suits, added a dash of himself with a dolphin tie. He calculated that it would take him an hour and a half to get from Wimbledon up to Highgate, and he still had to buy a bottle of wine.

In the off-licence, a small slender man with a turban watched in silence as Larry looked at the specials in baskets at the front. A Bulgarian red, a Portuguese rosé, a Chilean white. He was not a drinker. In his youth he had known only Mogan David sweet red wine, the drink of Seders and High Holy Days. Later he discovered Mateus Rosé for romancing his women;

27

something about the rounded squat shape of the bottle and the blush of the wine filled him with ardour.

He had learned to be careful. There was the time his Scottish girlfriend invited him to dinner. When he had reached Hendon where she lived he rushed into a shop to buy wine. An emaciated Hassidic Jew with wispy side curls and beard nodded to him from behind the counter. He kept on nodding, and Larry saw that his whole body was vibrating and a low singsong came from his lips. He had been so mesmerized by the man, even finding his own body beginning to undulate, that he picked out a bottle without noticing where it was from. His Scottish girlfriend handed back the Israeli wine and began talking about how he had colluded with the oppression of Palestinians.

He picked up the Portuguese rosé. Not Mateus but did it matter? Then he turned to the man: 'Is this good? I'm going to a dinner party.' He felt like a fool. What did this man in a turban know about wines and dinner parties? What did Larry know? He knew what it was to nosh at someone else's house, but a dinner party?

The man came forward. Larry thought his expression sardonic but maybe that was just his face, his narrow eyes and lined cheeks, his lean dark elegance. His voice was friendly enough, cordial even. 'Take the Bulgarian,' he said. 'It's very dry, very good. Just what's needed.' But would James Carrington, the banker, drink wine from some obscure and probably poor country? He imagined the whole population stomping on grapes. 'You think too much, Larry,' Talia used to say. 'Larry lamb chop. You think too much and none of it smart.'

Larry peered through iron bars. Once he had spoken his name to the lighted box and the gates opened, there was no time to think of where he could throw the bottle. For James Carrington lived in a mansion. Stairs led up to what looked like the front of a Greek temple, but once inside the columns he saw a massive brick façade with rows of latticed windows, yellow lit like teeth in a giant's mouth. They would wash their feet in his Bulgarian grape juice.

James came out on the steps dressed in a white suit. 'Welcome. You must be?'

'Larry Greenberg. I teach the law. I mean...'

'Of course. Larry. Please come in.'

But Larry was fiddling with the wrapping around the wine bottle. It had come to him in those minutes spent gazing at the fluted columns that he had forgotten to pull the price off.

'How naughty of you.' James prised the bottle from him.

As he followed him, Larry tried to remember if it had been £4.99 or £5.99. His impression of the hallway was darkness: dark wooden floors, dull oil paintings of men in swirling waters. Only his face was bright with shame.

'Everyone's in the library.' He felt a gentle push and he stepped into the glare. The others stood with their drinks before the flames unaware or unconcerned that they were reflected in the giant mirror above the giant fireplace, but he could not avoid his elongated face. Black and white rugs were scattered almost carelessly on the burnished parquet floor, and at the far end of the room where nobody stood were books, shelves and shelves of them. Somehow between the door and the library, James had managed to rid himself of the bottle of wine.

Larry was handed over to James's wife, Mandy, a tall rangy woman, one of these people who could speak with their teeth shut. Only her lips curled and uncurled over her large front teeth like a talking horse.

'Now.' She surveyed the room. 'Whom shall we introduce you to?'

Larry nodded to Charles Thomas, a small mossy man who taught English at Eureka. He stood with his even smaller wife at the fringes, trying to smile, but his small mole eyes looked frightened as if he had not known that he would emerge from the underground of his daily life into this terrible brilliance. Larry longed to stay with them; they could cling to each other all evening. But Mandy held his arm tightly, and he was confronted by two large people, a man and a woman with very

29

white faces, almost identical dark suits and large glasses. He never caught their names, only that they were big cheese at Penguin. They told him that Mandy was publicity director at some new publishing conglomerate, some recent merging.

'Mandy was lucky to survive the purges,' the female penguin said. She seemed to be addressing not Larry but some elusive person who moved about the room, but was never seen. Twice in their conversation Larry turned to see who she was talking to, but there was no one. He was about to say to them, 'Look, you don't have to stay with me,' when Mandy was upon him again, her arm around a young woman. The penguins moved off discreetly.

'Carla's our designer.'

Carla grasped his hand and held on beyond the shake as if she were drowning. 'It's all right,' he wanted to say, 'just a bad dream.'

Her face was all bone and stretched skin. She had the bright staring eyes of a consumptive, the haircut of an ex-skinhead. She was taller than him but so slouched she was on his level.

'So what do you design?' he asked.

'It's so hot in here,' she said. 'So hot.' She was not wearing much for October: a sleeveless black silky blouse with a neck cut low enough to show her protruding collarbone, and see-through shiny black pants. He thought he saw goose bumps on her arms, but said nothing.

She put her hands to her cheeks. 'Am I very red?'

'Not as red as me when I came in here.'

'You're still red.'

He thought maybe this was the moment to escape her but she had grasped his hand again.

'Why don't you take off your jacket?'

'I'm not hot. Okay? I was just embarrassed.'

He began to explain about the Bulgarian wine, stopped when it seemed she was not following him. But she said, 'So what if it's Bulgarian?'

He tried to explain how if he had known he wouldn't have bought any wine, how he had been unable to rip off the price in those dark moments in the hallway.

'You mean you brought plonk?'

'The guy told me it was good, but then that's not the point. This isn't some street party, is it? I mean, who brings wine?'

'Don't you think this place is tacky?' she said suddenly.

'I wouldn't say that exactly.' He looked around the room and noticed for the first time two small exquisite chandeliers. 'Tacky is not the word.'

She ignored this. 'Mock Tudor fireplace, mock Mondrian rug, mock Doric columns. Unreal.'

'You think maybe the books are fakes too? You open them up and find chocolates.'

She stared at Larry as if noticing him for the first time. This was always happening in this country. He would have to meet someone twice, even three times before they acknowledged his existence. Sometimes they never did, and he felt like jumping up and down and waving his arms before them.

'You don't even find chocolates,' she said slowly. 'No. Just empty wrappers.'

They were being ordered into the dining room. Larry took Carla's arm as they moved in a slow procession of couples through the doorway into a long room with French windows along the side, a table quivering with silverware and glasses, all of it reflected in a large gilt mirror. Carla went first, was shown to her seat at the far end of the table by James. Larry tried to follow but felt a tap on his arm. Mandy's hard face was smiling at him. Still he tried to go forward, for wasn't Carla his date for the evening? Even if she was peculiar, he needed to sit with her. But Mandy placed a friendly but surprisingly firm hand on his arm and one of the penguins took the seat by Carla. Carla looked at Larry like some star-crossed lover, and he, held back by a talking horse, could do nothing but return her look with a beseeching smile.

Larry finally understood that James was placing them all in some preconceived order: married couples neatly divided, men and women alternated. Everyone had waited to be seated; everyone knew to wait except Larry. Now he stood back while the table filled, James and Mandy gesturing and pulling out chairs like seasoned waiters. He, like some lone diner, some vagrant, was finally slung between a curly-haired portly man and his equally hefty wife.

'Hello. Clive Berman here.' He shook Larry's hand. 'I work with James. And this is my wife Julia.'

'Have you been before?' Julia asked. 'He gives a nice dinner.'

Larry turned from side to side addressing one then the other, his head nodding as if he were some mechanical dolly. There was something familiar about Julia, something about her tone of voice, her large bosom like a shelf, the sympathy in her face for him a single man living all alone, the critical eye she cast on the food brought out by a young woman who looked like she came from some South Sea island. That something made Larry want to recline, though this he could not do on the stiff-backed chair.

Clive asked about Eureka, factual questions about degrees, numbers of students, differences between American and British universities.

'It's not a real university,' Larry said. He had picked up Carla's word. He couldn't stop now, she had infected him so.

'How's that?'

'I mean it has no academic standing to speak of. It's just an imitation of what a real American college would be like.'

Clive looked at his face, then down at his suit, then back again with a nod of recognition. When he smiled, Larry thought he might place a fatherly hand on his head. Even now Julia stared into his face, as if she were poised to feel his forehead for fever or at least say how cute he was.

There was some concoction on his plate of shrimp and avocado. The others had begun, but Larry was not sure which of the four forks to use. Clive had chosen the tiny fork on the outside and was picking shrimp out of the green glob, carefully putting them down on his bread plate.

Julia said, 'I don't bother.' She pointed to Clive's fork work. 'I think that whatever the shrimp touches isn't kosher either. But Clive loves avocado pears.'

'I'm not that strict,' Clive said.

'Me neither. I mean not at all.' Larry loved shrimp but he felt nauseous at the sight of the pink and green glob. Still he dug his fork in. They said nothing while he ate, but Julia gave him a sad, questioning look as if to say, 'Is it so good you should spit on your ancestors?'

James was pouring white wine into one of the wine glasses in front of Larry. At least he did not have to say which color would go where. The appetizer plates were removed and there was a gap before the next course.

'Do you know Nigel and Deborah?' Clive asked him. He nodded to a man and woman sitting across the table. Between them Charles Thomas, who had done nothing but feed his mole face and was even now reaching for a bread roll, shrunk back into his seat.

'Larry teaches law,' Clive called across to Nigel, a pale, pimply man with thick glasses. His wife Deborah, large and bloodless, looked bored as introductions were made and went back to her conversation with one of the penguins.

'I'm afraid we're both stockbrokers,' Nigel said, shaking his head with mock grimness at Larry. 'You work the coal face, we're—' He waved one long white hand at his wife whose broad back was half turned. 'We don't do anything important. Parasites really.'

James at the head of the table heard this with a grin. 'Nigel, I've never heard you sound quite so self-effacing.'

Deborah was having a heated discussion with one of the penguins about hanging baskets. 'They moved in,' she said, 'and immediately there were baskets of geraniums everywhere. I loathe them.'

For some reason Larry could not let this go. He remembered the geraniums that bloomed every year in clay pots along the windowsill in his favorite café near Harvard Square. He had met Talia in that basement room fragrant with espresso and

33

incense, the waiters sashaying around them. 'How do they live with so little light?' she had asked, pointing to the blood red of those hardy flowers. He imagined Deborah stockbroker cutting off their heads, Madame Defarge with pruners. He could have cried for his loss.

'What've you got against geraniums?' he asked. The table grew quiet. Deborah stared at him as if to say, 'Who is this worm with a mouth?'

Then Nigel said, 'She just has this phobia about hanging baskets.' People around them laughed, but Larry could see disappointment in their faces. Something had almost happened.

Larry leaned forward and for a moment caught Carla's eye. He felt like a solitary prisoner whose door had suddenly been left open. Then she was hidden again when one of the penguins reached over to grab a bread roll.

The South Sea waitress brought plates of duck, and red wine was poured. The talk was of what to read on holidays. Nigel clasped his hands. 'Trollope. I always take my Trollope.'

Julia served Larry some potatoes. 'Do you miss your parents?' she asked. He longed to rest his head on her shelf. 'It must be hard at holiday time.'

'There's only my mother.' Larry hadn't meant to sound forlorn. He remembered his grandmother hugging him on the day of his father's funeral and wailing, 'Now you're an orphan.' His mother stood by looking confused. Maybe he was a foster child, his mother just some woman put in charge of him.

'Oh. You mean she's alone too?'

Clive shook his head at her and gave Larry another of his kind and wise smiles. 'It's the experience of being in a foreign land and meeting new people that counts, isn't it? While you're young.'

'You see, I'm taking a break from law. I got jaded.'

Clive nodded and Julia squeezed his arm. But could they understand what it was like not to have fun?

Across the table, Nigel said, 'We don't even realize we're jaded, do we Clive?'

Clive said, 'I don't feel jaded yet.'

34

'He's so involved in his work,' Julia confided to Larry, 'he has no time to be bored.'

'That's wonderful,' said Larry. He leaned forward to catch another glimpse of Carla but saw Nigel's gummy face and his own flushed one paired in the mirror.

'Lost something?' The jaded Nigel grinned at him, his lips gleaming from duck.

The table had gone quiet again. Everyone was involved with the duck. Fork and knife, fork and knife. Larry hated the way these English ate, the economy of their movements, their elbows raised, their hands lightly but expertly manoeuvring. Not for them the slow swing of the fork from left to right hand, the ungainly American habit like a Southern drawl. They were like surgeons.

The duck was no youngster. As Larry sawed through some stringy meat, he wondered if he dared pick up the leg and eat from it.

'Are you struggling?' Julia gave his elbow a squeeze.

Tears came to his eyes. He wanted to ask, 'Can I come home with you?'

He had forgotten which was the last glass of wine poured and was drinking from all three. He felt himself shrink as the wine went down, till he was a little boy begging favors at the big people's table. When the chocolate mousse arrived he looked at Julia, and she nodded as if to say, 'even though you haven't cleaned your plate, you can have this treat.'

Nigel loomed like a cartoon character. 'So what do you think of this country anyway? We're terrible, aren't we?' Larry was choking on the thick chocolate and could only stare back at him. 'We like our little ways.' Nigel looked down on him, for he was shrinking again; with every sip of wine he lost two inches.

James announced coffee in the library. There was a slow rising. Larry felt damp at the seat of his pants and for a moment thought he could smell urine, but it was only the dark taste of wine. The drinking, the sitting in a hot room, had made his pants cling to his ass. He held the sides of chairs as he followed the others. Clive and Julia waited for him. Julia took his arm and

35

walked him into the library, then excused herself: 'I'm going to spend a penny.' Clive was taken up by James, and Larry was left clinging to the back of an armchair wondering what Julia meant. Could there be slot machines somewhere in the house? Then he understood that she was powdering her nose, going to see a man about a dog, but the thought persisted: did James really charge people to use his bathroom?

The South Seas maid appeared before him with a tray of demitasses. He shook his head and the walls of books began to move in a steady orbit around him. He tried to focus on the fire which had been fed and stoked in their absence, but his own face flared. He had to look away and once again the hollow books circled around him, slowly, their covers open like wings. He shut his eyes and tried to remember his Bar Mitzvah portion, something about the decoration of temples in the desert. When he opened his eyes, the books had flown back to their shelves, the room was still and Carla stood before him: 'Let's get out of here,' she whispered.

'Where?'

'Just anywhere.'

'Can't walk.' He wondered at her pale calm face, the cool hand she placed on his. Only in her eyes could he see some of his own frenzy.

'I can,' she said. 'I stuck to the mineral water.'

She tucked her hand in his arm and drew him first to James who was still talking to Clive. They were leaving too early, he could tell by the hurt look which James quickly covered with a wink and a giggle. Julia had come back. She looked at Clara and Larry, then gave him a searching worried look. 'I would go home with you,' he wanted to say, 'but it's just not possible.'

'You take care of yourself, Larry,' she said. Then squeezing his arm, she added, 'And remember about Shabbat. If you're ever in Finchley.'

Clive shook his hand. 'Make the most of it.'

Not even his own parents had understood him so well.

Mandy came with their coats. She gave Larry and Carla a look which said their pairing-up was too obvious. Larry stumbled along the hallway where he had given up the wine of affliction, so dark after the brilliance of the library, the touch of Carla's icy fingers like the hand of death in a fun house. Under the porch light Mandy gave Carla a quick hug accompanied by mock kissing noises. Then she extended a limp hand to Larry before shutting the door on the two of them.

Thrust into the cold, he felt like a grizzled tramp. Carla was walking him to her car. 'I couldn't breathe in there,' she said. 'It was foul.'

He was suddenly aware of how late it was, how far he was from Wimbledon, how far from his self. He could not ask her to drive him all the way.

'I know,' she said. 'We'll go to the heath.'

'But I gotta get home. I don't live around here. I don't live anyway near here.'

Her face seemed implacable. 'It's just what we need.'

'But I have to go all the way to Wimbledon.'

'Stop bleating.'

'Who's bleating? I just missed the last train.'

'We'll clear our heads of all that poison.' She had a way of staring as if she had just had a visitation.

'But look...'

'Then I'll drive you home.'

Carla pulled him through bushes, and then she was running across a field into woods.

'Wait,' he called out in the gloom. 'Wait for me.'

There were movements in the shadows as if they had disturbed some wild animals, but the shapes which stirred and even walked between the trees were men. Larry grabbed her hand and pulled back. 'Don't you see them?'

'They're just gays cavorting.'

She led him to a small pond. They sat at the edge on damp grass. He reached inside her coat. Like embracing a skeleton. He felt ribs, hipbone, softness in places as if she allowed herself to lapse in moments.

'You feel wonderful,' he whispered and blushed at his lie.

She was like one of those abstract metal sculptures: 'Untitled in chrome and wire'. She snuggled up to him like some scraggy bird and he felt pity. 'How d'you get like this?' he wanted to ask. And such a beautiful face. He continued to explore, finding pockets of flesh, places she might be called a woman.

'Should we do it in my flat?' she whispered. 'I'm just afraid of getting grass up my bum.'

Why are you always so matter-of-fact, you people? What's wrong with euphemism, lies even? But he was shivering in the light rain and wanted only shelter.

'Okay, we'll go then.' He calculated he had maybe three hours of warmth before he was kicked out on the street again. His resolution had come to nothing. Once again he was hooked only to be thrown back. The wrong fish, or maybe, in the light of their bedrooms, not a fish at all. He sighed just thinking of the chill darkness, of the winding streets.

She lived in what looked like a warehouse off Chancery Lane, a noisy walk up metal stairs to the fourth floor, then a heavy metal door slamming behind them like a prison. She switched on a series of spotlights and he saw a large white room, bare floorboards, a kitchen nook but nothing cosy about it. He took off his jacket and looked for a place to hang it, but saw only a futon bed and a drafting table, a swivel chair hung with clothes, one long twisted black metal floor lamp.

'So when did you move in?' He stood shielding his eyes from the spotlight, his coat over his arm.

'Oh about. Let's see. Maybe two years ago. You wouldn't believe what it was like.'

He noticed the walls were not as bare as he had first thought. High up were small black and white photos of vegetables, at least he thought that's what they were.

'You got some place I could...' He held out his jacket.

She was busy shedding clothes. 'Just throw it. Anywhere. I don't have hooks or wardrobes.'

When he turned around, she was in bed already, the covers drawn up to her neck.

'Can I switch off the lights?'

'Oh,' she said, as if she had just noticed the glare.

'See I feel like I'm being filmed.'

But with the lights out the room was still not dark, a street lamp flooded the bed with yellow light. He realized what was bothering him. Nothing on the three long windows, not even those cheap hotel shades which never go back up again once you've yanked them down.

'Don't you feel exposed without curtains? Everyone can see everything.' He sounded like his mother.

She had shut her eyes. 'Who's everyone?'

'You know. Neighbors. Weirdoes. People you don't want to know your business.'

'I love the streetlight. It's like a friend.'

There was at least one advantage to being thrown out of here. He would not have to sleep like a hobo with the streetlight full on his face in a room that looked and smelt of nothing.

She was silent, passive, almost dead under him. Like one of these people who had their vitals removed but still functioned. 'Are you all right?'

'It's wonderful. I'm pretending you're a total stranger.'

He waited in the minutes after they finished for her to yawn at him, rub her eyes as if he were an unwelcome mirage and ask if he would put the kettle on. This was the sign like the quickening music at the end of a cowboy film that he should get on his horse already and ride into the dawn. But Carla fell asleep, not even an exploratory tap stirred her.

He slept only to wake with a curious fear around his heart as if someone had been yelling at him. The black twisted lamp raised its head like a cobra. 'You, you, you,' the voice hollered. 'What are you doing here?'

He was having his office hour. In the first year he had waited in his room with the door open every day, for how could the required three measly hours a week give them what they so desperately needed, these castaways? But only the Americans came to talk up their grades. They lounged in his office in their baseball caps. He imagined they thought he was a good guy until Kenny came along, stocky Kenny of the toothbrush hair, frank blue eyes and run-on sentences.

'Larry, I know I could make a B if you just gave me one more chance. I mean, I know I could do it. You know I could do it. Like, I've just had so much going on but if you just, like, let me retake that last test.'

Larry shook his head. 'Kenny, how many more chances?'

'I promise, this time really.' He looked Larry straight in the eyes, so how could he lie to him?

'But Kenny I don't even know if with another chance your work would improve.'

The boy's eyes, those wide pools of blue emptiness, seem to fill. 'Are you saying I'm stupid?'

Larry did not know how to answer him. He was used to the twists and turns of the courtroom where no one asked a question merely to hear the truth.

Kenny had gone straight to the Dean, who told Larry that students were more tender than he thought. It was also true that Kenny had a father, and that father was the owner of a national chain-link company which gave regularly and generously to Eureka.

'What's that supposed to mean?'

'Larry.' The Dean shook his head with what looked like a smile. Larry finally understood what was meant by 'mirth playing around the lips'. 'He just wants another chance.'

'But he's had another chance. Several times. Why is he a special case?'

'Larry, don't you think you're being hard on him? This isn't Harvard, you know.' The Dean had always been forty-five. His white flabby face and sparse yellow hair dyed the color of his checked suits made him look like a clown, but his real face protruded from the jowls like the head of an iguana, watchful and cold-eyed.

Larry opened his mouth. The Dean reached for his pipe and began to pack tobacco hard into the bowl. After he lit it, he looked up at Larry, the smile gone from his face. His expression seemed to say, 'What are you doing here, you?' Larry heard his father speak through the pipe smoke: 'Not everyone is like you, Larry. You are a boy not of this world.'

Now he offered the Americans one hour on Monday, Wednesday and Thursday afternoons. He kept the door shut. Only the small sign with his schedule let them know that he might be inside putting comments on the margins of their papers, tilting his chair to see his corner of the Thames. The others approached him after class, though he told them over and over again about his office hour.

'But that is your time. That is for you,' Omar said.

'No. It's for you.'

Omar smiled. 'You work hard, Professor Greenberg, much too hard.'

'Really. It's what I'm here for.' But he had not convinced more than a handful of the United Nations to creep up the stairs to his sulphurous corner room.

Now few came by. The Americans decided he was no soft touch. But since his talk with the Dean he could be persuaded to do anything, couldn't he? How could high ideals matter, once you had fallen?

Someone knocked, then turned the handle without even waiting for his voice. Hair in the doorway and the lips of Gershom Fish.

'So you're really here?'

'Not really.' A hint Gershom would never understand.

'You are conscientious, Larry. I don't bother. I mean, if they need to speak to me, let them make an appointment. I'm not

41

hanging around so some half-wit from Idaho can try talking me into a better grade. They bug you when they know you're around for them. Like you're their mother.'

'Maybe we are.'

'Maybe you are.'

Silence with Gershom grinning from his nest of hair. Larry shifted one pile of papers from left to right and then sat up suddenly because large gossamer wings were growing from his spine.

'Larry. This isn't what I came all the way up here for. Why'd they put you up here anyway? I'm on the main floor. This is weird. Like the undead live up here.'

The wings were still wet but Larry could test them by flying around the low ceiling to the amazement and envy of Gershom: 'No shit, Larry. You really are something else.'

'I've been wanting to tell you about our group. I think you might be interested. A bunch of us got together. Americans who have lived here, oh, for years, some of us. Sometimes we meet up to go to a demo to show that not every American supports George W's adventures in Iraq. Or just to be social. We feel like we miss home, but not enough to go back. You know what I mean? We kvetch about the English.'

'I do that enough as it is.'

'But this is different. We call ourselves "The Un-Americans". We've even got a mention in *Time Out*.'

What do you need me for? Larry thought. Leave me out of this. 'So you've got lots of lost souls.'

'Not lost. Just homesick. You know what it's like. You remember.'

'Do I?'

Gershom ignored this. 'We're pretty big now that *Time Out* noticed. I thought you might want to come along. We've got lots of women, but not enough men.'

Larry shook down his wings so they formed a neat fold at his back. He had Carla. An actual date with an Englishwoman.

'Just come along if you can. We meet about once a month. Actually we're going this Saturday to the anti-war demo.'

'I'm busy.' This sounded curt. After all Gershom didn't need to invite him, did he? He'd come all the way up here just to stick his hairy face in the door. 'I mean, thanks, but I don't think—'

'Well, whatever.' Was there just a trace of something like annoyance on his hairy countenance? 'You never know when you might need the comradeship.'

Gershom left the door open. The wind which lived on this top floor banged it back and forth, but Larry did not move. He felt good. Being able to say no, to treat Gershom like some supplicant, had boosted him. He stood up, stretched, shook his head from side to side. He flew high above these sour Americans on the march.

'Do I disturb?' Kalifa appeared at the door, had slipped in smooth as his silken words. Had he seen Larry grinning and nodding to himself? 'I can come back.'

Had there been a knock? Or had Kalifa lurked in the hallway listening and watching?

Larry shook his head, pointed to the chair. Nobody ever seemed to sit there. They preferred to stand over him.

But Kalifa sat down, his back straight, his hands on the arms of the chair like some Egyptian statue.

'So what can I do for you?'

At this Kalifa grew shy, almost looked as if he might stand up and leave. 'You're sure I do not disturb?'

'Kalifa. This is my office hour, I told you. This is for you.'

'Thank you.'

'Is it something to do with the homework?'

'No, you explained that real well. You see, I am wondering if you can help me in another way. I graduate this year. My visa is finished. I want to get a job here, but—' He shrugged and looked at Larry with tragic eyes. 'They say always no.'

Larry tried to remember where Kalifa came from. Pictures from Arabia floated through his mind: elongated people in white robes wandering in the desert, Abraham with his knife above his son, the one humped camel he'd seen at the Franklin Park Zoo.

43

'Won't they renew it if you tell them you want to work? I mean, you'll have an American degree.' This was pathetic. He deserved the look Kalifa gave him almost of scorn.

'It is very hard to work here. You know they say "we have not enough jobs for our own".'

'And you don't want to go back home just yet?'

Kalifa leaned forward. He spoke in a passionate whisper. 'I would want to go to America. But they make the Green Card very hard. Especially now after the Towers come down. Some do, but they have help. I thought, you are a lawyer. I could pay.'

Larry shook his head. 'I'm not that kind of lawyer, Kalifa. For that you need someone who specializes in immigration law. I'm not the one.'

'But what do you need to know?'

'I wouldn't know where to begin. You wouldn't be getting the best help. The right advice. Even if I was taking on outside work, which I'm not, I couldn't just take this on. It wouldn't be fair to you. There are other lawyers in London who do visas all the time.'

'But I know you to be honest. And that is more important. That is everything.'

But I am not. Larry lifted his shoulders as if to shake Kalifa's words off his back. His father always said, 'I know an honest man by his silence.' He himself had been the wordiest of men, a loudmouth who bullied so many people into buying insurance policies that the company had given him a ranking of his own and a trophy in the shape of a handshake. 'You and your father are so alike. You just love to chat,' his mother said.

'I appreciate your asking me, but really I can't do it.'

Kalifa gave him one of his sad, knowing smiles.

Larry sighed. 'I don't know. Perhaps I can recommend someone.' He could think of no one but Gershom. How could he deliver Kalifa to that shaggy dog, his mouth drooling lies?

Kalifa was on his feet. 'I'm sorry I have disturbed you.'

'No, you haven't, of course you haven't. I'm sorry I can't help you.' But he wanted to shake Kalifa hard, to say, 'Stop staring me into stone.'

44

Kalifa reached out his hand and Larry shook the bony fingers.

Half an hour remained of his office time, but Larry pushed student papers into his scratched brown leather briefcase, the same one he had used in high school and law school and had dragged up the stairs to the offices of Rosen, White & Abbott, a firm of corporate lawyers where he worked during his first years following graduation. He had never been depressed before, not for more than a day, and that was when he discovered that Cary Grant was no longer alive. But each morning as he mounted the narrow high steps of the firm's brownstone in Beacon Hill, he began to feel that someone had pinned him to the earth, drained him of the fruity wine which ran in his veins, and he could see himself grown grey and hoar like some character in a Dickens novel.

He had made his parents happy, had gone to law school and done well. He had the gift, his professors told him, of turning everything to his advantage, including the arguments of his opponents. He could tease out a fine legal point until his professor had forgotten why he had brought it up in the first place. He himself could never be pinned down for he was constantly changing his tactics, hopping and ducking to avoid punches till his opponent dropped from exhaustion. But Larry didn't care about winning; it was the game he loved. Nobody but he saw how funny it was, the judge in his high chair, the lawyers with their briefs under their chins like bibs.

'Larry's still finding himself,' his mother told her friends when he decided to go off to the old world to teach law in an American college. 'Larry's not settled yet.' As if she knew as no one else did how like a dragonfly he was.

He would not see Carla till Sunday night for she had gone to visit her father in Southampton. Two whole days stretched ahead when he might end up speaking only to the dry cleaner. There had been the summer Bank Holiday weekend when he had been between girlfriends and practiced talking in front of the mirror. By Monday he was ready to speak to anyone: the deaf fruit and vegetable man, the phantom who paced the pavement. Yet even he had a Bank Holiday and made no appearance during those dusty three days. Once when Larry, curious to hear his voice, asked him for the time, the man continued to walk fast with no sign on his worn melancholic face that he had heard.

Larry paused on the street, like Alice with two halves of a mushroom. One way was Waterloo and the commuter train back to Larry's mansion, his railroad apartment in the sky. The other led across the river into a cumbersome grey city so like one of these suited men who rushed past him in the morning. Standing there before the slow turning cars in the beginnings of dusk, he felt outside himself, as if Larry could be shed on this side of the bridge and he could walk naked into the city.

He loved the bridge, the way several things could be happening at once: sightseeing boats coasting, trains slowly rumbling across, beggars and poets selling bits of themselves. When he touched the handrail he thought he could feel vibrations from the train and the wind and even the footsteps. Yes, he was part of this, one of the crowd going up the hill of London with his Boston high school briefcase. Better to have no destination than to go in bitterness. His father's motto.

The yellow streetlights he had seen first from the airplane flickered as if they had not quite connected with the approaching night. He walked into Trafalgar Square, looked up to see the great columns of the National Gallery illuminate themselves. He climbed further, past a tiny park he had never noticed where men lay bunched up on benches, and reached a street market where lights dangled over barrows of oranges and tomatoes, and men sold bruised melons. Pushcarts, real pushcarts on huge wooden wheels. Now his grandma walked with him, gathering cucumbers, beets, potatoes. He left her there arguing and entered an alleyway where arms reached out to him, girls with silky hair and Egyptian eyes on high stools in black doorways or pushing aside a beaded curtain. Floorshow, peepshow, but he wanted more than an eyeful. He shook his head and smiled at them so that they would not feel rejected. But already they were calling to another man.

'Let's have an adventure,' his mother used to say. 'Let's take the bus to the last stop where we've never been.' But when they reached the end, she would never get off. 'Now we've seen, let's go back with him.' As if only that driver could take them back because he knew where they had come from. The night sky was soft to him and he rose like some fabulous bird, his small heart beating.

He was thirsty but the pubs were full of people with beer mugs and after-work faces looking him over, knowing him to be a stranger. 'They don't really know each other.' Whose voice? His own. Finally.

He found a quiet pub: brown carpet, brown wallpaper, a broken dartboard, one man working the handle of a fruit machine. All the light contained in the cosy horseshoe bar with its glowing bottles and glasses.

'Whisky on the rocks,' he told the barmaid. His grandfather's drink; his drinking, smoking, card-playing, adulterous Russian grandfather who looked like Lenin.

She grinned at him. 'When did you come over?' Like he was some turn-of-the-century immigrant in the hold of a ship going the wrong way.

He wandered away, then back again. The third drink made him feel larger, too large for the dark room and so he was out on the brilliant street again, carried forward as if all the faces of the people were his face.

He found himself again at midnight when the woman he had picked up at the Savannah Cocktail Bar threw her arms around him and cried. She was a big red-faced girl with flaxen hair, the bone structure of an Aryan archetype who had come all the way from Colorado Springs to study at the Royal Academy of Music. She had searched him out in a crowd calling out orders for 'Golden Dreams'.

'I can always pick out the Americans. They have such a baby look.' Then she had crumpled up for no reason. He had started to ask what instrument she played.

'I haven't. For five months. Five months. Whenever I get near the piano my fingers start to shake. See?' She showed him her large white hands.

'They look all right to me.'

'Can't keep them from shaking.'

They were completely still, the hands of a big strong girl panning for gold on the Colorado River or holding down a frisky horse while she saddled up.

'You need to relax more. It's an adjustment coming over.'

She was shaking her head.

'You're probably homesick, aren't you? You miss your family.'

'I hate my mother. Really. Don't get me going.'

'Then your friends. You miss them.'

This made her cry again and when she finished, with her arm in a stranglehold around his neck, she said: 'It's the air. I knew it the minute I got out of the plane. Just that funny damp feeling. You know?'

He didn't but ordered them another round of a murky concoction called 'Atlantic Drift'.

Then they were out on the street driven by the crowd into Leicester Square, she singing, 'You made me love you, I didn't wanna do it,' her arm tight around him, her large bony face alight. Suddenly she looked at him with beseeching eyes, her face gone pale as she staggered away to the railing and began puking.

'I'm going home,' she whispered, still clinging to the railings.

'Shall I take you? I mean just to make sure you're all right?' He wanted her to know he had no designs on her.

'I mean home home. You've made me realize why I can't play.' At this she puked again. 'That's it. I've got no more in me.'

At three in the morning he found himself alone in Waterloo station trying to read the destinations of trains but the words had turned to Russian. The only other person he saw, an elderly woman pushing a battered shopping trolley, had stared at him

48

when he asked if she could read the board for him, and then told him in a voice which thundered through the empty station, 'Go to hell'.

A train driver with his going-home bag told him there were no more trains to Wimbledon till morning. Outside it had begun to rain, the waiting black taxis wet and shiny as baby hippos.

'I'll have one of those,' Larry whispered to himself, then drew open the door of the nearest.

'What's an American doing in Wimbledon?' The driver, a small grey-haired man with glasses and the philosophical air, the knobbly nose of his Uncle Reuben, turned to smile at him. 'I went to New York once.' He shook his head.

Larry was falling into sleep. The taxi driver's voice seemed to slow down and muffle itself as if some mechanism had begun to wind down. 'Far, far from home, my boy. You've lost yourself again.'

'Yes,' his mind spoke to itself, 'but it's really not bad. In fact, I like it more than being found.'

CHAPTER 6

'I've never been to Wimbledon,' Carla said.

He searched her face for mockery. Could this be what was meant by 'a blank look'?

'So it's an adventure,' she said.

'You might say so.'

They sat opposite each other looking out at a stained grey building. On one of its concrete balconies, a little boy stood watching the train, his mother behind, her arms drawn round him. The ancient train was having its usual ten-minute break just beyond Waterloo as if to catch its breath after pulling out of the station.

It had been a mistake to invite her there. She would shrink into herself in Wimbledon. All those normal people shopping in their normal stores: Sainsbury's, the bakery, Ely's, the department store left over from the 1950s where he once heard a woman ask for a 'foundation bra'. Ely's had become 'Eli' for Larry, the name of an uncle who sold carpets from a store-front in lower Manhattan. And beyond, always in half-light, the long windy street of hardware stores, kebabs and second-hand furniture, huge wooden wardrobes out on the street like ancient bears. Only the lanky melancholic man, the pacer, would make her feel at home and he was never around on Sundays.

The train began to move. The little boy waved. His mother seemed to hold him more tightly. He waved and waved. Larry raised his arm but felt like a jerk. The kid couldn't see him. 'Does he know? Does he know how little he has?' Larry felt something like depression coming over him. It was the lack of sleep, waking after a late night with a head full of song – it was that, wasn't it? The kid probably had a better life than he would ever have. His mother looked nice anyway.

Carla seemed not to have noticed the boy. She was smiling out the window, all cheekbones and chin. Someday her skin would not stretch far enough and then everyone would see what was inside.

When she turned back from the window, she wiped her eyes. 'Isn't he wonderful?'

'You mean?'

'He's living on some crap estate, but he sees the beautiful train and thinks he's lucky, he's got the train in his garden. Just for him.'

You're not just a pretty face, Larry thought.

She was like some weird creature, some prehistoric bird let loose in his apartment, walking back and forth in the long hallway. 'How did you find this? It's like some Agatha Christie mystery. Can we sleep in separate rooms and then change in the night? We won't know where the other one is.'

'I live in a mansion,' Larry had written to his mother after he moved in. Why did they give these crumbly Victorian apartment buildings such glorious names, if only to fill him with despair every time he rounded the corner and saw the dirty white bricks framing misshapen windows, the broken wall where an estate agent had fixed a 'For Sale' sign and forgotten to take it down? The front door lay open, the door to his flat was half glass. But he was at the top; by the time the muggers had stumbled over the cracked black and white tiles in the hallway and climbed four flights, he could fly away with the seagulls who congregated on the roofs below him. He might live down in the plains of Wimbledon, but when he lay on his bed beside the high windows, he could see only clouds.

She slept through the night, through his 4am waking and milk drinking, through the birds and the slamming of doors downstairs. She lay like an enchanted being, a naked sylph of a woman.

'Just coffee. I feel sick if I eat in the morning.'

'You should always eat breakfast,' he said, but he could barely finish his usual toast and Rice Krispies. He felt nervous with her there and something else too, but he couldn't put his finger on it, like some patch of light which looked solid till you tried to touch it. He had the jitters. 'You got the heepie-jeepies.' His dad spoke to him there in the kitchen. He was fourteen and

51

the girl he'd been looking at all year in the school lunchroom suddenly came up to him and asked him for a cigarette.

He watched her take little sips. Then she raised her head and looked at him. Her pale eyes seemed to see some idea behind his head, or maybe he had disappeared.

'We'll go to the park,' she said.

'What about your job?' It was Monday. Even if he had had no class and he did – an Introduction to Corporate Law in the afternoon which always left him with a sour taste in his mouth – he would still not feel right hanging around.

'I work at home mostly,' Carla said. 'I do my best stuff at night.'

He saw her in a long translucent smock drawing elves and fairies under the gaze of the yellow streetlight. She had been vague about the books she illustrated but he imagined she drew pictures for children's fairy-tale books.

'There's a sort of island in Regents Park. Whenever I'm down I go there. It feels like the park is a great sea around me.'

'So what's wrong?' It could not be, no he knew it could not. It was unknown for him not to give pleasure. Even Talia had said, 'In one respect you are reliable, Larry, and that is probably luck.' But it wasn't.

'Nothing. Nothing really.'

'You can tell me.' But don't tell me. The first woman he had failed.

She had this way of stretching her neck and lifting her head as if she were trying to release herself.

'Whenever I visit my father I need to go back to the island to get my bearings. That's all.'

He could see his own father shaking his head. 'They're all doing it now. Why can't they just stay and fight? That's what Jews used to do, now they join the goy bandwagon.' Poor child of divorce pulled one way and then the other. So of course she is the way she is.

The island could be walked in two giant steps. Little bridges, cute little Japanese-type gardens. He felt like Gulliver. Carla perched on a little hill like some awkward heron. She

52

had taken off her jacket and now raised her bare arms. It was a day summer had left behind. The air smelled of dying flowers, cut grass and duck shit and something else, a funny scent like sandalwood and incense which could disappear in a moment.

His father had said: 'If you're not sure which way to go, always taste the air.' But it was her he tasted.

Then she looked at him, and they had one of those long serious glances he'd seen in movies. Probably this was the first time they actually exchanged quality eye contact. What was he supposed to be thinking?

'Aren't you cold?'

She shook her head and turned.

He walked to her and put his arms around her. Why did he never feel that he was grasping her?

'Gotta go,' she said after some minutes spent in his arms.

He felt almost tearful as he stepped off the island, turned and waved at her.

His Corporate Law class went badly, as usual. They were a dwindling bunch of boneheads and beginner crooks. Almost all Americans. Each week he had a new dropout. They wanted to learn how to feed on the fatties and he hadn't shown them. He didn't even know himself. 'What's with all this honesty shit?' one of his students had said.

He sat in his office and thought of Carla's bare arms. It really didn't matter, any of it. Today a kid raised his hand: 'Can you tell me what we're doing in here? Because like, I don't see the point?'

He smelled sulphur again, or was it disinfectant from dead bodies? He opened the window and tried to remember her smell. But it was the wrong way around. The smell made you remember, you didn't remember the smell.

Soon they would start to complain. The Dean would notice the low numbers on the register. 'You're not giving them what they want, Larry; this is a business, not just school.' Probably they were down there now with the Dean good-guying them. 'He's weird,' they were saying. 'You ask him a question and he just asks you another question.' He was choking from the smell. Maybe it wasn't decay. Maybe it was all the hot air in the school rising.

He took the back stairs, the 'body dump' they called it, where years ago, in the very early morning so that the living would not know, the dead were counted and carted down. But this way he could take the back exit and avoid passing the Dean's office.

He saw the baby face first, then her hands deep in grey frizzled hair. Gershom with a kid on his shoulders. 'Hey, don't pull,' Gershom said.

'Escaping?' Gershom looked at Larry, then reached up and pulled the kid's hand out of his hair.

Larry stared at the baby. She was almost a toddler, her face smeared with food and dirt.

'Meet Shayna.'

Larry continued to stare. It was as if a piece of a puzzle had been jammed into the wrong place. He just could not put this yellow-haired child and the shaggy-haired charlatan together.

Gershom grinned at him. 'I'm not a pervert. She's my kid. Isn't she beautiful?'

She was the ugliest child Larry had ever seen.

'Shayna keeps me centered. You know what I mean?'

A line of yellow dribble came out of her mouth and descended down to his hair.

'I think she just threw up on you.'

'Yeah, she does that. It's not really throw-up. It's like she's giving something back to me. Her productions. Like her do-dos.'

'I didn't know,' Larry said, as if Gershom had told him about a death in the family. He willed himself to say, 'she's cute', but nothing came out.

'After she was born, Katherine and I separated so I didn't feel like a father. Now we're re-engaging. Katherine lets me have her once a week. We have a creative separation which I think will eventually bring us closer.'

Gershom never cared what Larry thought. Never even waited for him to speak before he went gallivanting on, but now he looked at Larry. 'Don't be so shocked. Even you could be a father.'

Their conversations always ended the same way, with Larry feeling choked by Gershom's words. He continued down the stairs. His child would emerge from him light-footed as a chaste goddess.

'You sure you can't come to our Yankee shindig?' Gershom called after him.

'Gotta date with an actual woman, Gershom,' he called up the stairwell.

'Well, bully for you.'

Larry stood on the corner of Old Compton and Wardour with his *A to Z*, turning the maze of streets around in his hands. Who could read this? The art gallery where Carla was meeting him was in some passageway between two obscure little streets deep in the twisted heart of Soho. She had given him directions but he didn't like to follow them. It meant he had not navigated himself. He might become like some child left in the forest without a trail home.

Where were those streets? The page was like some crazed brain. He ran his fingers along the gridlines. Even if he were a tourist he would not ask. These streets were a dialectic; if he could identify their argument, however tedious, he would find where they led. Not that they led anywhere really. There's no beginning or end. He thought of Scruffy the toy tugboat heading for the open sea. A hand plucked Scruffy just before he was blown across to Europe. 'Let that be a lesson,' his mother said after every reading, for there was a time he would hear no other story. And when he asked what the lesson was, she looked confused and then smiled: 'Not to leave your own bathtub.'

He found streets, the Tweedledee and Tweedledum, but their linking arms, the passageway between them, was not marked. Perhaps it was a secret shared by only a few, or Carla's joke on him, for she was an odd bird. Even over lunch smack in the middle of the day she had managed to seem ethereal, picking at grains of rice with her chopsticks in a crowded Chinese restaurant.

But there it was, as narrow as a Venetian back street, dark but for the small lit window of the Opal Gallery with its poster of an empty bowl turned on its side: 'A Still Voice'. Inside the talk was loud, people in huddles, their backs to the paintings, a table of half-full wine bottles, dirty glasses mixed with clean, a bowl of peanuts. He went from group to group. No Carla. He could not breach the huddles so he began looking: a gleaming white canvas with a realistic painting of an empty table, an egg made of something like jello, and in the corner on the floor, protected by ropes, was a sheet of water. This attracted some of the crowd for the artist had managed to balance an inch of water on a large concrete and metal square. So precarious was it, that Larry believed even the slightest movement of air would send the water over the top.

A woman bent down and put her finger in. 'It's real. It's really real.'

Just leave it, Larry wanted to say, let it be a miracle.

On his neck a cold hand. 'Let me show you my favorite,' Carla said. Never 'hello' or 'how are you' or 'where've you been', but as if they had never been apart, she took his hand and led him to what looked like a silhouette of a man. But the face was a wooden door, a silhouette with a small knob.

'Pull it. You're meant to,' Carla said.

He didn't know why he hesitated, expecting somehow to tear away a skull, but inside was outside, a deep blue sky with the tiny figure of a man or woman, too tiny to know for sure, running towards the flat horizon. The artist had etched words around the frame: 'Eternity is in love with the productions of time.'

He closed the man's face over the great plain. 'There's such a thing as too much space,' his mother used to say.

He tried not to look at her. 'It's interesting, but don't you think, it's sort of pretentious?' Not what he meant really.

Carla pulled at the face till it was wide open again. She turned away. 'Actually,' she said, 'actually I don't like it.'

'Don't let me influence you.'

'I hate it.'

'Probably it's too obvious. If you compare it to the others.'

'These paintings make me feel so hungry,' she said.

'Don't you ever have a real conversation? I mean where someone says something to you and you say something back and they say something else and so on.'

'Aren't you hungry?' She took his hand in her bony one and pulled him through the crowd which was now so thick that

57

people were forced to face the paintings. Laughter came from the corner as a man staggered into the sheet of water.

'Too bad,' Larry said, but she was too busy pushing through. He followed her out the door and had to move fast to catch her twists and turns. The sombre street led to what looked like a dead end but was really the secret entrance to a path alight with peepshows and the glittering letters of a strip club.

'Do you know where you're going?'

'Trust me.'

Why? he thought. Why trust you or anyone? Then she turned from the brightness into a skimpy little street where the sound of cheering and shouting blasted from a tiny Italian café. When he looked inside he saw two men on stools watching a huge video screen. She headed down a dim, dirty stairway.

'Where you taking me?'

'I said trust me.'

He sighed. He wasn't having a fun night.

Inside the windowless room, a heavy, grey-haired woman sat behind a counter peeling potatoes. Old men, some of them with faces like large encrusted rocks, wearing what looked like dishcloths over their shoulders, sat at separate tables smoking. All stood up when they saw Carla and Larry and began to approach.

'Here or here?' They gestured towards the empty restaurant.

'Isn't it wonderful? When I came here for the first time I thought I was back in Greece. Actually they're Cypriots.'

Larry handed a full ashtray to one of the waiters, a courtly ancient. He inspected the glasses for lipstick and nose hair. His mother was screaming, 'Dive, dive.'

'It doesn't bother you that there's no one?'

'I love it here.'

You could not die from what was here. Probably not. Although if the food was as ancient as these men, it might harbor some microbe which had survived from prehistoric times. Something scientists hadn't even named, much less cured.

58

'They used to take me back to the kitchen to pick out what I wanted. Just like in Greece. Then there was some health inspection. They said you couldn't allow the punters back there. Anyway I always get the same thing. Moussaka.'

'And you survived.' He was only joking but she looked at him with what he thought to be scorn.

When she went to the bathroom, he wiped all the glasses and silverware with the paper napkin. The waiters, situated once again at separate tables, watched him. The nearest one handed him another napkin.

'You never told me what you paint.'

She said nothing to this but began to wave her hand. 'I'm starving.' All the waiters stood up and looked as though they would move towards them, but in the end only one ambled across the room with his pad and stub pencil.

'Get what I get,' she said, 'you'll love it.'

At least, he thought, after the waiter disappeared into some festering caldron of a kitchen, at least we'll die of the same bug. He reached across and grasped her hand, and this seemed to get her attention. She became almost shy, as if these men and the one woman were her family and he her suitor.

'So tell me what you paint.'

She seemed to hear him for once. 'I told you, didn't I?'

'No, you didn't, not really.'

'I'm an illustrator. I did tell you. I do books.'

'But you never even told me what kind of books.'

'You know those little drawings of purple testicles and kidneys? And the embryos. I love doing them.'

Why should this bother him? So what if she had cheated him with her weirdness. She wasn't a real artist, just a technician, that was all.

He had noticed for some minutes the slow approach of the oldest of the waiters, a tiny white-haired grandfather type. The large carafe of red wine filled to its lips shook in his hands. Larry stood up and stretched out his hands, and the grandfather waiter held out the carafe like a baby. The wine dripped across the table and on his hands.

'You have to get the balance right,' Carla said, and began eating a piece of pitta bread.

'I did my best. The guy's probably about a hundred. He's not exactly steady on his feet.' He was wiping wine off his jacket; the tablecloth was spotted with it.

She paused from chewing. 'The embryos, I mean. It's like they're always just about to tumble.'

'But do you paint other things? The embryos, that stuff is your bread and butter, but you—'

'I'm happy. Why shouldn't I be?'

'Sure. I mean I wasn't trying to demean what you do. Someone has to do it. D'you have to read up on biology first?' He could see himself walking deeper into the shits, her fine nose quivering from the smell.

He drank the wine though it was too warm and vinegary. Perhaps it would act as a disinfectant for whatever was in the food.

'I'm so tired of everyone trying to be an artist. So many posers. That's what I hated about art school. You can't just be ordinary.'

'So every time I see one of those cute little kidneys I'll know it's you.'

But she would not be teased. She stared out at the room. The yellowish light made it look even dirtier than it was. When she looked back at him her eyes were wet. 'Our insides are very beautiful, don't you think?'

'I wouldn't know.'

'I used to think that inside was where things could go wrong without you knowing it.'

'You'll know about it all right.' He was thinking about later when his insides would let him know what they thought of this place.

She smiled at him for the first time that evening. But perhaps not at him, for the grandfather waiter stood before them holding two plates overflowing with food: huge square wedges of moussaka and roast potatoes. Already his stomach rebelled

60

against his good sense, screaming that it was ten o'clock already, demanding he eat, eat.

'Wonderful,' she said, looking up at the waiter, who patted her head.

She picked at her plate, eating corners of the wedge, while Larry dutifully ate his way through. In a suicide pact the partners had to keep their promise. He would die first, that was clear from the pathetic amount she ate before sitting back in her seat and declaring herself well and truly full. Perhaps she had consumed just enough microbes to paralyse but not kill.

They emerged at the top of the stairs, his face flushed from the wine and the heat of the place, Carla hanging on to him, a reed woman swaying in the blue-green night. She said she felt strange and needed to be home fast. He left her clinging to a streetlight while he stood on the corner searching for a taxi. Soon he was darting into traffic with others as if they were all in some elaborate dance, arms out, body flung to one side, face beseeching. He lost two black taxis to men who ran straight into the middle of the road, arms out like traffic cops. Another went with a woman who snuck inside while he was talking to the driver. In the end he said yes to a soft-spoken man from Honduras whose car had neither meter nor shocks.

When they reached her flat she went straight to the sink, drank three glasses of water fast while he stood, jacket still on, waiting to be dismissed. Maybe for the best. He was too ordinary for her.

Then she curled herself around him. He was staying wasn't he? He hadn't said he wouldn't, but... She gave him one of her big-eye looks.

They were in the futon bed when she said couldn't they do something different for once, as if they were an old married couple, not two strangers beached in a barren room. She wandered over to the one chest of drawers, really a file cabinet which stood sentry by the window of the hooded yellow streetlamp.

61

If only she were not so thin, he was thinking as he watched her pull out the drawer, fumble around. She had legs, but the rest of her.

What was she looking for? Some new kind of diaphragm, maybe with spikes? One of these black nylon underpants with holes in the crotch? He stretched and put his hands behind his neck. At times like this he was grateful for his gift. 'Like a machine,' Talia had said. They could be fighting, she could be winter yellow, fluish, wearing a shmatte, but given the command, he performed. 'A trouper.' In her way Talia appreciated him.

'Shut your eyes,' Carla called from the file cabinet.

When he opened them again, the spotlights were on and she was beside him, a black and grey British Airways sleep mask over her eyes. She held out three scarves.

'What is this some kind of?'

'Take,' she muttered. Just what his grandma always said: 'Take, take,' urging him on to his plate as if he were some hungry workhorse.

He examined the scarves, one of them a large square green and blue paisley with Liberty written in one corner, the other two just plain sashes, one green and one purple.

'Can you give me some idea?'

'Don't be so feeble. I want you to tie me up.'

'With these?' He laid the scarves out on the bed like some haberdasher.

'Ropes hurt.'

'I just don't think...'

She continued to lie there speaking so low he had to bend his ear over her face. 'Otherwise it doesn't happen for me. You see? It's the one way I've found.'

'Do we have to have the spotlights on too? I feel like I'm on an operating table.'

'I just put them on so you could see what you're doing. They have to be tight. I thrash around a lot.'

'Really.'

A deep sigh. 'Can't you be serious? It's what I need.'

'I just never had to.' He meant to say his girlfriends wanted no extra-curricular activities. He satisfied them with his song and dance. 'I haven't done it that way before. I'm a traditionalist, you see. A man of the old school.'

Another deep sigh. 'The trouble is you're innocent.'

'Ignorant maybe. Has anyone ever been tied up to a futon bed?'

She stretched up her arms. 'You tie my hands together over my head and then each ankle gets tied to one of the little feet. See?'

When he had finished and turned off the lights, he felt suddenly bereft, as if he had just lost his best friend. She lay there waiting, impassive in her mask. He made several forays, then sat on the edge of the bed without speaking.

'What is it?' she said.

'I'm – I don't know. I've never –'

'Will you stop wittering?'

'Who's wittering? What do you mean by that anyway? I've never understood that word.'

'Just start.'

There was a silence in which he attempted a few manoeuvres with himself. 'Never. Never had this happen.'

She sighed. 'Just forget who I am.'

'I'm not working.'

'Doesn't it excite you?'

'Just the opposite. I feel like an oaf. I've never felt like an oaf before.'

'What'll we do? It's my only way. Otherwise I'm not in control. Anything could happen so nothing does.'

A corpse would have more control than you. Yet, when he was with her he felt confused, as if his brain was some glass snowstorm she shook and shook again.

'What if you tied me up?'

'But then—'

'You haven't tried it, have you?'

'No one ever suggested that. Everyone's happy to be the master.'

'Maybe if you had total control.'

He untied her and turned on the lights. She worked half-heartedly, the scarves loose around his ankles, his hands barely restrained, but by the time she switched off the lights, he felt himself again. As they moved together, she a silent wraith over him, first one and then the other of the sashes on his ankles slipped, but he pretended to be tied, protesting with little cries at his bondage. Suddenly she fell back against the bed.

'It's hopeless. I'm numb down there.'

He shook off his remaining sashes and removed the mask and began to kiss her. But she was passive. In the end she wanted only to sleep while he lay awake staring at her still face, then out to her friend, the yellow streetlamp. In all the Sunday afternoons, all the lone nights in Wimbledon, even the moment when he knew he was no longer wanted and had to fend for himself on the street, even at those times he had not known such loneliness. Maybe he was actually depressed. If he left now he would never have to see her again. The way home would be difficult at this hour and maybe he would spend the rest of the night walking, but he could not bear the mask beside him, the malevolent yellow street lamp. He slid carefully out of bed and searched the floor for his clothes. As he reached for his jeans, his house keys fell to the floor. She mumbled, then sat up in bed.

'Larry? What are you doing? You're not leaving?'

'Just looking for something.' He let his clothes drop to the floor and returned to her. Her face as a woebegone as a child's.

He kept watch on the night, whispering the *Shema*, then the Bill of Rights, remembering corporate disputations, even logarithms. He had only to sleep for a moment and he would lose himself, his soul snatched just like hers.

CHAPTER 8

'Anyone seen Joel?' he called to the back of the room. Two weeks of zeros next to his name. The sneer had gone. No wonder he had been feeling relaxed in class, almost a natural teacher.

The American baby boys shook their heads. Bobby called out, 'Look under the table.' The others laughed and someone said, 'Yeah. He's like fucked somewhere.' Clapping and horsing about in the back, the sound of chairs tilting. The golden youth lost in the sooty alleyways of London.

Chin in the front row looked at Larry with an uneasy smile. Omar as usual with his cordial expression, Kalifa deep in himself, turning a pen around in his fingers.

'Okay, shush.' His voice sounded feeble. He still felt groggy from the weekend.

Suddenly Sarah Ogunio stood up. Stately Sarah draped in gorgeous fabrics was like some Greek hunter goddess. Only she was Nigerian. 'You're too flamboyant for the law,' he wanted to tell her, but she was one of the best in the class. She had an implacable practicality; every time he lost himself in the beauty of some law, she broke into his dreaminess: 'But Professor, I want to know. What do you do with it?'

Today she wore purple and gold: headscarf, long dress, enormous gold ear hoops. Her voice was low but carried better than his had. 'Boys. You be quiet. We are here to learn.'

They giggled but she stood facing them until they stopped. Then she turned to Larry. 'They're just children. Sometimes need a good slap.'

All the years in court Larry had danced before the judge, never stumbling. He blamed Carla. 'What's your hurry?' she had called to him from the futon.

He had walked the Sunday streets, a fog settling around his head. Back in Wimbledon he lay fully clothed on his sofa and slept, only to wake with the shivers. The lady of the scales had handcuffed him naked to his teacher's desk. One by one his students filed past as if at a state funeral. Yet their faces were indifferent.

'He's gone AWOL.' The Dean looked down the registers for Joel's other classes. 'The others are still coming. You've got a full class, so?' He looked at Larry. 'One brat gone.'

'Shouldn't we call him? Keep track? I mean, he's in a foreign country.'

'Leave that to me. Some of these kids suddenly go ape when they're over here.'

'He seemed unhappy.'

'Joel Kurtz is what we call an underachiever. I doubt he would ever have got into the overseas program if it hadn't been for his dad.' He gave Larry a knowing look but Larry just stared back. 'His dad is one of our illustrious alumni. He runs an optic company. See?'

'So does that make Joel expendable?'

'No. But it means go easy when he shows up.'

'Suppose he doesn't?'

'That's my problem. He'll show. He's just testing his freedom.'

'How can you be so sure? For all we know he could be lying in some opium den. Seriously. He could be in real trouble.'

'Look, Larry, I appreciate your concern but quite frankly this happens all the time. You've been lucky. Sometimes a class just haemorrhages. The Americans go to Barcelona or just stay permanently stoned. The others can't see the point of it and leave quietly. The lecturer looks up one day. He's got three kids in the class.'

'So that's it,' Larry said, 'the kid disappears. No one's seen him for three weeks and you do nothing.'

The Dean had been smiling, but now he was the iguana again, cold-faced and leathery. 'You don't really care so much, Larry. You just feel guilty.'

'Guilty? For what? I really object to that.'

'You're not in court. Anyway I've got someone coming to see me, so.'

66

Back in the hallway he saw Gershom talking to a student. He turned and tried to get away but heard his name.

'Larry. How was the date?'

Larry shrugged and kept walking, but Gershom caught up with him. 'Hey, slow down. So, how was it? I'm dying to know. Do people really have dates any more?'

'How should I know?'

Gershom looked into his face. 'So it didn't go well. You gonna see her again?'

'What are you, my mother?'

'Don't get so, you know. Just making friendly enquiries. We had a wonderful time, the Un-Americans. We decided to join the Palestinians on the march, and then we went out for Chinese. You really should join us. We got a demo next weekend. American women, Larry. The best in the world.'

'I'll see.' Larry turned again. He had not thought about next weekend or the one after. All of them stretched out before him like paper dolls, featureless, one leading inevitably to the other. Carla was his last hope, the one native woman willing to keep him and she was crazy.

'Don't be too long in seeing.'

By the middle of the week Larry felt like a sinner about to break his fast before sundown. He sat in his kitchen looking over the red chimneys of Wimbledon. Never before had he known what this sad little feeling must be. Melancholy. Surely Carla would not want to be tied up every night. Like God she might have a Sabbath when she was released from bondage to have ordinary sex. One day in seven. Let her find other men for all the rest, he would not be jealous. But when he picked up the phone to call her, he remembered the creepy feeling which stayed with him all through last Sunday as if he had made love to one of Dracula's daughters.

What he needed was a real woman, not some fey creature out of Alice in Wonderland. He thought of Talia, big-boned, big-hipped Talia. Talia, who liked to say of him, 'There goes a man forever shedding his skin.'

67

'Larry, I thought you were in England.' Talia always sounded like herself.

'I am.'

'You're calling me all the way from there. That's sweet, Larry.' Then, more businesslike: 'So what's up?'

'Nothing really. I'm wondering how you are.'

'I don't hear from you for a year and you act like it's nothing. Just like a wave in the street. Do you even remember the last time?' She had thrown a law book at him, missed and broke her clay self-portrait. 'That's what you do to me,' she screamed, then began to cry, so unlike Talia to cry. He had picked up the pieces of her face, two clean halves. 'You can stick them back together, can't you? What about superglue?'

'You're there. Then not there. Back and forth. Then you say let's have an arrangement, let's be together but not really. That's your middle name Larry, "not really".'

'Talia, I'm the sad man.'

A sigh on the other end. 'Did someone give you the shaft?'

'No, not really. I just miss you.' This was true. He missed her because she was far away. If she were right in front of him shaking her hair at him like some lioness, he would not miss her.

'You got a girlfriend over there? You can tell me. I'm serious with someone now, I can take it.'

He shook his head; actual tears formed in his wondering eyes.

'Larry. Larry,' she shouted over the phone.

'I told you I'm the sad man. The women here, well, there's no one like you.'

'You gotta give them a chance. You've been there what, a year? Don't be such a wimp.'

'Over a year.'

'So it's a foreign country. They do things differently.'

'You don't know, Talia. They're like another species. They may look like us, even talk like us, but inside beats the heart of a reptile.' He thought of telling her about Carla, but was too embarrassed. Already she'd called him a wimp.

68

'Maybe they're too grown-up for you.'

'I can't get close to them. Only the weird ones open up.'

'Larry, I'm not your mother so stop whining. If you can't hack it come home. Or bond with other Americans.' Her voice softened. 'You're just not like other men. Probably they don't know what to do with you.'

It's what they do with me I don't like, Larry thought but kept silent. He could not imagine Talia tied down.

'You all right?'

'I'm better already. Just hearing your voice. Like a cup of sunshine.'

'Don't bullshit me. Okay?'

But he could feel a smile breaking out on his careworn face. 'I'd like you right here so I could squeeze you. And do other things. You're adorable.'

'Larry, please. Like don't muddy the waters. Get yourself a nice Jewish girl already. There's got to be some airhead from New Jersey who's finding herself over there.' She sighed. He loved her sighs. 'And if you want to call me again, you can.'

Larry sauntered near Gershom's office and then strolled around the canteen, then wandered back to the hallway. He didn't want Gershom to think that he was searching for him. But when he turned up as he always did, Larry was going to drop into the conversation about Saturday, how he was going to be coming into central London anyway so why not meet up with the Un-Americans. Of course there was always a chance he might not make it. But he would. All week he had turned and turned again; now it was Friday and still he had not called Carla.

It wasn't Gershom he saw, but the Dean coming back from the bathroom. 'Larry, I've been looking for you. You got a minute?'

A minute's an hour with you. Larry followed his brown and white checkerboard back into the smoky office. Why did a man with so corrupt a heart dress like an innocent from Ohio?

He watched the Dean push tobacco down into the cup of his pipe. The pipe was someone else again, the English gent, kindly, wise but shrewd. He looked at Larry with one of his smiles. 'Helps calm me down.'

Larry made a bridge of his hands. 'Whatever makes you feel good. We all need to relax more.' Was that really him speaking? These were the sort of homilies his mother exchanged with their next-door neighbors.

'How true.' Then, 'I had one of your students in here. Your Monday class.'

'You mean Joel? He's come back?'

The Dean shook his head with a smile almost of pity. 'No, Larry, forget Joel. What I mean is, a student was very upset about something that happened in your class.' He let that sink into Larry. 'So I told him I'd speak to you.'

Just getting me back. Nobody said anything, nobody would. They love me except for the boys at the back and they don't care. Even they think I'm a good guy.

70

'He felt the students were playing around too much. They were disrespectful to you. I quote him there.'

'Who? Who is it?'

'You know, Larry, we have students from all over. Some of them come from cultures where teachers are like gods. They just don't understand.'

'You're not going to tell me?'

'I can't. It was said in confidence. Of course we've never had any complaints before about you.'

So now it had turned into a complaint, one student's whine. The Dean leaned back, his iguana face calm as if he was now toying with some potential dinner.

'I'm treating this as if it never happened. Just a blip in your untarnished career here.'

'Thanks for that. Your confidence in me, I mean.'

The Dean smiled up at Larry who raised his hand to his eyes as if to ward off the Medusa. He had remained standing, had resisted the iguana's cushioned armchairs. Like being caught in his soft mouth.

'I just wanted you to know. You might want to, I don't know, discuss it with the class. Or review your class management plan. I leave it to you for now.'

You don't care, leatherneck. But Larry was hurt. One of his students had told on him.

He stepped out of the Dean's office into a crowd of Americans who just finished a class. He let himself be pushed along, bobbing like a rubber duck in their chat, their swinging limbs, their milky upturned faces. Oh to be them surging towards Friday night. In the distance he saw Gershom and waved at him, actually beckoned for the hairy monster to come and lick his face. He would be with his own kind this weekend.

The house sagged, seemed to draw the rest of the terrace down with it, a little row of modest white Victorians in a crescent off Camden Road. The cracking maroon door was open. Barking and the distant sound of voices. Larry knocked, got no one, knocked again, the barking more furious, the dog reached the

71

door, nosed out. An ancient black and white mongrel with a handkerchief for a collar, tail flapping. Still no one. Larry checked the info Gershom had given him, his 'bolt hole' he'd called it. He pushed the door and found himself in a dank little hall laden with rags, but still no Gershom, no nobody. He walked further in, followed by the dog, who licked first one and then the other of his hands.

He jumped when a white face appeared in a doorway leading off the hall. The face was attached to the body of a very long woman with short curly hair. He tried not to stare at the pair of child's antennae on her head.

'Is this...? Are you Un-Americans?' Or the undead, he thought, looking at her pale face.

She looked through him.

'Does Gershom Fish live here?'

'He's in the bathroom. We're all—' She waved her hands towards the end of the hall.

The dog nudged him. He followed the woman's bobbing antennae into a small humid crowded living room. Faces looked up at him from the floor, two women and a stringy youth with long greasy curls and mottled T-shirt with the word 'scum'. On the sofa draped with Indian bedspreads, a small crabbed man in what looked like a cravat sat talking into the hearing aid of a long-headed fellow, an elderly Fred MacMurray. The bobbing antennae joined a group sitting around a table in the far corner, and he was left standing.

From the floor came the only sounds of welcome, an old woman with red painted cupid lips and sparse hair. 'Hi there,' she said and Larry put up his hand like an Indian chief.

'I'm Edie, that's Devorah and Graham. You wanna make a poster?'

'But I can't draw.'

'Don't worry. Nobody can.'

But he'd looked down and seen the dove she had outlined. 'Really I was never good at it.'

'Don't be such a perfectionist. What you say your name was?'

72

But he hadn't. Once he said his name, he had to stay. Gershom hadn't even appeared. If he left now no one would be able to report him.

Edie had made a space for him beside her, near the now grinning youth and young woman who had looked at him briefly with half-closed eyes before turning back to her poster. 'C'mon. Don't be shy.' She patted the floor.

There was a smell when he crouched down on the floor, different from the dog and mildew he had been inhaling since he entered the house. He sniffed and followed his nose a few inches to the grinning youth now sprawled over his poster. Not so young. The greasy corkscrew curls sprouting grey. He was coloring in the large words on a white sheet. He looked up again grinning.

'I nicked it. The sheet I mean. From the home.'

'The home?' Larry stared at his mouth crammed with crooked yellow teeth like the scream in a horror movie. Where had he got to?

'Home for old gits where I work.'

'Graham is what they call a care assistant. But he does much more,' said Devorah of the sleepy eyes.

But he's English, Larry wanted to say, why d'you let him in, this is supposed to be a haven from them. He's English and he smells.

'Larry.' Gershom appeared on the threshold. 'I never thought you'd make it.'

Larry didn't like being down on the floor with Gershom above him. He tried to rise but since he was still crouched, he fell back on the old youth.

'Take it easy.' Gershom put out a hand which Larry ignored as he rose once more.

'So is this it?' He gestured around the room. 'I thought you said—'

'People come and go in the group. It's like a drop-in centre. But yeah at the moment, we're pretty solid.'

He could have killed him. Where were they, all those American women? He counted three. One was at least seventy,

73

another was a Martian and the third, well she was determined not to notice him. She could be a lesbian for all he knew.

He would have left then and there, if it hadn't been for Edie, the non-stop talker, mouth moving as fast as her little fingers. She was the only friendly person in the room. 'No more Bush fires', she had written on her poster.

'You coming on the march later?' Gershom asked.

'I don't think so.' Larry searched for an excuse. He had forgotten the group's agenda, that it even had an agenda.

'Whatever, Larry,' Gershom said. He turned and sat down beside the Martian at the back table.

'Larry, why don't you do a poster at least. We'll carry it for you if you can't come,' Edie said. She had not abandoned him even if everyone did.

He crouched down again. He remembered the banner he saw once in college back in the days of the Gulf war.

'There is no just war,' he wrote in large stylish letters on the cardboard.

Edie looked over his shoulder. 'I like it.'

Devorah read it. 'You're a pacifist then.' She stared at him. He realized she wasn't sleepy, just her eyes were permanently half-closed. A full woman draped with scarves, a blue feather dangling from one ear, she reminded him of someone, maybe, maybe not, maybe she was just another of these adorable Rubens women. Only her skin was a yellow shade of olive, and she hated him.

'Not really. I just don't like to fight.'

'Sometimes you have to. If you were in Spain during the civil war what were you supposed to do, let the fascists kill you?'

'I'm just not a fighter. I like to dip and dive.'

'We should kill them all,' Graham said, still with a grin on his face.

Larry thought, my whole life has brought me to this point. He bowed his head and began coloring in the letters, trying to keep within the lines he had drawn. When he finished he could leave.

CHAPTER 10

He had never expected to hear from her again. Weeks had gone by, too late now to call her up and casually arrange a meeting. His silence had spoken to her and she in her warehouse room had responded in kind.

'Larry, Larry, is that you, Larry?' Carla shouted into the phone as if she were next door testing Alexander Graham Bell's new invention.

'Who do you think this is? Godzilla?'

'I've been thinking about next weekend. You see my mum called and she wants— you with me Larry?'

Time was not the same to her as it was to earth people. Three weeks was a wink of her eye. He was still her datelet.

'Sure. I'm just adjusting my eardrums. Do you have to yell?'

'I'm not hearing. I have this ear infection so I'm all cotton wool inside. I'm on antibiotics. Have to sleep with my head propped up on a suitcase. It's killing me. Like someone's twisting a screwdriver into my ear.'

So she had been missing him after all. 'I'm sorry. You want I should make you some soup?' He tried to remember her ears, little and close to her head he reckoned. Everything about her was neat except her mind.

'You want to come down to Witherns? My mum's at me again.'

Ever the mistress of the non sequitur. 'I need some help with this. Could you give me the first letter of one of the missing words?'

Carla said, 'She just keeps on even though I've been in the summer and probably I'll be the one who has to do Christmas. "Carla," she says, "I want you to see my viburnum."'

'Maybe she misses you.'

'I thought you might come with me.'

Ah, so she was actually bringing him home. He stood by the phone waiting.

'What?' she asked.

'I didn't say anything.' She only ever heard him when he was silent.

There was a pause. Then she said, 'Unless you're busy.'

Maybe she does understand, maybe the cotton wool is only in her ears, and she knows how I fled from her, how, desperate for females, I went to a coven of expatriates.

The Un-Americans were meeting again at the weekend, 'a social' Gershom had called it. He'd not gone to the demo, had never gone back to the sad sack house. Edie's face turned up to his as he left that time. 'You'll come back?' If only she was not an old woman. No one else would remember him.

'It's so boring down there. Coffee mornings. Old farts getting high on custard creams,' Carla said.

'Sounds attractive.'

'I feel buried. But if you come, it won't be so bad. We'll go down to the beach. If it's not raining.'

He was trying to remember where she came from. Somewhere south of Wimbledon. She talked so little about family, not like him. Her father was some kind of engineer, an unreliable guy who walked out when Carla skidded into teenagehood. He imagined Carla's mother like one of these lean Yankee women who served skimpy portions of food. He'd met enough of them in Massachusetts: white hair they never bleached, curled or crimped, a frame built from wire hangers and a smile bright with craziness. An aunt of his had never forgotten her one and only Yankee lunch: three shrimp on a bed of iceberg lettuce. A weekend with Carla's mother would finally kill him.

'Mum's used to me bringing home boys. I mean we'll sleep together.'

You bringing your ropes? Larry wanted to ask, or do I have to tie you up with your mother's apron strings? But of course that sort of woman never wore aprons or dirtied herself in any way.

'I've trained her. But I should warn you. They're so backward down there. English in the worst possible way. Going

76

to an Indian restaurant is a cultural shock for them. I always think how did I keep sane?'

You never really knew them until you entered their house. Only then would the glass barrier roll down.

'Probably you'll want to leave as soon as you get there. When you see what I mean.'

He hadn't even said yes yet. 'It must be pretty by the sea.'

'They built these mock Spanish villas on the front. Makes me want to puke. They tore down all the interesting bits. It's all shitty bungalows.'

'So your house doesn't have a thatched roof?'

All week he had a case of the dreads. In a dream hundreds of elderly Yankee women flowed past him over London Bridge, heads upright, long flat arms swinging.

He felt like a bride waiting for her at the platform's entrance. Waiting and waiting. The train was leaving in ten minutes, then five. She appeared dragging a purple bag, walking fast, almost walking past him through the turnstile and down the platform.

He had to run a little to keep up. 'Shouldn't we get in?' he asked.

But she kept walking, looking into coaches as she went.

'We have two minutes it says. The guy is about to blow his whistle.'

They had nearly reached the front of the train when she stopped and pulled her bag up the steps.

'Perfect,' she said. The coach was empty. Well, nearly empty. A youth with headphones sat in one corner moving his head and shoulders and uttering little cries.

She cuddled up to him the minute the train pulled out of Waterloo, and for a moment he thought they could be normal together. But she was pulling at his zipper.

'Here?' He looked out the window. The train had paused before the grey council building, a woman leaned out of one of the balconies smoking. No sign of the little boy.

He watched the woman, who seemed suddenly to look in his direction. 'People can see right in.'

77

'It couldn't be more perfect. No one will come in till Clapham Junction. We've got at least ten minutes.'

'What about her?' but the woman on the balcony turned her back on him and went into her apartment.

He whispered, 'That boy is just over there. And the ticket collector could come through. Anyone could.'

'Please. I've always wanted to be caught like this.' She gave him one of her pale beseeching looks.

'I don't know.' He glanced at the seats, the cushions stained and grimed with the asses of thousands. Suppose he picked something up? And then there was the narrowness of the seats. He would have to perch over her like some insect.

Already she had shed her pants and was lying there, her head against the window, eyes shut. He had become a stranger taking advantage of her in an empty carriage caught between stations. Even he could see the beauty of it.

He untied his shoes, all the time looking down the aisle, then took off his pants and hung them over the back of the seat in front of him. Just get it over with and then you can relax, what his mother said when he couldn't face homework. He tried to move on top of her grasping the top of the seat with one hand, one of his knees wedged against the back. She said nothing as he struggled to position himself. He was nearly there when the train jolted and he was thrown into the aisle bare-assed.

'Larry? Larry, are you okay?' She rose from the seat and stared down at him.

'What d'you say we give this a miss?'

She shrugged, then spent the rest of the journey staring out the window. It was going to be a fun weekend, he could see that. Him with the skeletal mother and daughter, rations for food.

It was only when the train was slowing down just outside Witherns that Carla said without any sense of urgency: 'Here we are.' He grabbed at the edge of the door, for there was no handle, then pushed and pushed. People were getting off and soon the train would leave. One of her tricks. They'd be locked in for eternity, rolling through Britain with no one to know, and he a corpse having sex with another corpse.

78

'Let me. It's tricky.' With her tinny arms she managed to pull down the window of the door, reach outside and turn the knob.

'Whoever heard of a knob on the other side of a door? Why didn't you tell me?'

'I just assumed you'd know how to open the door.' She walked ahead of him dragging her bag.

So it was one of these rites of passage. Something kids here learned that made them bond with their trains.

Larry looked for Carla's mother as they walked through the gate. She'd be tall and rangy, walking briskly, hand thrust out for a shake, a smile straining the bone structure. But he saw only a heavy white-haired woman ambling towards them, glasses on a chain, big smile. Carla fell into her hug like a young deer caught by a polar bear. Then a large hand crabbed with rheumatism stretched to Larry.

He'd heard about magpies choosing sparrow nests but this was something else. What it was Larry could not say; anyway he did not need to speak much for Carla's mother chatted all the way home as she drove. She kept going, fed with only a few words from him about their trip: how annoying these doors with outside handles could be, how she was nearly stuck on one herself, how she had to go a long way around because traffic in the village was impossible. The weekend was promising to be wet but down here, well, you never know. Did they have rain in London? Carla sat beside her staring at her hands, wan and slender beside her mother's rosy talk.

Perhaps adoption, but then how to explain Carla's brother. She could be one of those big-hearted women who take in discarded children. Which could explain the ease with which she accepted him, sending the two of them upstairs to share the guest room.

They had entered through the back door into a crowded kitchen: flowered wallpaper, spice bottles on a windowsill crammed with pots of parsley. Plates with white towels over them lay in pools of sunlight.

Carla came alive. 'Mum I told you not to. I told you.' She began lifting the edges of the towels and Larry standing by the door with his silver suitcase, the cute overnighter his law office had given him as a send-off, wondered if her mother was not who she seemed. The towels conceal some moldy growth; beneath her comfortable flesh was the twisted soul she had bequeathed to her daughter.

'You know I don't eat puds anymore. They give me headaches and I don't feel right in myself.'

She had left one towel askew and Larry saw the edge of a pie.

'I just thought.' Carla's mother caught Larry's eye, smiled and seemed to nod encouragement.

'I love pies,' he said. 'Did you make them all yourself, Mrs Sanderson?'

'What do you think?' Carla turned to him. 'And you can call her by her first name for God's sake. Rowena. She was named after an iron. But her mother couldn't spell.'

Rowena turned to Larry. 'My mother read the name in Ivanhoe.'

He had never seen Carla like this. Actual emotions showed on her normally fey face. Irritation. Disdain. She left the room and Larry heard the television go on.

He glanced at Rowena, who stood beside one of her creations. 'Would you like to see?'

One by one she took off the towels and named her pies: gooseberry, apple, blackcurrant, and steak and kidney.

'I wasn't sure what you like. Carla wouldn't say. You know how she is.'

'I won't know where to start.'

'Put the kettle on, will you?' she said as she slipped one of the pies into the oven.

He could see this would be his job for the weekend while Carla sulked. Soon he was carrying the tray of tea things: flowered cups and saucers, a heavy brown teapot, silver strainer and milk jug, and blue and white knitted cosy. He who had been weaned from a bottle to a mug now fingered bone china.

80

Back and forth he went, refilling the teapot, cutting himself slices of pie, more pie. On one of his journeys back he paused to listen to them:

'Don't be so thick. He's not one of those.'

'But darling, you never know.'

'I know. I've been to restaurants with him.'

'But they have special foods don't they?'

'Mum will you please. I've seen him eating a bacon butty.'

He approached tapping the lounge door. They turned, Rowena with one of her sunlit smiles.

'We were just discussing you. Do you, I mean are you all right with eating my food? I never thought to ask Carla.'

'Mum please, this is really unnecessary.'

But she ignored Carla and turned to him: 'I wondered if you had to eat specially prepared food. I don't think we can get it down here. There aren't many, well, many Jewish people living here.'

'I don't eat kosher if that's what you mean. Never did. My mother used to but ...' He shrugged. His father liked shrimp and crispy bacon. Larry beamed back at Rowena. 'I eat everything but broccoli.'

'You have a different way of cooking, don't you? I once heard a programme on the radio about Jewish food. I tried to make one of the recipes. It was a kind of potato pie.'

'I'm sure anything you cook would be wonderful. Especially pies.'

'I knew it wasn't quite right. I was in a bit of a hurry. They asked for rendered chicken fat which I didn't have. I didn't think it mattered much. So I used lard.'

He said nothing, just continued to smile benignly. Lard. Wasn't that something you washed with?

He could see she wanted to know everything, down to the ceremony where they cut off a bit of his foreskin. She would eat his Jewishness while he had her pies.

In the morning there was a knock and when he finally made it to the door, he saw a tray of mugs on the landing.

'Hope I haven't woken you,' Rowena called out from the foot of the stairs. Such discretion. And such kindness.

He had been cold all night for the upstairs had no central heating and Carla had said the space heater smelled. She herself gave no heat in bed even after he labored above her.

He drank his tea, warming his hands around the mug, while Carla lay with her head under a pillow. Then he washed and shaved at the little sink in the bathroom, one of those irritating ones with separate faucets for hot and cold. When he returned she had moved to the far side of the bed, the duvet over her face. He bounced on the bed but she did not move. It was nearly 9:30 and he was hungry. He tried to pull the duvet off but she clung to it. 'Carla,' he whispered.

'Just leave me.'

'It's breakfast time.'

'Stuff breakfast.' The muffled reply. This was entirely unlike her. 'I never sleep,' she once told him, 'I just shut my eyes and let the darkness shade me.' In those mornings in London when he turned to her, her eyes were wide open as if she had been waiting all night for him.

He went down alone. Rowena sat at the long wooden refectory table with a cup of coffee. The table was set with tiny juice glasses, plates with pretty little houses on them and a group of jars: a large brown one and three with hand-written labels: quince, gooseberry, orange marmalade.

'I hope they're all right,' she said, 'the gooseberries were a bit runny.'

'You mean you made these yourself?'

She insisted on getting the coffee and putting on toast. 'I'm sure your mother wouldn't let you do it.'

He sighed.

'You must be homesick.'

Everything his mother cooked came out of the freezer. She once told him that she worried that fresh food was dirty.

While Rowena was in the kitchen he inspected the brown jar. Inside was a shiny chocolate-colored paste which gave off a strange aroma, something like the inside of shoe mixed with

82

anchovies. Perhaps some medicine or a variation on the brown sauce bottles he saw in train station restaurants.

She had finished her breakfast but sat with him as he ate. 'What do you normally eat in the morning?'

'Oh this is fine. Just what I'm used to.' He spoke quickly, afraid she'd start on Jewish food again.

'I asked Carla, but you know what she's like.'

She watched him eat. 'Is she coming down soon?'

'Well, she wasn't up when I came down.' He felt embarrassed to be talking openly about sharing a room.

He wanted to say, 'We haven't done what you think we have', but strictly speaking it wasn't true. She had allowed him but he felt afterwards as though nothing had happened. Since Carla touched home she had become a child who eats, sleeps and shits without a care for anyone.

'Because her godmother called. And I didn't know if Carla had plans for this weekend. Somewhere she wanted to take you. She's invited us for tea today. But of course if you have plans.'

What plans could they have here? A visit with the newsagent, a stroll through John's grocery, John, a lank glowering man with fiery cheeks who stood guard over his empty shelves. Perhaps a session getting his hair blue at Helen's Hair Dreams. They had walked by the front in the late afternoon, past square new flats with bare gardens and the occasional staring face in the picture windows, then out to the eroding cliffs with their warning signs, all the wilderness below in the grey thrashing sea. It was going, this place, bit by bit.

'Margaret will understand of course. Only it's been a while since she's seen Carla. Last time Carla didn't go around there. I think she didn't have time.'

Tea in an English house with a real godmother. He'd only ever heard of godmothers in fairy stories.

'I don't see why not.'

'Margaret would enjoy meeting you. She really doesn't get out much. You know how it is.'

He nodded, not knowing but hoping to imagine so.

'She's never met—'

83

Here he interrupted, because he was worried she'd say 'a real Jew, not just some Shylock'. 'I mean, it's up to Carla, but personally I'd be in favour. I really can't see that we'd be doing anything special.'

'Shall I phone her then? Because she likes to go out in the morning.'

She left him eating and was on the phone to Margaret in an instant, her voice gone high and full of 'Oh dear. Really. Are you sure? Yes, they've just come yesterday. Well then. Shall we say?' He realized that he had become part of her plan.

She came back into the room, a cardigan pulled over a dress which barely contained her. Larry couldn't remember a time when his mother wore dresses. She lived in pants suits all of the same crisp colors and artificial material. What would she make of this affable stout woman, a dowager without a lace mantilla? He felt that if he allowed Rowena everything, he would always be welcome in her house.

Carla emerged at noon, a figure in a sleeveless black tank top at the door of the sun lounge where Larry and Rowena had ensconced themselves with cups of tea. There could never be enough cups of tea here and biscuits and jam tarts. He lay back in the soft old chair, the sun turning his pallid cheeks rosy. He felt like a schoolboy with a favourite aunt.

Rowena turned, smiled up at Carla. 'Aren't you cold in that?'

'Aren't you hot?' She continued to stand there in the sunless border between the living room and the sun lounge.

'Dear. I hope it's all right. Margaret asked us to tea this afternoon, and I've said we can come. Larry said you didn't have any plans.'

'So you've been roped in.' Carla looked at Larry as if seeing him for the first time. 'Your face looks like a furnace by the way.'

'She hasn't seen you in a while and I thought—'

But Carla had left the doorway. Rowena looked at him with a smile; maybe it was triumphant, he couldn't be sure. They could hear Carla in the kitchen, and when she returned it was with a mug of black coffee. She sat down on the sofa, picked up a *Daily Mail*, flung it down, stared out the window. Rowena tried to maintain her indulgent mother's smile.

Carla turned and with a face full of fury, a face he had never seen before, she said, 'She's boring. So boring.'

'You hardly ever see her. In fact I can't remember the last time.'

'You got him to say yes. That's how you did it. You always find a way to make everyone do what you want. Did you ever think that maybe he doesn't want to spend hours talking to some dim old woman?'

Rowena blinked back what looked like tears but could equally be moisture in an elderly woman's tired eyes. 'If you feel that way, you don't have to go. I can call her and make excuses. If you really feel that way.'

'You're always making excuses. You spend your life making excuses. We'll go then. What else is there to do? Look, it's pissing down.'

Margaret was a giggler, and if she was boring she did not know it. The door opened to reveal her and a large blue china frog. 'Oh I'm so glad to see you.' She hugged Carla and then gave her hand to Larry with a shy almost girlish smile. She was one of these tiny old ladies with neat coiffed white hair, but her narrow blue eyes were full of wonder.

'Come into the lounge. You must still be exhausted. I hope it's not too much for you coming here. You don't want to overdo it.'

Carla said nothing. Larry was preparing some pleasantry when Rowena spoke: 'They came up yesterday, so they've had a good rest. But of course the air down here—'

'Yes, it always makes us sleepy doesn't it? But then we're used to it.'

'I expect they'll have an early night again.'

What was this all about? Carla had raised her eyebrows and looked out the window. He understood that Rowena was preparing the way for their eventual escape.

85

Larry lifted up a small pink beanbag frog and sat in the soft florid armchair. He began to have a nervous feeling as if they might suddenly come alive: the tiny frogs on the mantelpiece above the gas fire, the large grinning ones on shelves around the room, even the painting of frogs cavorting on a meadow.

'May I borrow him?' Margaret said to Carla.

Larry followed her into the narrow kitchen where he noticed that even the sponge was held in the gaping mouth of a yellow frog.

First he brought in orange squash, and then a plate of tiny crustless white bread sandwiches filled with the thinnest fillings he'd ever seen. Then a tray of cookies and iced cake she pulled from plastic wrappings.

'You sit down now. He's been made to work.' She turned with a giggle to Carla who gave one of her fey smiles. No sign of the angry child now.

'Very nice, Margaret,' Rowena said, 'you always had a way with sandwiches.'

'Once you cut the crusts properly, the rest soon suits itself.' She caught sight of Carla slumped on the sofa cushions. 'You're not slimming? Not in my house dear. Have a Jaffa cake. I know they're your favorite. I asked Mother.'

'Actually I don't—'

'Carla had a tummy upset this morning,' Rowena said, 'she'll probably not be up to much.'

Margaret seemed not to see through this and looked genuinely concerned. 'What a shame. Our sea air is not for everyone. Don't you think?' She looked at Larry who had been nodding throughout her words, nodding to give reassurance to a kindly crazy old woman. He reminded himself of the bobbing head of the frog that sat beside him on the glass table.

Carla slumped further, her face full of bitterness.

'Mother's looking well.' Margaret turned to Carla.

'She always does,' Carla said, and Rowena blushed.

Larry poured the tea from a teapot which wore a blue sweater into flowered cups with fluted edges. Finally he was having the real experience of England in a room filled with flowered bulky cushioned sofas and armchairs. It was like having tea with a group of dressed-up matrons, the sort who appeared on the pages of his children's books, comfortable women with aproned laps like large verdant fields.

'I love having it here instead of the dining room. It's like a picnic.' Margaret held her teacup but did not drink or eat. She gazed benignly at each of her guests.

Rowena smiled back and seemed to wink at Larry. He knew he was doing well here and felt his heart swell with his own goodness. 'You are a mensch,' he heard his father say.

Only Carla could ruin it, the shadow slipped between blue and pink ruffled cushions, the cockroach in the corner. He tried not to look at her. If I want to be an American tourist, let me.

'Are you struggling?' Margaret said. Larry was trying to cut his cake and manage the teacup on his lap at the same time. 'You probably don't have tea like this where you come from.'

He knew where this would lead and searched for a detour. 'I like your frogs.' He didn't. Frogs gave him a queasy feeling.

She giggled. 'My son thinks I'm a bit off.'

'They're really something,' he said.

'You want to see the others?'

She took him back to the porch to see the minute glass frogs and the ones made of stone. Then they went upstairs to a room like a crowded bower. Everything was flowered: the wallpaper, the bedspread, the chairs. A large green and yellow stuffed frog lay across her bed and beanbag frogs stared from every chair and from atop the chest of drawers.

'You can pick him up,' she said, 'he won't bite.'

Larry held the stuffed frog, whose glass eyes gleamed at him.

'You like him? He's my naughty boy. Up to no good.'

Larry stared at her.

'When my grandchildren visit I bring them all downstairs to meet them. They love them.'

He wasn't sure who she was talking about anymore. The frogs, her grandchildren? He dropped the stuffed frog on the bed but it continued to give him a sinister look. He'd wandered into some demented fairy tale, and yet her face was guileless as a child.

'You must find us very peculiar here.'

He shook his head and blushed at his lie.

'I met an American boy once at a dance. I couldn't understand a word he said. I had to say "could you speak English please". He didn't like that one bit. It must be very difficult for you. Do you get homesick?'

There's no one like you there, he wanted to say to her upturned face.

'But then you have Carla. She's never brought a young man down before. You must be special.' She squeezed his hand. 'Isn't she lovely?'

'Why do you lie?'

He was stretched out in the bathtub but he heard Carla. She had come back from Margaret's with a headache. While she lay in the darkened bedroom, he and Rowena had played Scrabble. And then Rowena had insisted on running a bath for him. He had felt like a prince.

'Always. You could not live without your lies... Oh sure. That's what you would say. When Dad left you lied. Even then... No you didn't. You didn't.' She was shouting now. 'You just tried to cover up. It's always the same with you... I don't care. I really don't care. Let him hear.'

He could not hear what Rowena was saying back, but knew it could not temper Carla. What had happened to this silhouette of a woman who spoke only to herself? He slid down in the bath so that the water covered his ears.

In the darkness he felt her cold fingers on his face. They had made love once, but so quickly on one of the chill narrow beds that it may have been a dream. He thought she did not want to in her mother's house. He had tried to be sensitive, but now she was whispering they should creep downstairs.

'Why not here?' He pulled back the cover and made a motion towards her. 'Just tuck in.'

88

'I hate it. These puny beds. Like I'm in a nunnery. She always sends me up here to sleep. She makes me feel like a kid.'

'Come. You're so skinny. It's like having one and a half people.' He reached out to touch her bony waist and shivered.

'I always wanted to do it in the lounge.'

'But she's right next door.'

'We'll do it on the settee. That horror. She hangs on to it just because of Dad, to spite him even now. You know what he used to call the lounge? The dinosaurs' sitting room.'

Daddy's girl. At least she was somebody's daughter, her face in the reedy, uneasy looking man in the wedding portrait. He had left years ago for no reason, except, if you believe Carla, that he was bored.

'Carla, she'll hear. She's so close.'

'She'll never. She sleeps like the dead. Listen.'

Through the damp dark spaces he heard only the belch of the refrigerator. Then a low whistling sound like a defective kettle.

'That's her. Once she starts, you could do anything.'

'I can't. I can't do that to her.' He thought of Rowena removing the cloths on each of her pies. His grandma lifting the satin cover with the Star of David after she had blessed the challah bread on Shabbat. Rowena the righteous gentile.

'You're not doing anything to her. She won't even know.'

'She'll know. On some level she'll know. Look, I'm in her house. It's like... I don't know.'

'You don't know. And she won't either.'

'What's the point of this anyway?' He almost said, 'Why don't you grow up?' But wasn't he the boy? And yet.

A sigh. Carla let go of his hand. She went back to her own monk's bed under the slanting wall. Then in a whisper, 'Why don't you get in with her? She'll never know.'

In the morning Carla either pretended to sleep or was so deep in dreamland that none of his movements woke her. But Rowena was there waiting with her homemade jams, her bright smile. After breakfast they went to the only shop open in the village to get her a *Sunday Telegraph*.

'Shall we take a walk? I don't know if Carla showed you everything?'

Everything? He looked around at the drawn shutters of Helen's Hair Dreams, the dark windows of John's grocery and a storefront selling bungalows. A wind blew up from the sea and shook the bus sign where nobody waited. Beyond the row of stores was the flat grass of the cliff top and across the street, a line of modern flats and squat houses. How had Carla come from this blandness?

Rowena took him the other way, along a similar cliff top, telling him the story of Witherns, how there had once been big houses along the front which had been knocked down and turned into flats and bungalows for retired people. 'It's quiet now but during the war they had dances for the soldiers. We had our refugees too. They all lived in that house.' She pointed to a tall red brick building across from the cliff top. 'I used to play in the garden. We called it "gypsy house". I don't know why. They weren't gypsies.'

The house looked strange in the midst of the low bungalows like some awkward large child.

'Some of them still live there. You want to go in? They like having visitors. Of course they're all very old now.'

A brick archway beside the building led to a garden at the back where a tall gaunt old man bent over a patch of soil with a hoe. A woman with a flowered scarf around her head sat on a bench watching.

Rowena smiled at the man. 'I wanted to show our visitor your garden. He's from America.' He paused to stare at her. His beard looked as if it hadn't been cut since he left home.

'You came from Russia, didn't you? You've been here a long time.'

Again no answer, but a smile. The man had not been here long enough to learn English.

'I think she's Polish but I'm not sure because she only speaks her own language.'

The woman on the bench nodded to them but said nothing. She had a face he'd seen on ancient newsreels about the Second

90

World War: deep in the folds of her babushka were hooded eyes, narrow lips, probably no teeth. When the woman turned her dry lined face to stare at him, he thought 'Jew hater'.

'I used to see them around the village; they looked strange in their clothes.' She turned to him with a look of apology. 'You see we weren't used to foreigners. I thought they were so exotic. But now I never see them. I guess they're too old to go out much.'

'Why didn't they go back?'

'I don't know. Once they stayed here and saw how much better it was, they probably didn't want to go back. It must have been terrible where they came from.'

'You have a beautiful garden.' Rowena spoke loudly as if that might penetrate the man's incomprehension.

There was something about the garden which made him feel that he was no longer in the bland little town, something about the line of skinny bare trees which bound the garden from the bungalows of ordinary folk, the tall grasses beyond the plots of soil, the broken wall. Something which made him shiver.

The old Russian had resumed his digging. The woman got up and with an odd jerking movement began to walk towards the house. Larry thought he heard her say 'Goodbye.'

'Hello,' he murmured, 'hello, hello hello.' His heart filled with guilt.

'I think we disturbed them,' Rowena whispered. As if it mattered what she said. They were like extinct animals.

In the afternoon Larry sat in the sun lounge sipping tea with Rowena. They would have to go back to London in a few hours but Carla still hadn't come down. When he peeked in she was under a pillow doing her teenage act.

'I'm sorry to leave,' he said. It was true. He was not sure what he would miss: the pies, Rowena, the cups of tea, the idle talk. It did not matter what ridiculous comment he made, Rowena turned it into a conversation in which what he said was fascinating.

'Let's go to the beach.' Carla stood in the doorway. Did she never want to cover her arms?

91

'But it's started to rain.' So what if he sounded like a kvetch. He did not want to stir from his soft chair.

She raised her arms and glanced out the windows. 'Only spitting.'

Rowena sat ignored but smiled anyway. 'But darling, you haven't eaten anything. There's some cold chicken and—'

'Oh please. All you think about is food.'

Larry sipped at his tea and took another slice of lardy cake. It dripped with fat and syrup and even as he felt his veins clog he wanted to go on eating.

'Haven't you had enough tea?'

You're a killjoy, thought Larry. 'Okay so we'll go out. Okay already.'

They were sitting against the rocks watching the sea crawl towards them.

'She took you in there? I don't believe it.'

He was thinking that he preferred Carla when she wasn't listening to him.

'Our local colour. Don't believe her hard-luck stories. Most of them were white Russians who came because they hated the Communists. The refugee story is crap.'

'But what about the others? The Polish woman who looks like a peasant.'

'There was this tall Russian guy. He looked weird, like Tolstoi. But he was actually a pervert.'

'You mean the one—' He stopped. There could have been another tall Russian.

'Every time I'd walk by he had his prick out. Every time.'

'Did you tell your mother?'

'Do you ever tell your mother something like that? We called him the Russian sausage. He'd just stand there with this creepy smile and his thing dangling.'

Larry just couldn't let go of the man with his gentle demeanor. 'He was probably freaking out. He'd left his country. He couldn't speak any English. Maybe he didn't even know what he was doing.'

'The first one I ever saw. And it had to be his. He used to beckon with his bony finger. We just ran away laughing.'

She began bouncing stones off the boulders. 'My mother knew.'

He shook his head. 'C'mon. If she knew she would've done something.'

'Can't you see what she's like? How everything has to be smoothed over. I know she knew but she wanted to think how kind we were taking in refugees.'

'You really think your mother would cover up, collude even. With a flasher?' Poor Rowena.

'You're so naïve Larry.'

'But not all of them were perverts.' He was thinking of the Jew-hating Polish woman. She would simply put a stake through his heart.

'They weren't the real refugees were they? The real ones nobody wanted.'

She was not becoming serious? This troubled Larry. The one advantage she had for him, the one compensation for her bag of bones body and odd ideas was that she was, well, not exactly shallow, but a visitor who only barely spoke earth language. This could be difficult sometimes, but it meant he did not have to pretend that he thought deeply about matters which, had he thought about them, would depress him.

'You think maybe you're exaggerating?' he said.

'She always wins everyone over.' She spoke to herself. 'Should we have a paddle?' Before he could answer, she was pulling off her shoes and socks, rolling up her jeans.

He watched her walk over the stones and then into the greenish waters.

'You're crazy. It must be freezing,' he called out. She would not drag him in.

'No, it's just cold.' She turned and gave him one of her stretched-skin smiles. Forgiveness? Was this what the smile said? I forgive you for eating my mother's cakes.

93

He had no friends in that class anymore. He walked in just on the hour, no more hanging around exchanging pleasantries with Chin in the minutes before. He let his books drop loudly on the desk to alert the baby boys at the back, then gave them a look. He'd stopped smiling, though inside was another him who laughed at his stern face: 'Who're you kidding?' The face answered, maybe more sad than stern: 'I'm not kidding anyone, kidding's what got me in trouble in the first place.'

Sarah had said to him at the end of the last class, 'That's right, Mr Professor, they should respect you.' She clicked her tongue. 'Trouble is they have too much. Their mothers give and give. Never say, what you going to do for me?'

He avoided Sarah's approving eyes, the apologetic face of Chin, Omar's uncle smile. He looked into the space between the United Nations and the baby boys when he spoke, as if that middle distance of empty tables and chairs contained his real students.

Into the space came Joel, the lost boy with drooping forelock and bloodshot eyes. Why didn't he sit with his friends? But Larry did not comment on this or the kid's pallid face. He only observed that the class had started half an hour ago.

'I'm sorry. I've been wasted,' Joel said. An actual apology. Maybe the drugs had done major brain damage.

'I mean like I just couldn't get up.'

The boys at the back laughed. One of them called out, 'We told you he was out to lunch.' A loud whisper, 'He's so fucked up, I can't believe it.'

Joel turned. 'Shut up you assholes.'

Whistles from the back. 'Joel, you better watch it.'

'That's enough.' Larry felt almost like crying. 'You talk to me afterwards, Joel.'

'Ooh. You're in trouble.'

'Boys, be quiet.' Omar's deep voice stunned everyone. Something about a quiet man shouting. Had it come to this?

Suddenly he knew what he had to do, should have done long ago. 'You have to leave.' He spoke to the Americans but the boys gazed back still with triumph on their faces. They did not believe him.

'I mean all of you. You come back when you're ready to shut up and listen.'

They stared at him without moving, the grins gone from their faces, the petulance of spoiled little boys.

'Come on.'

Bobby spoke: 'You're not serious, Larry? Maybe you're just in a bad mood.' He looked almost concerned and Larry wanted to strike him.

'I said get out.'

Slowly, slowly they rose. They could not leave without knocking over someone's books. When the last of them was out the door the class heard an explosion of laughter in the hallway. He shut the door on them and when he returned, he saw Chin looking at him with fear. Or was it amazement?

'Joel, why don't you join us down here?'

Joel looked like he might refuse but then gathered himself and moved next to Omar. It was something.

'As I was saying.' But what was he saying?

Afterwards Joel lurched past with the rest of them.

'You all right?' Larry asked.

'Yeah. I'm okay, why shouldn't I be?'

'Because you look sick.'

'I'm just like spacey. You know?'

Should he pursue this? The kid was probably high on something. Only he did not look high. He looked like no one was home.

'No I don't, Joel. You'll need to tell me.'

'Like I was walking by the river and I thought which river? The Thames, the Mississippi? Was I in England or the States? Actually I've never even seen the Mississippi. It's just we were always having to spell it.'

'You're going to be all right?'

'Maybe. Maybe I need to go home and sleep.'

95

He turned away, then back again. 'Did you ever have an out of body experience? Like where your spirit takes a walk?'

'No, Joel. I'm saving that for my death.'

'It's like I'm here not here. You know what I mean?'

Larry shook his head. He was remembering his mother's favorite expression: 'It's neither here nor there.' This about a sofa or when he moved in with Talia.

High was not the right word for this floppy-haired kid with the vacant red eyes. He drank some potion that had not worked properly. Probably he should send him to the office before the kid took an overdose. But if he told Joel to see the Dean, his face would once again twist into a sneer, the 'teacher is nerd' look he could not bear, and he would rejoin the bad boys. Larry had kidnapped their mascot, would not return him till they behaved themselves.

'I'll see you when I see you,' Joel said.

'You mean next week to be exact.'

'Who knows?'

Joel swung past Kalifa, who waited at the door like some refugee.

'Can I speak now or do you—?'

'Now's okay. I'm just going up for my office hour.' He felt like an asshole saying this. What was he, some doctor? Nobody came to his office hours; he kept them for the phantoms who lived on the sulphurous top floor.

'I'm sorry if it's not good time.'

Kalifa was always sorry. Like bowing or saying 'you're welcome, don't mention it' when someone thanked you.

'You said about the other lawyers. Maybe you know someone who could help in my situation. It is always better to know someone. If you cannot I understand.'

Larry sighed. He knew no one who finagled Green Cards but Gershom.

'I'm sorry to stop you going home.'

'It's okay. I told you it's my office hour. I'd like to help you.'

'You see I really cannot go back. It's impossible. It's really. I cannot.' He actually touched Larry's arm and then withdrew his hand. The sorrys weren't real but this was.

Gershom could not hurt him, only waste his time and money and give him false hopes. Larry looked at Kalifa's gaunt Pharaoh face. He would not be fooled. If Gershom's words were empty, if all that was there was the fool, Kalifa would know to walk away.

'You know he does this? I mean I do not doubt you. My friend takes a course with him and I know he's very good.' Kalifa gave him a funny look when he mentioned Gershom Fish as if he began to wonder whether Larry was really someone he could trust. It takes a fool to know a fool. 'I'm not, I'm not like him,' Larry wanted to say.

'He's the only one I know in London who does Green Cards.'

'I'm sorry if I questioned. I've taken so much of your time, I'm sorry.' The sorry man, but I'm the sorry one.

Larry climbed the back stairs to his office. Nobody came up there but him and the cleaners. Not even ghosts. Only ghosts of ghosts, dead wisps like the wings of moths.

Metal desk, walls of porous white, the high window with its muddy sky. He had left nothing of himself here; even after a year he could think of no reason to decorate the walls. 'You love to feel sorry for yourself,' Talia used to say, 'poor little boy.'

He stood by the window. Yes, one room was like another. What did it matter? In a few days he would sail to the island of weekend where he could live for days with pleasantries. He thought of Rowena's Saturday: a coffee morning with arthritic women, an hour arranging flowers in the church, tea with Margaret among the frogs, several hours of serious pie making.

'I'm retreating,' Carla had said. All weekend she was staying in some converted almshouse where she wasn't supposed to talk or make eye contact. She could be herself and nobody would find it strange.

'You're allowed to eat but everything has to be round,' she said, 'so you don't think about ends.'

97

Larry imagined long tables with oranges, eggs and melons all lit from within like they were radioactive. Maybe that's what ailed her.

'I'd invite you but they're full up. People book years in advance.'

'Don't worry,' he said, 'I'll have my own personal retreat.'

'It's what I need after a weekend home. I always have to purge myself.'

But what if it was him she was retreating from?

Only halfway into his office hour but he was going. If he took the back stairs, the body dump, he would meet no one, no needy students, no grinning Dean his loins probably sated on American girls, no one to see his crestfallen face. What was Carla to him? It wasn't love, his father would say.

Down at the bottom of the staircase, a head moved. The Gershom dog: a draggy walk, tongue lolling out of rubber lips. But he did not have his usual pleased with himself look.

'You rushing off?' Gershom asked, 'because I wouldn't mind a drink. I feel like shit.'

Larry said nothing. His hand remained on the banister, his feet poised for escape.

'Just a quickie. Please Larry, you may be preventing a potential suicide.'

Larry went to the bar once in his first year when he still regarded his students as chums. It was a low windowless room down in the basement with brilliant white walls, grey vinyl floors and round Formica tables. Once, bodies had been wheeled down there and kept overnight until burial. The students called it 'the morgue', but its real name blazed across the top of the serving hatch: 'The Melting Pot'.

The metal grille was just going up as they arrived. Gershom pushed his way into a group of students and arrived back with two large beers. 'Should we stand like the Brits?'

'Sure,' Larry said. If they stood it was easier to get away. But Gershom ignored him and placed the two beers on one of the tables.

'I never understand. Why do they like being uncomfortable? Have you noticed in every situation they'll choose the unhappy option?'

'Don't you think you're generalizing?'

'Maybe. Maybe I'm just overreacting. You know what it's like.'

Why did people always assume he understood when he didn't? He drank from the mug and kept silent. Let Gershom talk out whatever was inside him; let him talk it out without interruption until he had nothing left. But of course there was always something.

'My wife's giving me shit. She's talking about moving back to Wales with my kid.'

Larry remembered the kid. He thought Gershom had lucked out but all he said was, 'That's too bad. I thought you had an amicable arrangement.'

'We did. I got her alternate weekends, some holidays. We were just separating for a while. To get our heads together. But now she's shutting the door.'

'You've got rights.'

'You think it's that easy? I want to get back with her. This whole thing wasn't my idea. She needed a breather, okay, but now. She wants to go home. Which incidentally is bullshit because she hasn't lived there since she was in diapers. If she goes, I can't handle it. I just can't.'

He thought Gershom might cry. Not here, not with me. Instead he spilled beer down the front of his food-stained shirt.

'Shit. Just look at me. My karma.'

'Talk to her.'

'I've been talking. She says Shayna needs a real identity. Something solid. Not some Jewish-American half-breed. But she's got both of us inside doesn't she?'

Larry thought of the ugly little girl on his shoulder, her face smeared with throw-up. 'She looks like you.'

'Thanks,' Gershom said.

Was this a real thanks or had he actually cottoned on to Larry? Gershom, who seemed the blindest of men, who could

99

stare into an abyss and see only his grinning face, could sometimes find the hidden pictures.

'I'm putting a lot on you. I was just feeling like I couldn't go home.'

Larry nodded. Home was where he wanted to be, not in this beery bunker listening to a potbellied dog howl.

Gershom rubbed the corners of his eyes. 'So how are you these days?'

'Okay I guess.'

'You don't give much away, Larry. How's your girlie-friend?'

Larry shrugged.

Gershom grinned at him. 'If you're free, remember the Un-Americans. We're meeting every Saturday now. People remember you. They've been asking where you went to.'

His father would say to Gershom: 'You're walking knee deep in it, knee deep.' He said, 'C'mon, Gershom, I was hardly there.'

'Really. You made an impression.'

Larry sighed.

'Devorah asked after you. Remember her?'

Bedroom eyes full of hate.

'You doing anything Thanksgiving?'

Gershom took him by surprise and he shook his head, then tried to cover his tracks. 'I don't plan that far ahead. I could be busy, who knows?'

'So you're free to come? That's great. We're planning a special dinner. Everyone's bringing something I guess.'

'What's the point?' Larry said with a bitterness he hadn't intended. 'We're not home are we? Thanksgiving's a sham here.'

'You sound like my ex-wife. She was the most dreary Irishwoman I've ever met.'

'You said she was Welsh.'

'No, this is the one before.'

'You have two ex-wives?' Two women in possession of their minds had given themselves to him.

100

'I'm a serial marryer. Anyway Larry.' Gershom held out his arms as if he expected Larry to run to him. 'You have an open invitation to Thanksgiving dinner. We're having it the Saturday after the Thursday. You know the date. You haven't forgotten your roots really.'

'I hate Thanksgiving,' Larry said, looking straight into his reddish face and seeing a look of amusement. 'I hate it.'

'Don't we all, Larry?' Gershom patted him on the back.

'Why do you need me? There're a million Americans in London. Why me?'

'I don't know a million Americans.' Then with a sly look as if he only pretended to be a jerk. 'You're normal, Larry. A normal American is like gold dust in these parts.'

I do, I do, I do hate it. Larry thought of the wet slap of the cranberry sauce as it slipped from its can into the bowl. The sweet potatoes with their yellow crust of marshmallows. The dry bird still strutting at the centre of the table. His normally cheerful father poured his wife's thin gravy over his food and talked about the death of the year. Once when he was a kid, he couldn't remember how old, but old enough to hope, his father tried to convince his mother to go out for Thanksgiving dinner, but she felt shamed by the other mothers: 'I gotta be busy like them.'

It was pre-rush hour in Wimbledon, a languorous almost warm air blew over the station. A group of schoolgirls all in identical blue blazers and skirts appeared in a rush of noise then disappeared down onto the District Line platform.

He could have a Wimbledon weekend: Friday night listening to the refrigerator concert, Saturday morning small-talking the dry cleaner, Sunday all day watching the sky from his bed like he was practicing for death. There was nothing to stop him. He could just go along to the Un-Americans on Saturday without committing himself to Thanksgiving.

He could see him a block away, the tall gaunt man, the pedestrian walking fast as usual, head bobbing above the others.

So fast when all he would do was walk to the end of that street, turn around and walk back. Larry watched him once from the doorway of a newsagent. Over and over, but each time as if it were the first, each time as if he were desperate to reach his end.

Now he drew close, the usual smile on his tormented face, thinner perhaps, all cheekbones and shadowed eyes, jacket beginning to shine. His shoes, Larry suddenly noticed, were of course white sneakers. 'Running shoes,' Larry whispered as the man strode past. 'I'll call you "running shoes".' Like some lost American Indian.

CHAPTER 12

The dog was at the door again, tongue caressing Larry's fingers. 'You remember me?' Larry touched the top of his old head. He didn't really like dogs, though he had lived with one for a year after one of his girlfriends brought home a stray, a short mongrel traumatized to silence by life in the streets. He had a large white face, wide spacey eyes and perpetual worms. She called him 'Orphan' but it became clear to Larry who really wore that name.

Deep inside he heard the Un-Americans, those refugees. Was he not one, a stray American parched as a cowboy? He had tried Friday night out in the local hot spots. The first was a wine bar called 'Wimbles' where everyone wore tank tops and he was the oldest and hairiest person. He walked up to Wimbledon village in search of something more classy, stepped in horseshit before entering a pub of twosomes, threesomes and foursomes. Me lonesome. He leaned against an antique bellows and discreetly wiped his feet, but the suited backs shaking with laughter did not turn or even notice him.

They were gathered in the living room. On the sofa he recognized the two elderly men in conversation, the peevish cravat and Fred McMurray with a hearing aid. What was that smell, like a hundred derelicts had relieved themselves? He did not see the old youth with his yellow grin and grey corkscrews. The Martian was sitting on the arm of the sofa; without her antennae she seemed almost normal except she stared right through him as if she were watching a film in the wall behind him. A bad film, he could tell by the grimace on her face, but she couldn't take her eyes off it. On the other arm sat Devorah: 'Welcome back,' she said with what looked like a sneer. As he moved towards her he stumbled and fell over a child.

'There you go again.' As he picked himself up he saw Gershom lift his daughter. Beneath her was a pool of pale yellow. 'She's training,' Gershom said. The little girl, whose face had grown larger and more grotesque since he last saw her, looked down at her pee with something like pride.

'So you're back with us?' Gershom said. And in a whisper which everyone could hear: 'Didn't she work out? Your girlie-friend?' Then to his daughter, 'Next time in the potty. Let's go clean you up.' The girl began to cry and Gershom could be heard comforting her. 'No, no, your pee-pee is very good.'

Larry didn't answer him. He was too busy looking on the floor for a dry spot. There were no free chairs.

Devorah watched him. 'Don't bother, there's pee everywhere. You either stand or sit in it.'

'Come sit with me. I won't bite.' Edie, the kind old woman with nimble fingers. She patted the big old armchair. Larry sat on an arm. He was trying to breathe without smelling.

'We missed you,' Edie said. 'We don't have enough of your kind.'

She grinned at him and mouthed the words 'young men'. 'Now you'll have to tell me your name again.'

'Larry, wasn't it? Larry the lawyer,' Devorah said.

'You see I'm cramming so much into my head nowadays I don't have a place for names...You're from California.'

'He's from beantown.' Again Devorah. So maybe she had noticed him.

'You see I should tell you I'm writing a novel,' said Edie, 'a Victorian romance. There's a heroine and then about a million characters and I have to describe their clothes and manors. It's so complicated I don't have room up here for much else.'

'But why?' Larry began.

'Why write a novel? Because it's going to be a best-seller. I'm having fun with it. I spent five pages just getting her out of bed. Another five she's in bed again, but not her bed. I just don't know where to go next. I can't really let her be seduced because then it's all over.'

'I mean why set it in Victorian times? It must be hard.'

'I get to describe all her clothes. I've been researching at the Victoria and Albert. They wore such complicated underwear you could spend five pages just getting off her slip. It's all sex these days. I find it so boring.'

Gershom returned holding the child's hand. She was still bare bottomed.

'Can't we have a break while we're eating?' Edie said.

'It smells to high heaven in here.' The peevish man in the cravat. Then in an undertone to Fred McMurray: 'Why doesn't he just stick her in the bathroom and lock the door.'

Devorah said, 'You could put a diaper on her.'

'Then she'd get the wrong idea,' Gershom said.

'She won't, she'll be fine.' Devorah gave Larry a wink.

'Okay, if that's the consensus.'

He diapered the child on the floor in front of the sofa. The peevish man averted his face from the spectacle.

Edie went on as if nothing were happening. 'I'm taking three courses. I'm reading five books at once, so how can I remember?'

'Just take it one at a time,' Devorah said.

'But you see I've got to make up all those years. If I'm going to be a writer.' Then turning her face up to Larry, 'I never went beyond high school. Never read anything. I'm an ignoramus.'

'Talk less, Edie,' said the peevish cravat man. 'That's the answer. Talk less and write more.'

This silenced Edie for a moment. Then she said, 'I know. I know I'm a chatterbox. I'm taking a course in listening. But it goes against the grain.'

'Don't you think Americans like to talk about themselves,' Larry said. 'We're a garrulous bunch.'

'You're my defender. But I'm hardly an American anymore. I've lived here for forty years. I even married one of them.'

Gershom stood the little girl up. 'Before she shits on herself, I think we should eat.'

There were newcomers to the group: a New York lawyer who wore an English accent over her Manhattan drawl and a tense, red-faced professor from Ann Arbor who spent six months of every year with his lover in London.

'Maybe that's the way,' Larry thought. Always halfway across the Atlantic. Half-assed his father would say.

Ralph, the peevish man with the cravat, was a prep school English teacher who came over in the 1950s because, as he said, he had to leave or 'they' would get him. His Fred McMurray friend, whose face when seen up close was even larger and lozenge-like, turned out to be a genial mid-westerner named Clark. He arrived in London after college for a European tour and never left.

Larry sat between Edie and Devorah eating everyone else's pot luck. 'I feel like a freeloader,' he said.

'Just eat, Larry,' Edie said. 'We're sharing your company.'

Gershom paused from spooning yellow muck into his daughter's mouth. 'Want to redeem yourself? Bring the turkey to our Thanksgiving dinner.'

'I'm not sure I'll be there.' He trailed off.

'Just kidding.'

Devorah grinned at him. She was larger than he remembered, rounder, truly a Rubens woman but with cropped hair and olive skin, eyes always half closed. Did she do it on purpose, the low steady stare? She was adorable if only she'd stop laughing at him.

The Martian woman whose name he had managed to forget was arguing for a vegetarian meal. 'Turkey's such a symbol,' she said, 'like a burnt offering to God. It's as if we're blessing the Puritans for the rape of the land.' Larry looked over at Gershom who was nodding at all of this. The Martian continued to speak as if to nobody: 'Turkey's a symbol of the type of proto-fascism which America represents so why collude?'

Ralph interrupted: 'If this means nut roasts and soya beans, I'm not coming.'

'It won't be Thanksgiving, will it?' Edie said. 'That's why we're all here because we miss it, all of it. I get so lonely thinking about who I am and where I've been.'

'You know what to do,' Ralph said, 'you've been here long enough. They'll make you a citizen. I did it five years ago. I became one of them.'

'But you never are. Not to them.'

'Who's them?' Devorah asked. 'You talk like they're aliens.'

'No, we're the aliens,' Larry said.

'Speak for yourself.' Devorah gave him one of her looks like he had been X-rayed and found to be missing an essential organ.

Edie patted Larry. 'I know how you feel. At the beginning I was like that. Then I stopped caring, like a nerve was cut. But that took years.'

Gershom wiped his daughter's face and gave her a wooden spoon to play with. Then he addressed the table, and Larry could see how he held it together, how his reddish eyes in that nest of hair missed nothing. 'So we'll have the turkey.'

Heads nodded. The Martian woman opened her mouth and then changed her mind and said nothing. Clark smiled his long-headed western smile and said: 'I'm such a slow eater I leave the talking to everyone else.' It was not clear whether he had heard any of the conversation.

Gershom began assigning each of them a food. When Larry couldn't say whether he could come or not, Devorah poked him: 'Don't be so wishy-washy. Of course you're coming.' Then to Gershom: 'He can bring apple pie. It's just so him.'

Ralph and Clark were going to make a pumpkin pie, and Edie offered chestnuts and candied sweet potatoes.

'Just bring the chestnuts, Edie,' Gershom said. He winked at Larry.

The Martian had decided that she would come, but with a salad.

'Who eats salad on Thanksgiving?' Ralph's aside to Clark, but heard by all.

'Graham would,' Edie said.

'But we're not inviting Graham are we?' Devorah said.

Who was Graham, Larry wondered, that he should be so honoured?

'A sad man. Really you have to say.' Gershom began.

'Every demo we got stuck with him. Me and Edie. Last time I thought I was going to throw up from the smell of him.'

It was then that Larry remembered from his first visit with the refugees, the old youth of hectic teeth and wild words, the one Englishman.

'Graham left us,' Gershom explained to Larry. 'He was in the wrong group. He thought he could belong with us, but actually—'

'He was a mental case,' said Ralph.

'He scared me,' Edie said, 'and it wasn't funny.'

Gershom shrugged. 'The group is fluid, people come in when they need to.'

Larry grew impatient with Gershom's singsong spiel: 'You mean you told him to leave?'

'He disappeared, him and the clothes he lived and slept in,' said Devorah.

Gershom's daughter had manoeuvred herself from her perch on several pillows and stuck her spoon into a large bowl of what looked like chocolate mousse. 'That's for everyone, not just you, Shayna.' Gershom stroked her head.

'It was for everyone.' Devorah under her breath.

Then Gershom said: 'I think he was off the streets you know, and all that stuff about old people was bullshit. So he could feel part of us. Purposeful.'

Is that what we are? Larry looked around. Only the child knew what she wanted.

They left in pairs and singles, gradually, as if they were some secret cell watched and preyed upon, not a group of sad-eyed Americans. Larry waited around, waiting for what? For Devorah of course, adorable Devorah.

Clark and Ralph went first in a minicab. Then the Martian rose abruptly, looking around as if for dry land. Gershom said, 'Hey, you don't have to leave now. You can help with the dishes.' She seemed not to hear this. She spoke, but only to herself, 'If I don't leave now when can I leave?' and pushed her way through the living room as if it were crowded with people.

'What's her problem?' Larry asked.

'Not everyone can be a smiley boy, Larry. She got stranded. She came here a million years ago on a Rhodes to do her

108

doctorate and she's still doing it. Only there's no money left. So she gets depressed.'

'She's always like that,' Devorah said. 'Someone should send her home.'

'She can't leave. Not till she's finished and she never will. Every morning she looks at what she did the day before and crosses it out. Every day she's beginning again.'

'That's really sad,' said Larry

But Gershom turned his back on Larry and wandered into the kitchen. 'Edie, you're not doing it all?'

Devorah actually smiled at Larry and he followed her in, even picked up a dishcloth and stood waiting for instruction. He would stay as long as she stayed. Gershom lounged in the doorway, his daughter climbing up his legs.

'I saw your student,' he said.

Larry had to think a little. 'Oh you mean—'

'The Egyptian. He's a nice guy. But—'

'You can't do anything?' This was a relief for he did not want Gershom tampering with Kalifa. Even if he could do something, especially then. He wanted Kalifa to remain pure.

'I don't know. He doesn't just want a visa. He says he's never returning home.'

Larry nodded but wondered why Kalifa had never said this to him. Maybe he had fallen for Gershom's spiel and really believed he could become an American.

'That's tragic,' said Edie. 'Imagine feeling that about your own country.'

'You never returned,' Devorah said.

'I meant to.'

As they walked together down Kentish Town Road, Devorah in her long ancient fur coat wheeling her bike, Edie with her worn Marks and Spencer bags, he remembered going home in the dark from the playground, he and his best friend Harvey talking about the friends who left them.

The Martian had been a spectre in the group from the beginning. She talked only to Gershom, and only when no

109

one else was around. Devorah thought her doctorate was in something like 'transmutations and gender'.

'But I can't understand it,' said Edie. 'She doesn't like women. Not us anyway.'

Ralph and Clark seemed a couple, but no one was sure. 'You can never tell,' said Edie. 'I once spent a year in a creative writing course with a woman who had been a man. Clark is so sweet. What's he doing with that sourpuss?'

When they reached her bus stop, Edie said, 'Don't bother waiting. It can take forever. I'm used to it. I think up my plots at the bus stop. Writers call it empty time.'

Larry would not have left his own mother there in the dark where the only normal person waiting was a woman with green hair. But Edie turned her small face resolutely to the traffic which streamed towards her like a school of glowing fish.

'She's a tough old lady,' Devorah said when they turned away.

'Tough is not what I'd call her. She's sweet. A sweet little old lady.' He looked at Devorah. 'Why not?'

'She drives me crazy. Haven't you noticed, she's a non-stop talker?'

He thought maybe Devorah was not his type after all.

'I'll have to leave you here.' They were across from the tube where a man was speaking to a small group whose faces were upturned and lit by a torch. He pointed to the book he cradled in one arm and said: 'Look no further for your soul.'

'Can I see you again?' That sounded pathetic but the look she gave him made him chilly and hot at the same time.

'Don't you feel like you're not supposed to date in the group? Like we're in therapy together. You know what I mean?'

He wanted to say that the only reason he put up with Gershom's face and his smelly child was to find her. But he said, 'I'm sure no one will mind.'

'They will you know. Gershom is weird about that.'

'So we'll keep mum.'

Then she was laughing at him again. 'Larry lawyer. I don't even know your last name.'

110

'I don't know yours. Does it matter?'

'Listen Larry lawyer, I've got dance classes all this week, so I don't know when. Should I call you?'

He nodded. This was usually a prelude to nothing. They never called, said they lost his number, forgot his name.

'It's just at the moment, dance comes first.' She took out her phone and tapped his name and number in.

'Greenberg. Larry Greenberg in Wimbledon. There's only one of me there.'

She kissed him on the cheek and he could smell soap and old animal fur. He watched her mount the bike in her long coat. He thought, 'bear on a bicycle'. She turned on her light and as she rode off he heard her shout, 'Bye Greenie.'

He hadn't thought of Carla the whole time, but now he imagined her rising above them like some startled fairy.

CHAPTER 13

'I'll come there,' Carla said.

When she called on the Wednesday after she returned, he felt uneasy during the whole of the conversation. He hadn't done anything with Devorah. She was what he was used to, his own kind, that was all.

'You must be kidding. A whole weekend in Wimbledon.'

'I love your apartment. The rooms are so nothing,' she said.

'Thanks.'

'For me it's like going on a holiday coming down there.'

At least she sounded happy. In Wimbledon she'd forget about bondage. The dullness would be enough of a frisson for her. And Devorah hadn't called. Those ladies of the left were too busy righting the world to do right by him.

Carla arrived late on Friday with a soft overnight bag and a large black portfolio.

'You moving in?' he asked and was surprised to see hurt on her face. Maybe the retreat had changed her. He imagined a Gentile Yom Kippur with Carla fasting and flagellating herself. 'And I will put a new heart in you,' God promised on that day of Jews swaying with hunger. Maybe someone had.

He woke with the sun striking his face.

'Don't move,' she said.

She'd pulled back the curtains and was sitting naked on the floor beside him sketching. He shut his eyes. He had thought of them waking together, then going out for breakfast just like he did Saturday mornings back in the time of Talia: onion bagels and a fermenting smell from all the sated couples.

'You want me to open my eyes?'

'Just don't move.'

'I thought you only drew insides.'

'Your talking's ruining everything.'

He fell asleep to the sound of her pencil. When he woke again, the room was empty. Had she ever been there? He

112

wandered down the hall in his pyjamas looking in rooms but no her, no sound of a living creature. Then he found her dressed in the kitchen.

'Let's go somewhere,' she said.

'What about breakfast?'

'Let's just go. I'm not hungry.'

For once he ignored her. He put some water on for coffee, pulled out the Rice Krispies and two slices of brown bread. She shook her head to everything he offered except coffee.

'You should eat.'

'You and my mother.'

'You should in the morning. You need to boost the blood sugar. Otherwise you slump.' This he learned from Talia who ate huge farm worker breakfasts: cereal, three eggs over easy, toast, home fries and a glass of some milk and brewer's yeast concoction called 'pep-up' which she needed like a hole in the head.

'I like that hungry dizzy feeling,' Carla said and for once he thought she was joshing him.

She watched him eat Rice Krispies. 'Okay. I'll have some of that.'

'Don't do me any favors,' he said. But he shook the cereal into a bowl, then started to pour in the milk. She grabbed his hand. 'I hate milk so much.'

'You eat it dry? I've never seen anyone—' He'd watched his father eat herrings in cream sauce for breakfast, but this was something else.

'I like the crunch. It's like eating snow crystals. And then there's the sugar rush.' She gave him a smile, the second one he'd had in the space of five minutes. What was with her?

'She likes you,' a voice whispered. He felt uncomfortable with her, not the usual reaching for thin air, but as if she suddenly grasped him and would not let go.

He spoke gruffly: 'So where do you want to go?'

'They gave us this book of walks. Let me just get it.' She was off her chair before he could say anything.

113

He took it from her, a sky blue leaflet unfolding like a row of paper dolls. *Endless Walks.*

'It's not what you think. They're all circular so you don't retrace your steps. You begin where you end.'

The last time he'd been on a walk in England was with some group called 'The Ramblers'. From the name he had imagined an easy-going stroll through the woods with the sun glinting, a bucolic day. But these walkers in gaiters and hiking boots were like gnarled soldiers, their leader a stern-faced old woman with a map and compass hanging from her neck, a pole in each hand. They never noticed that he had stopped to retrieve his loafer from some cow dung. He'd be there still, crying like lost Hansel, if a farmer hadn't come by on his tractor.

But he was reassured by the leaflet's soothing words. It described the walks as easy, a few miles through gentle country, what he had had in mind for a ramble.

'There's some not far from here, down in Surrey,' she said.

He was nodding but ignoring her. For once he would choose the way.

They had to take a train and then a little bus and soon they were walking through half-naked woods.

'I like November,' she said. 'Just the bareness of it. You see so much better what things are.'

He picked up a sad orange leaf. He was remembering the loud foliage of Massachusetts in the fall, the hectic apples, maple trees like burning bushes in the last sun. The best would be over by now.

They walked on in silence till they had to climb up a stile. He went first and helped her, though she said, 'I'm okay.' She wasn't. She'd worn ridiculous shoes, espadrilles which kept falling off.

They ate their lunch near a fast-running stream which he had seen gleaming through the woods as they walked. She kept to her retreat diet of spheres and balls: boiled eggs, grapes and oranges. He ate a tuna fish sandwich and a banana, while she pretended to avert her eyes.

'They said it takes weeks to wear off, the pureness.'

He said nothing about the Rice Krispies. Perhaps they were in the realm of round. He wondered if he liked her better this way than the sullen girl at her mother's.

'I feel a little spacey from it. Like sometimes I'm in two places at once or even coasting above it.'

'You sound like Joel, my out-of-world student.'

When he told her about the lost American kid with the fallen forelock, she said, 'He shouldn't be afraid to feel lost.'

'So what'll I tell him? "Joel, just continue taking the drugs. Make friends with your hallucinations."'

'Don't tell him anything. He finds the way,' she said.

'He should go home. They all should go home.'

'What about you?' she asked.

'What about me?'

The bleakness of this was too much for him. Larry stood up and walked to the edge of the stream. He poked a branch into a dusty leaf and threw it in. 'Gentle, gentle,' his father said. 'You upset it that way.'

Larry turned back to her: 'You wanna sail something?'

They made boats out of twigs, dead leaves and pieces of rotten bark she scraped from a tree and sent them down, one after the other, only stopping to free those caught by a rock. Once he looked up to see a horse staring from across the stream. He didn't know how long they had been there when he felt a change in the air, the smell of night. 'We gotta go on,' he said.

They came to another stile. He was beginning to like these steps to nowhere, like Jacob's ladder but no angel waited. A muddy path led out of the woods to a hill he hoped would be the beginning of their return, unless like Carla you did not believe in ends. She kept losing her espadrilles, so they climbed slowly through rusty ferns. And then the path twisted, dropped down again and went into a forest of gloomy Christmas trees and pines. He looked again at his map. What happened to the lake?

'Don't think about it,' she said.

'I wanna get out of here,' he wailed.

He had never hated pine trees till now, their dark stares, the way they stood crowded together against him. He longed for a stile, a ladder even, from which he would be plucked to heaven.

He walked fast, looking at the ground, so the gate seemed to appear out of nowhere. He pushed at it, but something was stuck or maybe they could never reach the other side. He pushed and pushed, until Carla came up and showed him the way to open it using a latch he hadn't noticed.

They'd entered a field of bare, skinny trees with headdresses of light, when he heard an eerie sound like crying. Maybe he had mountain fever, forest fever, fear of the unclaimed. As they walked towards the brightness, the sound grew louder, and he began to shiver. 'What is it?' he had to shout over the cries. But she had taken off her espadrilles and was running ahead of him. He ran after her into the opening. They were flying above the lake, then dropping down to coast in the smooth waters. Around and around, he grew dizzy looking up at them.

'They're coming home,' she said.

She stretched out on the grass to watch them circle. Geese, swans, who knows what? He started to say that they should go on quickly because of the night, but he lay down beside her. Before the birds appeared he had imagined a field of a million babies with their mouths open. He took her hand. They were like lost children who had only each other.

She stayed on through Sunday. The rain kept them indoors. He marked papers, while she sketched and wandered through the rooms. He was getting used to her, could imagine coming home and finding her there still. She took up so little space.

They were standing in the kitchen on Sunday night talking about going out to dinner when the phone started up. This was rare for him, someone actually calling. His mother had still not mastered the overseas code, and everyone else expected him to do the phoning.

'Greenie?' He knew that voice.

'See, I said I would call. You sound funny.' When he realized it was Devorah he stood up, sat down, stood up again.

'Why're you whispering?' she asked.

'I'm not.'

'Who's there?'

'No one.'

'Look, I'm booked up this coming week. I just got asked to an audition. I'm really excited.'

'Great.'

'What is it with you? These one word answers.' Devorah's voice sounded so loud he was sure Carla could hear, but she seemed to be reading her sketchbook.

'Larry? You there?'

'Sure, I'm listening.'

'Maybe I shouldn've called. You sound occupied. What are you doing right now?'

'Nothing really.'

'You're whispering again.'

'I got a sore throat.' He regretted his words immediately. Carla put down the sketchbook and sat staring beyond him with a peculiar smile on her face.

'Listen, I'll call you again when I know I'm free,' Devorah said.

Carla walked out of the room and down the hall. He heard a door slam.

'What was that?'

'Just someone slamming a door somewhere in the building. The walls are so thin you can hear swallowing.'

'Prevaricator,' Talia screamed at him.

'Adultery is never fun,' his father used to say, 'because you can't kiss in public.'

But this wasn't that. These women were like incomplete packs of cards; only by mixing them, could you play a game.

'So I'll hear from you in this life?' he said.

'What happened to your sore throat?'

He shrugged.

'You still there? Larry?'

She was beginning to sound like Talia. It wasn't that he minded her hectoring, just that now he was used to being ignored.

117

'You cured it,' he said.

'What?'

'Forget it. Just forget it. So I'll hear from you.'

He found Carla in the little room where he stored books. She sat cross-legged on the floor staring out the single window at the rain, still wearing that smile. She had it all through dinner and when they went to bed. Even in the dark he could see it, the smile of the betrayed.

CHAPTER 14

He should have stayed home. From the moment the anxious smiler paused in his stride up and down the sidewalk to stare at Larry, he knew the omens were not good. He did not just stare, but stood still for once, blocking Larry. Larry mumbled 'Excuse me,' said it again when the man did not move. He came so close Larry could touch him, could smell his parched skin, his sad odour of dead leaves and exhaust; only in his eyes was he not a ghost, his dark eyes of an eternal refugee. 'Take me from limbo,' the eyes said, 'take me from my whirling brain and set me among the multitudes.' And then, as if he had seen something in the beyond he had always been looking at, he walked off, catching his own stride.

On the train Larry was crushed against a woman who tried to move so that no part of her was touching him. Then his briefcase snapped open. Never before in all the years since high school had it failed him. When he tried to shut it, his ass brushed against the woman, who made loud disapproving noises with her mouth. The briefcase would not shut, so he lifted it up and clutched it to his chest.

'I'll have to get a new one,' he said, 'I've had this forever.' Nobody around him seemed to have heard. The woman had successfully turned her back on him.

Students loitering on the steps leading up to the heavy doors of Eureka, stared at him as he climbed up holding his briefcase in his arms. He thought he heard someone say, 'There goes goofy Greenberg.' Maybe they had said goon or good or god. Maybe Greenberg was in his head, what they said had only to do with their little affairs.

He felt small before the great oak doors, pulling at the large round knob with his one free hand like a child trying for the first time to enter his parents' room without their help. Inside, the large central hall made him think of some court with students in groups like plotting courtiers, the occasional lecturer walking fast to avoid them.

His first class was not for half an hour, time to drop the broken briefcase in his office and gather himself. He saw and then looked away from the Dean peeping out of his office like some malevolent fairy-tale creature. Gershom had told him that the Dean was really a tragic figure who had once been head of a physics department at a real university until he'd fallen for one of his students, a young Englishwoman. He left his wife and baby, picked up his present job so he could follow his lover to London. But the student had turned from him once she smelled the damp air of her native land. No one would take him back, not his wife, not his university.

'He's the original nowhere man.'

'Why'd he do it?' Larry had asked.

'He told me, "I was bewitched".'

Maybe he still was, she had turned him into a lizard.

'Larry.' He heard just as he had travelled beyond the Dean's office. 'A word please.' Vague smile. The Dean even put a hand on his shoulder as he led him beyond his little corridor waiting room to his office. Had he guessed that Gershom had told him about his fractured life? He even said 'How are you, Larry?' A preface for once. But Larry's dim answer floated away from him and became lost in the folds of the Dean's lizard neck.

'You know that student you were worried about?' Then, impatient when Larry looked confused, 'Joel Schwarz. In your American Law class.' Spacey, surly Joel, Joel of the forever forelock.

'What happened? He's not—'

For a moment Larry imagined the kid stretched out in some drug den, skinny arms pocked with needle marks. Larry had only smoked marijuana once at a party where a joint was passed around like a wine bottle. Later he saw people slouched and sleepy or munching from cereal boxes. A girl painted her fingers with alternate layers of peanut butter and cream cheese and sighed as she licked her hands. He wanted to talk and talk, but there was no one. All the others, including his date, a physical education student from Des Moines called Mary Ann, nodded their heads to some hidden beat in the noise coming out

120

of the stereo. He had so many words that if he did not speak his head might explode, so when he talked to the girl with the peanut butter and cream cheese fingers, he did not care that she said nothing back but only continued to lick and sigh.

'He phoned home and told his mother something about not knowing where he was and being afraid to go out. He didn't know if he was in his own body anymore. Sounds like a classic breakdown. Were you aware that he was hallucinating?'

Larry did one shrug and then another. 'He looked out of it sometimes but then they all do. I thought. I assumed.'

'Drugs. I know. He's taken some. So his roommates say. Maybe quite a lot. But the point is he's gone AWOL. Just disappeared from the screen.'

'Don't get slick with me,' Larry wanted to say.

'If he comes to your class, he has to see me. Right away. You understand me? Don't let him out of your clutches.'

'You really think he'll turn up? Just like that?'

'Maybe not. But his parents, you can imagine. They're ready to get on a plane. We're *in loco parentis*, which means anything happens to him, we're the fall guys.'

'So we're covering our backs.'

'Listen Larry.' The Dean's leathery face looked tired. Larry tried to imagine him lovesick over an English girl, one of those clammy ones with long matted hair, a look like she hadn't eaten a piece of fruit for decades. 'I had to identify a dead student once. I don't want to do it again.'

'Poor Joel.'

'Poor us. His father practically owns the school. Well, Joel will turn up. They always do.'

'Except when they're dead.'

'Even then.'

The Dean's manner had returned to reptile. Larry backed out of his office clutching his broken briefcase.

He headed up the back stairs to his own office, passing on his way Bobby O'Brien who, with cringing manner, if anyone that big and shiny can be said to cringe, asked if he and the others could come back to the class. A victory. Yet Larry had

121

hoped they would disappear forever. He said they had all missed going to his class. 'Really,' Bobby insisted, almost doffing his baseball cap.

It had been so nice without them. Nobody laughed except when he made a joke, everyone was with him all the time as if he were captain of some boat of refugees all eager to see the lady's outstretched arm and dry land.

He asked about Joel, but the big boy shrugged and said he thought he'd gone home. 'He got weird,' Bobby said, but wouldn't elaborate.

So really, thought Larry as he climbed the metal stairs, who cares?

His office smelled like a sick person's room. He dumped the broken case down on his desk, opened the high window. He hadn't phoned Carla since their Wimbledon weekend. On the Monday morning when they had both taken the train into work she had sat hunched over reading a copy of Genet's *The Maids*. She made no reply to anything he said. Only when they were just outside Waterloo did she look out the window at some grey council flats and say, 'The weather is ever so much better here.'

Devorah might just pick up the phone. Then again if he got involved with her it meant going along to the refugees week after week, eating their potluck Thanksgiving with Gershom's hairs on the turkey. Devorah was one of these women, the exalted ladies of the left. He had had them before. She would not forgive him if he dropped out of the Un-Americans. Already she had asked if he was going to the anti-war march and when he had hesitated, she grew impatient, almost like Talia when he could not commit.

Talia divided people into mensch and non-mensch. A mensch was a real human being, a person of courage and decision. 'You,' she had said pointing at him as if he were some insignificant insect she could not be bothered to squash, 'you will never be a mensch.'

He began to unload his case. He did not want to be a mensch. Real people got sick and old and bored. There was nothing for them beyond this world, no heavenly Beach Boys harmonies, no swish of wings. He imagined them a race of stolid, solid men, standing feet akimbo, their arms folded, their eyes upon today. 'A mensch is special,' Talia had said, but he knew himself to be gossamer.

Yet he felt heavy for the first time in his life as if his flesh had turned to stone. It made his square featureless room something to be dreaded. Maybe he should go back. Just like that, even it meant breaking his contract. He could say he had had some kind of breakdown, he could say anything. And if he disappeared it would be as if he had never alighted on these shores. He could go back and be who he was before he came here and knew what it was like to speak to no one for three days.

Since when did he wait for a woman to call him? But if he made a move he could see her face already, distrust in her half-shut eyes. He didn't even have her number or address. Gershom would know. Gershom had all their vitals. Probably he was working for the CIA, behind all that hair a little bald head like a fist.

There was hesitation on the other end of the line as if Gershom were considering whether he would give out Devorah's number. Larry remembered how Devorah worried about Gershom finding out they were seeing each other outside the group.

Gershom said, 'Watch out, Larry, she's a tough Theresa.'

'How would you know?'

'Don't worry. She wouldn't have me.' Gershom after her. Larry felt sick at the thought of his face on her face, his pot belly on top of her.

'Just joking. I'm married, remember? Or I was. Anyway we never connected in that way. That's not what the group's about. Actually I can't see you two together. She's too, I don't know.'

Just give me her number or let me die. But there seemed no end to this drawly conversation. He knew he could lose himself in her, burrow deep inside till he was safe.

'Do I even have her number?' Gershom started humming, so high pitched that Larry had to plug his ear.

He had to talk to her now. If he waited she might make other plans, she might forget him and then he'd have to begin all over again.

'You're in luck. She's on my phone.'

Gershom knew all along he had her number. He just wanted to torment Larry.

'I can't figure you,' Gershom said, 'she's too big for you.'

'I'm just calling her. Don't make a federal case out of it.'

But all he got was a woman singing opera, maybe not even her, maybe not even her cell phone. He left a message anyway, gathered a bunch of student essays on the right to bear arms and went down to teach.

When she called that evening her voice was impatient. 'I said I would call you. Couldn't you wait, couldn't you trust me?' She didn't know about the weekend, couldn't commit herself. 'Don't try to pin me down,' she said.

'Okay then. Okay so I'll see you when I see you which is probably in the next world.' Enough was enough. He had Carla. He sighed at the thought of her.

'Just give me a chance. I said I'd call again.' All this back and forth, this tangoing was wearing him out. She probably liked to talk through her orgasm. He shut his eyes, thought of how Carla reached a state of nothingness. 'Think of your own shit,' she said, 'there's nothing beyond that, nothing.' Where was Carla now? Probably binding her feet.

He had wanted to see Cary Grant, a leopard and Katherine Hepburn at the National Film Theatre, but Devorah turned up her nose. How could she not love Cary Grant? His feet barely touched the sordid earth of this world. Cary Grant and Katherine Hepburn. If he knew that they would attend his funeral, still bickering, he could die with joy in his shrivelled heart. Devorah said she had seen it on TV and wasn't it so old? For a moment he wanted to forget her.

She suggested they hear a Palestinian support group in Red Lion Square. 'You call that an evening out?' he said. Maybe she'd be too serious for him, a true lady of the left who counted orgasms.

In the end he chose the restaurant and she picked a dance performance. They sat on rows like bleachers above a bare wooden floor. The dancer came out walking, an anaemic-looking woman with lank hair and limbs, who stood for a long time facing them without moving.

Larry wanted to wisecrack but glancing at Devorah's still profile, he kept silent. In the semi-darkness she looked like the Pharaoh's daughter, a stone princess with short curls.

The woman began to move her arms, just her arms, slowly at first then with quick jerky movements as if she were some wind-up doll gone crazy. Her head, her torso, her legs remained still.

'How does she do it?' he heard someone whisper in the dark.

There was knowing laughter, even a lone clap as the woman moved faster and faster still with her head straight, the rest of her body motionless.

Devorah leaned forward. Larry put his hand on her back and whispered: 'Is this it? She's going to dance or what?'

Devorah turned and gave him one of her sleepy glares: 'Shut up.'

He focused on her back, doing a massage in counterpoint to the woman's jerks. Devorah did not seem to mind when he slipped his hand under her sweater. Hers was no Carla back with bony bird-wing shoulder blades. She felt smooth, fleshy, with muscles underneath like some hefty panther.

The woman stopped suddenly, bowed her head and left to the sound of clapping. 'You really liked that?' he asked, but got no reply.

Then a man and a woman dressed in what looked like cellophane came running out and began flinging each other around, the man throwing the woman, the woman even lifting him. If only there was music. He wondered what Devorah would say if she knew he'd gone last week to see a revival of *South Pacific*.

'That's more like it,' he whispered.

She smirked at him and pinched his ass so hard, tears came to his eyes.

The dancers drew close, twined arms and legs so that one could not move without dragging the other in his wake. They were like two grasshoppers he'd once seen at camp, so stuck together that even a hop could not separate them. Yet they seemed still to struggle as if their bodies might burst from their own coil.

'Yes,' shouted someone in the darkness.

Larry tried to read the program. 'What's it called?' he whispered to Devorah.

'First date.'

He had forgotten how empty Carla's rooms were. Or had she removed what little they contained? The bed was now just a mattress on the floor. He thought that at least there was nothing to tie her to. The place smelled musty, an empty waiting room on some outlying tube station.

'Oh it's you,' she had said.

'Who else has my voice?'

It was odd how talking to one woman made him appreciate the other. With Devorah he had to measure his words but Carla listened to what he never said.

'Just wasn't expecting...'

He had shivered from her tone. He was reminded of a brief affair just after he arrived in London with a tall square-headed civil servant who came at least a hundred times. Still raw from her gap-toothed love, he called a week later. In the voice of a schoolteacher she said it was not possible, no it was definitely not possible this week or the next. Very sweet of you but maybe sometime in purgatory.

'I don't know,' Carla had said when he mentioned going to a movie, then a play. 'Maybe we should just, I don't know.'

So stay mad. He wouldn't keep asking her. Not like some guys who think no could be yes. He kept silent.

'Why don't you just come over here?'

'You sure you don't want to go out?'

'I can make you dinner or something.'

'Okay Carla. That sounds great.' He could think only of the legs of her futon. She would want bondage again.

'You should open some windows.' He had come straight from class. He put his bag down on the metal table, the only unyielding surface left in the flat.

She stood watching him, not exactly friendly. Her arms were bare and she wore a short green shift which looked like a hospital gown.

'Should we get some takeaway?' she asked.

'I thought—' He was sure she had said she would make dinner. Perhaps this was some fantasy of his, that her mother's genes had finally made an appearance.

'I've got this brilliant Chinese place just around the corner.'

'You want me to go?' He remembered the satisfaction of Sunday brunches with Talia. After their struggles, they ate fiery green beans and oysters swollen in black bean sauce, shrimp glowing through their paper wraps. He always said he loved the audacity of Chinese food.

'You'll never find it.'

He wasn't sure why but he felt a kind of dread low down in him when she said this.

'Do you want the usual?' She turned towards him before she left. He was sitting on the bed. 'What's usual?' he said.

'Oh you know.'

'No I don't. Hey,' he called to her for she had started to leave. 'Just no ducks' feet or sea slugs please.' But she was out the door.

He should have known. It was not the exotic she brought back, the stir-fried dog and roast monkey of his nightmares. She was the kind of person who ordered set dinners and always had fried rice. But this was worse than even the egg foo young of his mother: orange chicken, glued-up noodles and what looked like old bandages in grey sauce.

She insisted on using the wooden chopsticks provided by the restaurant. 'You're not really eating Chinese unless you use them.'

But this isn't real Chinese food, he wanted to say. He struggled for a time with the slippery bandages, but when one fell on his pants he made a decision. 'Can I have a fork?'

'You are just so—' She was lifting individual grains of rice with chopsticks held like surgical instruments. It was clear to him that they would be eating all night.

'Just tell me where they are.'

He began to walk into the kitchenette.

128

'No, not there. I never keep them in the kitchen. Check the file cabinet. Second drawer, I think.'

There was a jumble of utensils from which he pulled a bent fork. He sighed. He'd had enough of this half-assed bohemian.

'Don't you ever cook?'

She kept lifting the grains of rice, her face close to the white box. Why have plates, she once said, we only have to wash them again.

'I mean it's not healthy the way you eat.'

She paused. 'I can't cook, don't you see? I'm just hopeless.'

'You should ask your mother to give you lessons.' Why couldn't he just keep quiet, why, when it was so obvious that Carla was not her daughter? Not anyone's daughter.

'Oh sure. I'm just going to sit around pinching pastry dough.'

'Just kidding.' Maybe she rose from the muted waves at Witherins.

'You and my mother.'

'Just forget what I said. Okay?' He wished back the vague girl, the nymph he had plucked from the director's dinner. Or had she plucked him?

'You and her. How could you? Like I wasn't even there.'

'I was being friendly. You're the one who invited me down. What d'you want me to do, glare at your mother?'

'Just go back to her.'

'Who? Your mother?' She couldn't be jealous of a voice over the phone. Didn't she know that Devorah could not exist in this room?

She shrugged.

'Now this is crazy.' This was again the wrong thing to say. She dumped the box of rice she'd been eating into the sink and threw herself down on the bed beside him, her face lost in the folds of the duvet. At least there would be an end to her eating.

He was patient with women who cried. Never did he use the word manipulative. He stroked her head. She had the fine hair of a child. She was a petulant child and he was? He was another child. Why couldn't she see that?

129

'You want me to go?' He knew she didn't.

She rolled over. 'What's that smell? I'm going to puke.'

He sniffed and collected the sour stench of her life, the sweet medicinal smell of the orange chicken and some flat odour which he could not name.

'It's vile.'

'You mean the food?'

She shook her head. 'I don't know what it is but it's something.'

'Well that's true.' He sounded cheerful, but was beginning to sniff himself. Sometimes really spicy Chinese food, the kind Talia said fucked her mouth, made his sweat taste different.

She sat up, her face paler than usual.

'Take deep breaths,' he said.

She shook her head.

'Lemme get rid of the food. I'm sure that's what you're smelling.'

She shrugged. He figured she was too embarrassed or too proud to admit how bad her choices had been.

He found a garbage bag and dumped everything in, including the abandoned rice and some soggy shrimp crackers.

'Now if we could just open a window.'

'Whatever you want. I still. Oh God it's horrible.'

He pushed up the window and let in rainy sidewalks and curious vapors, like old stone breathing. How stifled he had felt. Her response was to undress and bury herself under the duvet. He sat on the edge of the bed waiting for her to want him.

But she didn't say anything or even move until he moved.

'Where you going?' she said.

She went quiet and still when he joined her under the duvet, just as she had been that first time when he had thought she might have died on him. She didn't speak even when he reached for her; all the way through she was silent. He began to think she was sleeping.

Then she spoke: 'I can still smell it.'

She herself smelled of nothing, no hot female stink. He sniffed his armpits and tried to blow his breath up to his nose. A bit of the orange chicken had stuck to his teeth.

'You got a spare toothbrush?'

'I think you better go.'

'Can I at least brush my teeth?'

'Can you just go?'

'First you want me to stay. Now you want me to go.'

She was throwing him out before dawn. He wouldn't beg. So what if he had to walk home to Wimbledon.

CHAPTER 16

Eureka closed for Thanksgiving, as if the college stood on the Great Plains, the dark emptiness settling on the cosy clusters of turkey eaters. Some of the American students actually flew home for the week. In his first year in Eureka, Larry's mother was bewildered when he told her that they did not do Thanksgiving in London: 'It's just a day like any other.' He'd wandered around London that Thursday feeling as he had as a child in the first days of summer when he bared his pale legs.

'You're not lonely?' His mother had asked.

He had been, but that was the beauty of it in those days. Already his first year in London was like his childhood: distant, memorable in its pain. On Thanksgiving he had eaten prawn curry and something called 'dhal' alone in a bare bright Indian restaurant above the Strand. The small bald elderly waiter took his order with a gentle smile. There were pictures of Nehru and Gandhi on the yellowing walls between the large long windows which faced the street. 'This is good,' the waiter said as he ordered. He reminded Larry of his grandfather, the same sweetness, the same acceptance of everything that Larry was and was not.

Larry took the apple pie he'd bought from Sainsbury's and stepped into five o'clock darkness. Back home, as his students always said, back home the great meal was over. No, it was only midday there, time for the starving aristocrat and sated tramp to find each other. In his favourite O. Henry story the aristocrat always treats the tramp to Thanksgiving dinner. The tramp never questions why he eats while the other just watches. Then one year the tramp is waylaid by charitable nuns who persuade him to eat their Thanksgiving dinner. But he cannot let his friend down, so he goes on to meet the aristocrat, has another full meal and collapses from overeating. His friend does too, but from starvation, for he is an impoverished aristocrat. Larry's eyes grew moist as he imagined those two good-hearted innocents walking to meet each other on that day of days. He thought of the Americans setting out from different points of London. Pilgrims. Edie with her bags of chestnuts, Clark and Ralph with homemade pumpkin pie, Devorah cycling slowly through Camden, a bowl of cranberry sauce rich, dark and fragrant in her basket.

'You made it.' For once Gershom and not his dog was at the door. He wore a T-shirt with a turkey's head and the words 'some of my best friends are'.

He took the Sainsbury's pie from Larry. 'We're gathering,' he said. But inside there was only the Martian woman sitting at the dining alcove reading a newspaper.

'I thought I was late. I rushed. Nobody's here,' said Larry.

The Martian, who had not lifted her eyes from the paper until now, looked up. 'Thanks.'

'I mean...' But the Martian went back to her newspaper.

Gershom gave him a cross-eyed look. 'Susan's been helping me with the turkey.'

Larry turned to her, his hands on his hips, his mouth trying to shape a smile but ending up a simper. 'So you're no longer a vegetarian.'

'I never said I was. Never. I just wanted a vegetarian option, just in case. All of us aren't flesh eaters. Why do you assume, why oh why does everyone assume just by looking at me that I'm a vegetarian?'

Larry put up his hands in mock hold-up style, but she had gone back to reading.

'Strike two,' Gershom said. 'Larry, have a look at my beauty.'

As they stood before the open oven, Gershom whispered, 'She's completely fucked up.'

There was some commotion. Larry looked behind him to see if the Martian had heard, for she was sitting just beyond the kitchen doorway. He thought of the two lost children in the witch's candy house; had the witch pushed them in the oven or was it the other way around?

133

He saw Clark's long face emerge from the hallway, in his outstretched hands a pie which looked as if it had been patched together.

'We had a little trouble,' he said in his endless plains way, but with just a hint of Fred MacMurray's shrewdness.

'That's an understatement.' Ralph darted around him. 'It was hell.'

'Oh it wasn't so bad. It just broke and we had to fix it up a couple of times.'

'You said you could do pastry.'

Clark gave a slow wink to nobody and patted Ralph's shoulder.

'Now boys.' Gershom grinned at them.

Were they a couple, a couple of—? Larry looked from one to the other. He had thought they were mismatched pals.

By the time they sat down to dinner, it was well past the usual Thanksgiving hour. But Devorah reminded them that they were okay by New York time. In New York they were just settling down to it.

The Martian said, 'Who cares anyway? All time is relative, all relatives give me a hard time.'

You made a joke. You actually made a funny, like a toddler finally going in the potty after holding in. Larry wanted to ask her, 'What's the time in outer space?'

'You're quiet, Larry,' Edie said. She had come in dressed to the gills. Black and white checked suit with padded shoulders, red lips, reddened teeth, eyebrow pencil. She looked like some aged movie queen. Only she carried shopping bags, one filled with ancient chestnuts which all of them had spent an hour cutting with little dart marks.

'You think everyone's quiet.' Gershom said from the head of the table. He was carving badly; the table shook from his exertions. 'Shit.' He'd hit the bone, sending white meat everywhere.

'You want me to do it?' Devorah said.

'I'm all right.'

But she was out of her chair and pushing him aside. 'You don't know your ass from your elbow.'

Gershom patted her bottom. 'Yes I do.'

'I'll strangle him for that,' Larry thought and then felt nauseous at the sudden vision of Gershom's flesh on her.

Larry looked around the table. Would anyone care as long they got fed? The red-faced Ann Arbor academic was caught between Ralph and Clark, Ralph chatting about some paper he wrote for a journal the academic had never heard of. Journal of the unknown scholar. Clark sat waiting for food, his hearing aid beside his plate.

'Don't go eat it,' Ralph had said when he pulled it off his ear because it was ringing too much.

Devorah was quick and before long they were bent over dishes full of turkey and little else, for most of them had brought pies. Gershom had forgotten about the sweet potatoes, and the beans lay in a blackened pot at the side of the stove.

'This is luscious,' Edie said. How delicately she ate, like a spider monkey he'd seen at the Zoo. Fine fingered.

Larry poured more gravy on his plate. The turkey was dried out, the potatoes hard and the wrong color for Thanksgiving. Only the cranberry sauce, for once not out of a can, but made by Devorah with real berries from Massachusetts, gave him anything to be thankful for.

She was next to him but talking to the others. He didn't mind. Her nearness gave him opportunities to squeeze her waist, stroke her arm, even brush a wisp of a curl from her cheek. All this she endured without comment or movement, except once to cast one of her sleepy-eyed sidelong glances which gave him the shivers.

From the head of the table Gershom spoke to everyone, throwing out lines so that no one could feel left out or at peace. His lips and beard were stained with cranberries, his eyes had the oily shine of the gravy. He glanced over at Devorah and Larry: 'What's the matter? You're not eating.'

Larry had just pinched her ass, a friendly happy pinch, but it was enough to make her stop eating, grin at him and pinch him back. Had Gershom noticed? So what if he had.

'Are you my mother?' Larry said.

'Maybe I've got nurturing needs. My kid's with her mother this weekend. I said why can't she come, she's half American isn't she? But no, she's got to have her.'

'Thank God for that,' Larry heard Ralph say in a not-so-undertone undertone to Clark, who smiled in deaf ignorance.

They ate the pies in the living room, Ralph and Clark on the sofa, Gershom in the armchair beside them, Edie in a straight-back chair she pulled over from the dining table.

At least the pies tasted like pies, even Clark's patched-up effort. Larry thought they produced a feeling of goodwill in the group.

'Do you know this is the first time in thirty years I've eaten a Thanksgiving dinner? Thirty years. And the last time doesn't count,' Ralph said to no one in particular.

'I go back further,' Edie said, 'I go back so far I can't remember. It wasn't happy though, not like this.' She paused, looked in the middle distance as if her younger self were standing there. 'Anyway this is scrumptious.'

Down on the floor with his plate and fork, Larry remembered not a Thanksgiving dinner of long ago but his birthday party when he was five and the kids putting their fingers in the ice cream cake. He wished he were not on the floor with Gershom above him. He wished that Devorah, sitting in yoga position with her pie on one knee, and he were on some warm shore, naked of course, but far from the crowd.

'When d'you want to leave?' he whispered to her.

'Be patient.'

'I am. Amazingly so.'

He looked up to see Gershom staring. 'Did I tell you I saw your student again?'

Larry shook his head. It had been a mistake to send poor Kalifa to him.

'He's on some list. I had to tell him I couldn't do anything.'

136

'What list?'

'The thing is he's been involved in some left-wing political group. Maybe communist. Something old-fashioned like that. Nothing violent I don't think, but the US immigration doesn't like Arab troublemakers.' He shrugged.

Ralph shook his head. 'Oh yes, we know all about their lists, don't we Clark?' But Clark was edging his way to the dining table where the unfinished pies lay.

'I didn't know. He seemed just ordinary. I didn't think of him as political.' Larry felt a fool, his student had put one over on him.

'I told him to find an American girl to marry. He's a good-looking guy. Some dumb undergraduate at Eureka who wants to bring home a trophy foreigner.'

Devorah said, 'That's crass. Really shitty.'

'What's the guy going to do? If he goes home they'll probably arrest him. Maybe worse. He's not going to have a life.'

Larry wanted to leave badly but he saw Devorah straightening her back like a warrior.

'You're setting up two vulnerable people. You don't care do you?'

'The guy's got no choice. He can't stay here, he can't go back. Not really. Anyway I don't think he took me seriously.'

'It could be romantic,' Edie said, her face alive with plot possibilities. 'Their marriage is just a business arrangement. He doesn't mean to but falls in love. But does she love him? Can he risk it?'

'It could be pretty unromantic,' Devorah said.

'There's plenty of these marriages of convenience, I can tell you. I knew a girl,' Gershom said.

'Could you say woman?'

'Okay this woman who got paid to marry and divorce. She must have done it ten times before they caught on.'

'That's sad,' said Devorah.

'Not for her it wasn't. She made good money and she made people happy. You're too pure, Devorah.'

137

'She's like one of those Greek goddesses. What's her name?'
Edie shut her eyes. 'Maybe I'm getting confused between two
of them. One of them never had boyfriends.'

Gershom gave Larry a look which he pretended not to
understand.

'You don't see.' Devorah stood up. 'You're not serious.
Ever.'

'Let me prove myself.' Gershom held out his arms with a
grin.

'Gershom, shut up. Okay?'

Larry stood up. He was trying to finish a piece of pumpkin
pie fast. She might storm out and forget about him because of
that asshole.

'Is everyone going home already?' Clark said, his mouth
flecked with pie crumbs. 'A shame.'

'This is so typical,' Ralph said. 'Thanksgiving ends with a
fight.'

'We're not fighting,' said Devorah. 'I just hate him.'

'Nice,' said Gershom. He was still grinning but somehow
without his usual confidence.

Edie came between them with her thin arms outstretched.

'Make up. Say you're sorry. Have a pow-wow.'

'What's the point of all this?' Larry said. They turned
towards him. 'Kalifa would never marry anyone he didn't love.
He's the one who's pure.'

'So you think,' said Gershom.

'Why? You know different?'

'No, I just wonder how you can be so sure.'

'He's my student, Gershom. I had him all last year. I know
him.'

Devorah squeezed his ass, so he knew he'd said the right
thing. Gershom continued to grin, arms folded, but he looked
like the small hairy man he was. The group began to turn their
backs on him, Clark and Ralph with their empty pie plate, Edie
gathering her shopping bags. 'Byee,' she called out.

Larry clung to Devorah, his reward for enduring this meal.
All the way to her apartment on some dour side street off

138

Kentish Town Road, he would not let go, so she had the bike, her ancient racoon coat and him to contend with. 'Needy,' he could hear Talia saying. 'You're so needy.' So what if he was. Needy was how he had felt those Sunday afternoons with the damp sunlight on his face in Wimbledon Common, walking nowhere from nowhere, asking the time like some mugger in Central Park, but in his case just to speak and be spoken to.

The flat smelled like her: earth, musk and incense. It was in the basement of a Victorian house, two large dark rooms she'd made even darker with scarlet curtains, brown and white tapestries of peasants with baskets in their arms, heavy red and black brocaded Indian bedspreads thrown over every piece of furniture. Even the kitchen chairs were draped with pieces of Turkish carpet. Only the floor was left bare for her dance. Her bed held the only evidence she was American. A patchwork quilt she'd bought in Vermont, its clean cool squares of blue and white like a benediction over their bodies.

'I feel underground here. No one can find me.' He wrapped himself around her. But it was she around him like a cocoon, he bursting forth with fiery wings.

'Greenie,' she mumbled. 'Such a child. That's what I love about you.'

He hated her calling him that, 'Greenie', like he was some Yeshiva boy with pimples and eccentric facial hair. He squeezed her tight. He wanted to stop her speaking, to hear only what she called 'her revolutions'.

CHAPTER 17

He didn't notice him in the crowd moving down the road from Charing Cross tube. His mind was full of Carla, why she had called him. 'I have something to show you.' Sinister. So he was in a haze when the kid asked, 'You wanna find out who you are?'

'No thanks.'

'You just answer some questions. It's free. God picks up the charge.'

Devorah would have told him to fuck off. She did that to a Jesus freak who blocked their way in Leicester Square. Scared him so much the guy dropped his leaflets, then had to chase them in a sudden gust of wind. Larry had grabbed Devorah's arm and dragged her away, but the Jesus freak followed them: 'God will damn you to hell for eternity.'

'What would you know about eternity?' Devorah said.

The guy blinked at her. Larry pulled at her arm, but it was too late. The guy made a gurgling noise and spit. She moved and Larry got it in the face.

He hadn't even looked at the kid. Just a monotone American voice like the slow buzz of an insect he could brush off.

'Hey, Professor Greenberg. Don't you remember me?'

It was and was not Joel. Joel with short back and sides, minus his forelock or rather his forelock gone upright like some Elvis with electricity in his hair. But still with that febrile lost boy look in his eyes.

'Where've you been?'

Joel shrugged. He held a clipboard and was wearing a white shirt and tie like one of those English schoolboys.

'Aren't you cold?

'I'm always moving.'

The Dean's face appeared in his mind, just his face like some sliver of malevolence. 'You know they're looking for you.'

'Who? You mean—'

'Your parents, the school, me. You just disappeared.'

140

'I didn't. I've been like here all the time finding my goodness. These guys.' He pointed to some other jacketless youths with clipboards working the crowds around the station. 'Saved my life. I was walking like maybe to my suicide when someone came up to me and said "Do you know who you are?"' He looked straight into Larry's face for the first time. 'I know, you think what a load—'

'I think your parents will have conniption fits.'

'What do they know? "Little Joel's got no attention span. Maybe he's got a learning disorder. Hey wait, little Joel's got dyslexia. So that's okay then." These guys showed me nothing's wrong with me. I looked deep deep inside me with them holding the flashlight. They call it tunnelling.'

'They're not Moonies, are they?'

Joel got back his scornful look. Almost a relief to Larry to see the surly boy again. 'We're called the Natural Born Church.'

'But you're Jewish. A Jew is a Jew.'

'I was never Jewish. I mean we had bagels on Sunday morning, but the rest is just bullshit, isn't it?'

'You've got to tell your parents at least.'

'You're not gonna tell them?'

'Well there's the Dean.'

'Fuck the Dean. He's got his fingers up half the girls in that school.'

'Joel, you're putting me in a funny position. I don't like—'

'Please. Like my father will come over. I know him.'

'What if I just say I've seen you? I don't need to tell them where. I guess.' Suppose the kid's been brainwashed?

'It doesn't matter. He's like Dracula. He'll just stalk the streets till he finds me and spoil everything like he's always done.'

'Don't you think you're being a little melodramatic?'

'Just pretend you never saw me.'

'I can't do that. You know I can't do that. Why'd you stop me anyway if you didn't want to be found? I wouldn't have seen you.' The kid was putting him in a lousy position.

141

'I just got so excited seeing someone from my past. You were the only one I could relate to there. You're real.'

'Sometimes I wonder.'

The two of them stood there for a moment, pushed and moved by the current of people from the station, Larry with the new plastic briefcase he'd been forced to buy, the kid with his clipboard clutched to his skinny chest. *In loco parentis*. Only Larry had never fathered anyone, and his own father had been a joker.

'You wanna meet my girlfriend? She's Dutch. We're really close. I mean she saved my life.'

So that was it. These cults always used bait.

'She's down the Strand. We try to spread out.'

'Look, I've got to meet someone, I can't.' But Joel turned, began pushing through the crowds. Never around. Larry pushing after him was thinking: 'Hans Brinker, Dutch boy paints, girl with blonde pageboy. Windmills of your mind.' He hadn't done Amsterdam.

Joel was putting his arm around a black girl who also held a clipboard. Dutch, double dutch. She was some mix of Africa and the South Seas: long black hair, body like Dolly Parton, face like a flower.

'Rita, this is my professor. Mr Greenberg.'

When she smiled, Larry knew that it was no use. The kid would stay on the street.

'Rita's a natural healer. One of the gifted ones.'

Rita winked at him. Was she just playing along with Joel?

'We all can heal,' she said.

'So you won't tell?'

'I don't know.' Larry sighed. 'Joel, you're a big boy now. If your father comes to London, you can deal with him.'

'I'm so happy. I've never been so happy.' He held Rita close, and when he looked up at Larry his eyes were actually wet.

He remembered Joel in class, the aimless boy who looked like he'd just been forcibly weaned. Then he remembered Carla, who had actually told him not to be late. And he was, already.

'I've got to run.'

Joel grasped his hand. 'You're the only one I trust from that shit-hole.'

'Thanks.' Larry turned, then turned back to say something else, but the two were kissing, their clipboards held behind each other's backs, kissing with eyes shut in the swirling crowd.

Wish I had never seen you. He shook his head, made his way along the edge of the sidewalk and then began to negotiate the crossings to Trafalgar Square. It almost took the edge off seeing Carla again. She'd sent him out into the night, hadn't she? Before he could decide that she was just too weird. But grudges were for big people, water-balloon-belly men filled with indignation. 'You see this?' His father pointing to the swollen source of his indigestion. 'Thirty years listening to shnorrers.'

Why see her anyway? He had Devorah, or did he, did anyone? 'You never know.' His father's motto. He said it to elderly widows who wanted to stop paying for their life insurance policies, to the young couples who could not stop for death. Since he had left his parents' house, Larry made sure that a woman was waiting in the wings. Only in London had he had aloneness.

He saw Carla first and got a shock. Was she always so very thin? He felt cumbersome in his down jacket, like some inflated toy entering the ICA. He'd been there once to see a play about two women who would not let go of each other. Why had he gone? He reasoned that a play about women might attract women.

She stood by the bookstore, coatless, in some black shift, her reed arms bare.

'Aren't you cold?' He touched her arm and felt her shiver or maybe it was him. Her skin was like death.

She gave him a smacker on the lips which he decided was just for show, then led him past the guy at the entrance to the gallery who smiled and nodded.

'I can bring guests for free,' she said and wandered into the long white gallery.

He wanted to eat, but felt something like shame before Carla as if she were one of the hungry his mother had burdened

143

him with whenever his dish still held food. 'Think of the poor children of Europe. They don't have nice food and you, you leave over.'

He thought of them with their spoons in his chicken pot pie.

Or maybe he hesitated because of the look of the place, cold chrome and monochrome and a black-shirted guy with concave chest and ghoul head.

But he could not help himself: 'What about lunch?'

She kept walking, past a sign made in floating red silk: 'Women Voyeurs'. He ducked to avoid the sign but still felt it brush his hair. He passed a large photo of couples coupling, a life-size sculpture of a man inspecting his penis and a painting in which a man floated in a grey sea of sperm with screaming faces.

'Can't we eat first?'

He followed her, brushing past a mobile made of purple and green condoms. 'Don't you think it's a bit obvious?'

She stood before a small drawing in black ink smiling, then stepped aside to let him look. The man was naked, like so many around the room, drawn realistically except that instead of a left arm he had a wing.

Larry drew closer till he was nose length away from the drawing. He looked and looked, then turned and began to speak: 'Did you?'

She nodded, beaming at him.

He felt himself blush. The man had his face even down to the mole on his cheek. The man had his face and was naked in a public place with a wing for an arm.

'You could've asked me. At least. And why does he? I mean why do I?' He stopped, drew back from the painting. 'Why does he have a wing? I mean just one wing?'

'Do you like it?'

'I don't know. You could've told me. I mean aren't you supposed to ask permission? That's my body. Or some of it.' He stared at it. 'Why the hell do I have a wing?'

'You remember the fairy tale about the twelve brothers turned to swans? Their sister weaves cloaks for all of them.

144

Once she's finished she throws them over each swan to turn them back into men. But the youngest. She doesn't finish his in time so he has an arm and a wing.'

'Lucky him.'

'She weaves the cloaks from nettles. I can remember feeling the rawness in my hands. She can't speak the whole time or else the spell is broken.'

'You sure it's a fairy tale? Sounds like a masochist's dream.'

'I always loved that story. The way she gives herself up to pain and silence.'

He stared at her, remembering her still body and shut eyes.

Larry drew back from the picture. From a distance it could be anyone, couldn't it? He imagined his students coming in here and pointing to his penis. She had done it well. He never thought she'd noticed. Half the time she had a flight mask on.

She stood with her arms folded. Now he could see a shiver pass through her. She had blood in her after all. 'I always wondered what happened to him, the brother with the wing. I called this "Winged Victory". It's meant to be ironic.'

'At least something here is,' he said.

'You haven't said whether you like it.'

'It's not a question of liking it. I feel exposed. It's like those dreams everyone has. You've got no clothes on and nobody seems to care but you.' He looked again at the winged man's privates and blushed. Beneath the blush he felt something like pride, yet beneath that was shame.

'That's the point of all this I guess.' She turned towards the rest of the exhibition: the sculpted penises, the men in languorous nudity. 'People have said he, you, whatever, is beautiful. They've actually come up to me. I don't see why you can't—'

'That's just great for you.' He felt like a puffed-up fool in his down jacket.

'I saw something in you which just came out.'

Larry drew close to the drawing again. The boy-man held his wing up, his face joyful.

'I can't understand. Why the wing?'

145

'Sometimes I think the brothers didn't mind being swans. They got used to it. Maybe they were happy. And when their sister came to throw the cloaks over them, the youngest tried to get away.'

'But that's not what happened, is it? She didn't finish in time, so the youngest got a raw deal.'

'I'm starving,' she said. 'The café's super.'

'What do they have? Pickled balls?'

'It's all veggie.'

She walked away from him, a girl on a stick. He didn't know how to feel.

'You call this food?' he mumbled.

She ordered a seaweed salad, and he the very thin barley and cucumber soup.

'Is there anything in this?' But he spooned his soup carefully so as not to disturb the angry sperm who lurked at the bottom.

'My mother asks about you all the time.'

'You're gonna show her that?'

She shrugged her bony shoulders and looked the way he felt standing in front of a full frontal of himself.

'I made what I saw in you.'

'You made me a freak.'

'Someone who could fly if only...' She actually had tears in her eyes. As if she listened to him. She got up. He was still slurping his thin gruel. 'I've got to go.'

He paused, looked up at her. She had lost weight; her face was like some gorgeous skull. 'Wait. I'll walk out with you.'

'I'm going back in there.'

He spooned some more of the gruel into his mouth. 'Always finish your food,' he told himself or was that someone else speaking? Then he went in search of her, brushing past the condom mobile which he now saw had happy faces like gremlins. She was talking to the black-shirted ghoul, her skull face upturned, his arm around her skimpy shoulders.

When Larry touched her shoulder, she turned and stared at him.

'I'm going,' he said.

She continued to stare at him.

Don't let her go like that. But for once he didn't know what to say. All this swerving and stopping, it wasn't like him.

She waved him goodbye. Maybe she was too upset to speak. He started to follow, but it was too late to pull her back. She'd walked off with the ghoul, both of them so skinny and in black they looked like one.

He wanted to have a last look at himself, but that would mean going past Carla and her dybbuk. And he was already late for an office hour with nobody wanting him, followed by his class in Corporate Law.

He walked over Hungerford Bridge swinging his bag slowly as he eyed the Houses of Parliament. He had wanted to confide in Carla about Joel, she rather than Devorah, who would go tough and scornful about the kid's godliness. Joel was happy. Should he go and tell on him to the Dean with his lizard face and scorpion sting? His mother's proverb: 'Don't get involved unless you are already.' If he didn't actually see the Dean, that could decide him. He would walk past his office and if the lizard didn't appear, the Jesus kid could stay with his black Mary.

It was Gershom who filled his space in a duffel coat which looked like it had been washed with Styrofoam, and a racoon hat with flaps.

'Like your hat.' That was sarcastic but Gershom didn't react. Too subtle for him.

'What? I can't hear anything with these.' He pulled up the flaps.

'I said I like your hat. Is it Russian?'

'Got it in deepest Islington. My wife said she'd leave me if I wore it. So.' He shrugged. 'She left me anyway.'

Larry was only half listening. He kept watch on the Dean's door. If this mongrel kept him much longer his decision was made for him.

'She's moved back to Wales with my kid. I'm into loss at the moment.'

But why did he have to tell on Joel? The Dean didn't really care. Not about Joel. If only he could leave now, but Gershom had drawn him in again. He tried not to look at the Dean's office, not to see even a bit of him, but could not stop himself.

Gershom watched him. 'He's not around. I popped my head in. Not a whiff of him. Karen said he's out sick.' Karen was sometimes the Dean's secretary, sometimes the registrar. She was bad at both jobs and had phenomenal BO.

Well that was that then. But of course it wasn't. He had had a reprieve, or Joel had.

'How's Devorah?' Gershom raised his eyebrows a few times.

Larry stared at the bald patches in Gershom's hat. 'That hat's got into a few fights.'

'Something's started to live in it. I had to pick off the maggots. But I'm sentimental. It was what I was wearing when we got connected, Katherine and me.' He actually looked misty-eyed. 'Now she's so negative.'

'You think maybe she doesn't like worms?'

Gershom gave him a hard look. 'You know I wouldn've thought of the two of you, you know together. But then Yanks get lonely.'

He would not even acknowledge that Gershom had seen and pronounced on them. 'Gotta go. Got students waiting.'

'If you gotta go, you gotta go.'

Gershom waved a hand and turned. A coonskin tail twitched at the back of his hat like a live animal. But it was only Gershom's greying hair tied in a ponytail.

He had a measly four students for Corporate Law, who looked embarrassed for him. 'Christmas shopping,' one of them said. The class had been dwindling. His heart, that fierce little beater like some bird's breast, his heart wasn't in it and they knew. The class ran over that peculiar time from four to six; he began in the day and then in mid-lecture, looked around to see his face in the inky windows as if he too had departed.

Afterwards in his bright office with the tiny window like a blind eye he looked at the test he had given the four of them. They would have failed if he had marked straight but in Eureka nobody did. There seemed no reason to stay. He gathered the tests into his new blue briefcase. It was made of hard plastic and always felt and sounded hollow. Sometimes he forgot what it looked like. Once he had left it on a bench in St James's Park. A man came running after him. 'This yours?'

Larry had had to think. Did he really belong to this plastic box? He missed his old broken school case, the scratched brass buckle nosing out of brown leather worn like the coat of some aged animal.

He never wanted to be here. The room smelled funny. Always. He shut his eyes and tried to breathe in Devorah, but smelled disinfectant, or was it medicine?

Someone's door banged shut. Steps in the corridor. The nurses starched to the gills and masked, checking for death. Germs, his mother told him, germs are everywhere. For a moment the lights dimmed, then returned to normal.

A knock. So slight.

'Yeah?'

The door moving but nobody. He shivered. 'Come in.' Whoever you are.

Kalifa in a black suit, tieless, his dark face a solemn mask, only his eyes restless. Beyond him Omar stood smiling, his arms folded.

'Why don't you sit down?'

Kalifa shook his head and Larry began to feel unsettled. Who are these guys anyway? There was no one else around up here. The cleaners weren't due for an hour. In the meantime he could be bundled away by these Arabs. These Arabs. What it came down to.

'You are busy.' Kalifa eyed his briefcase.

'No, I'm just—' Larry's throat seemed to twist and he sounded like a strangled frog.

Omar waited at the door like some lookout while Kalifa drew close.

'So quiet. You are alone here?'

Larry managed to stand even though his toes were trembling. 'What is it, Kalifa?'

149

Kalifa cast him a weary look then a smile, the Kalifa smile, and Larry sat down again.

'I won't take your time. Just I want to say thank you. Professor Fish cannot help.'

'You're not leaving? The term hasn't ended yet.'

'I finish your class but who knows. My visa ends this term. So I thank you for helping.'

'You too Omar? You're leaving us?'

Omar came forward, shook his head. Kalifa said, 'He's engaged. To an English girl.'

'Well congratulations. I didn't think anyone got engaged anymore.'

'She is very English,' said Omar with a grin.

'Kalifa, will you be all right?'

'Depends what is all right. Professor Fish said why not marry an American girl. Just like that.'

'Maybe someone else can help. He's not the only lawyer.'

'He knows. Believe me. What do you think? Just to marry a girl so I can live in your country?'

'How bad is it if you go home?'

'I am nothing. They will see to that for what I have said and done here. They will. So.'

'I wouldn't do it but then I'm not you.'

Omar put his hand on Kalifa's shoulder. Larry wondered if Omar was marrying for love of one of the clammy ones.

'Try to be me,' said Kalifa. 'Think what you would do.'

'Kalifa, are you sure you've explored all the options?'

Larry thought about the argument they had had at Thanksgiving. He imagined Gershom lining up girls like a Miss America Pageant, and Kalifa, dark and lean, shoulder blades visible as he walked back and forth in front of them like some magical cat. A line from a distant service came back, read by the rabbi then sung in the high severe voice of the cantor: 'Choose life and be blessed.'

'You must think about yourself. And if your life is threatened in any way then I guess almost anything goes. But your life isn't threatened, is it?'

Kalifa smiled down at him like some sad, wise uncle. 'Don't worry Professor Greenberg. Don't worry about me.'

He saw them first before they could notice, the little group of Un-Americans with their bed-sheet banner: tall long-headed Clark under an umbrella with his little peevish friend Ralph, Gershom with his kid in a plastic-covered stroller, Edie in a see-through rain hat holding up a piece of cardboard.

I can leave now, he thought. But for the sight of Devorah's luscious curls. She wouldn't forgive him. No matter what he said, she would know the truth beneath his excuses.

'The things you do.' Beneath his frown was the smile for afters as they call it here. Afters in Devorah's humid flat.

'Wimbledon? You must be kidding,' she had said when he asked her home. 'Who lives in Wimbledon? It's like, nowhere.'

He never asked her again. He could not see her there sauntering through its cheerful drabness. Would she try to speak to the gangly anxious man as he looked for something over Larry's shoulder? She would have had to shed herself: her embroidered skirts, her long purple scarves, all her gorgeous drapery would drop from her in his flat, so like an airport lounge with wall-to-wall beige carpet and views of sky. No, she could not come there. It would be as if they were playing at being mommy and daddy, but without the clothes.

'Larry,' Edie called through the crowd. All of them turned to stare at him. 'Where's your poster? Didn't you bring it? Larry, it was so good.' Edie and her bags. 'What a shame.'

'I forgot.'

'Yeah, sure,' said Devorah, 'you're a reluctant picket.'

'How many animals you skinned for that?' A stringy youth, hair in black oily spikes.

Devorah turned to him. 'It was my mother's. I didn't—'

'So you say. Animal killer.'

Larry stood between them, turning this way and that. He'd pull the guy's spikes out one by one till his head looked like a bowling ball.

Devorah's face actually reddened and Larry thought, 'I've got to do something. I can't allow this guy to just—' He moved towards him without thinking what might happen, but Devorah caught his sleeve. 'Keep out of this,' she whispered.

The guy said something else but it was impossible to hear in the sudden noise from the loudspeaker, a cacophony of words and squeaks.

The guy disappeared into the crowd before Larry could make up his mind what to do.

Edie squeezed his shoulder. 'You were so brave. Like a knight.' But Devorah said nothing. She shrugged off the hand he laid on her shoulder and moved away.

'We're starting,' Gershom said. And the group of them moved forward into the march. 'We Hate Freedom – Americans Against the Bush War' their banner said, and people who noticed them grinned, even stuck up their fists.

Larry said, 'Don't you think it's a bit strong? They might get the wrong idea about us.'

Devorah sighed. 'You don't get it.' She was holding up one end of the banner, the Martian the other.

'I'm just the dummy,' he said.

He tried to stay with her, but there wasn't the room for the banner and three of them to walk abreast, so he straggled behind her with Edie and Gershom, who was pushing the stroller, his beard dripping with rain. He had pulled up the plastic cover, and his daughter's dirty face could be seen sucking a lollypop.

'I thought she was in Wales.'

'She was. She is. Katherine just dumps the kid when it's convenient.'

'She sounds irresponsible. Maybe you should have custody.' He knew this was a terrible idea; Gershom would ruin the kid if he hadn't done so already.

'You mean battle it out? Who needs shit like that?' Not like Gershom to be glum. Maybe he realized how ugly his kid was. She was crying now, her lollypop stuck in front of her parka like a badge.

'Larry could you help?'

153

Clark and Ralph paused, then walked around and in front while Gershom undid her harness and lifted her out. 'Hey there,' he said to her, 'you got the screamy meanies.'

Then, 'Shit, we lost them,' Gershom said. 'Take this will you?' He began running with the girl, Larry following behind pushing the empty stroller through the marchers.

Ahead he saw the high flat head of Clark, Gershom with his daughter now hoisted on his shoulders. Larry felt suddenly alone with the stroller. He tapped Gershom on the back.

'Am I pushing this for the duration?'

'Would it kill you? I mean I got my hands full.'

'I feel like a jerk.'

'Just for a while. She's getting tired I can see. In a minute she'll be out of it in the buggy, I promise you.'

The girl was bopping her father on the head with her lolly and giggling. She gave Larry a cold dark stare.

He pushed the stroller forward till he was walking beside Edie. 'Wanna a ride?'

'You look so cute,' she said, 'I can just see you as a father. A doting one. But then.' She paused. 'Then something happens.' He could see a story bubbling up in her.

'Then your daughter is taken from you by, I don't know, could be an estranged wife, but then that's what everyone would think. No, your princess, that's what you call her, she's taken by...'

'Edie. Talk less and read more.' Peevish Ralph turning.

'I read everything. I read and read.'

'I mean something decent. Real books. Not this romance clogging up your brain.'

'At the moment I'm reading the history of the Russian empire.' She looked hurt. 'Ralph, you misunderstand me.'

But Ralph had moved forward and did not hear.

Larry couldn't bear for her to be sad. Not her. 'C'mon,' he said, 'keep telling me.'

'Well, your daughter is taken by some woman who's mad because her daughter was kidnapped. You wheel an empty buggy all over London, grief-stricken, till, I don't know. You could find the woman and then the two of you.' She looked ahead at Devorah. 'Can you see her a mother? Can you?'

He shook his head but was thinking of Devorah's roundness, not soft, no, not with her dancer's football legs and arms like Olympic rowers which could and did wrestle with him. But still womanly like those smiling Madonnas he got so fed up with in Italy. Women with flesh they could only share with a baby. Not even a real one. Suckling a god.

Edie stopped, put her bags down. 'You wanna go on ahead with Devorah? You can. I need to catch my breath.'

'Why don't put your bags in here?'

'You sure?'

He felt ashamed he'd let her carry them all this time. When he lifted them up he saw bags within bags: a thermos, a book large enough to be about the Russian empire. They were heavier than he had thought. He pushed the stroller with effort while ahead Devorah and the Martian shouted 'Out, out, out' with the others. He did not shout or even speak to Edie who took his arm. 'I wanna go home,' he mouthed to himself.

There was a pause as the marchers began to enter the park. Devorah turned and smirked at him. 'You look like an asshole, Larry.'

'He's performing a useful function at least,' said Ralph.

Edie turned to him. 'Don't let them rile you.'

It had begun to drizzle again. Still with his daughter on his shoulders, Gershom led the refugees to stand beneath the bare branches of some stump of a tree.

'What's the point?' Larry mumbled.

Devorah heard him. 'Then go home.'

'No, I mean.'

'Just go home Larry. You've had a face the whole march. Like this is the worst thing you could be doing.'

Edie came forward, her face white in the darkening sky. 'Don't.' She laid a hand on Devorah.

'It's just. I hate the look. Like he's some victim. If you don't want to be here. Just don't spoil it for us.'

155

'First fight.' Gershom looked up from the stroller where he was strapping the kid in. His grin was back. The kid was making loud thumbsucks, eyes drooping like a drunkard. He handed Larry Edie's bags.

'Mind your own business.' Larry felt like a child. A very young one.

'Sorry, sorry.' Gershom put up his hand in a peace sign.

'I didn't say anything about not wanting to be here, did I? Did I?' He turned between Devorah and Edie.

'Will you be quiet? I can't even hear.' The Martian had spoken.

Maybe if you take those antennae off and stop listening for Martian tunes, maybe then. But she wasn't wearing them today and her pale face was creased with aggravation.

He stood with his back against a tree while the others shared umbrellas, Edie in her rain hat, Clark in a sou'wester, like a bonnet on a horse, Ralph in his silly beret. He had nothing but the tree. His hair and face were already soaked and he was sure that he had lost the use of his hands which held on to Edie's bags.

The speaker shouted, 'We've been fed lies for so long, we can't even trust the truth.' But the 'we' was dwindling all the time. Great gaps appeared between groups huddled under umbrellas.

'How long do we have to stay?' Larry asked. 'It's raining for God's sake.'

'Don't be such a whiner,' Devorah said, 'we're all wet. We just don't kvetch.'

If not for Edie and her bags, Larry would have left. He was shivering, his clothes heavy with rain, even his underwear.

'Poor Larry,' Edie said. She had a tiny red umbrella like a child's, but she tried to hold it over him.

'Don't bother. I have nothing to keep dry.'

'You wanna go home?' She tucked her arm in his. 'You go if you want to. You've done well.'

'Edie, he's not your son,' Ralph said.

156

But Larry felt like kissing her. She was his only friend. He would carry her bags through the flood.

Edie looked up at him, her lipstick smeared, smudges of black around her eyes, almost melancholic. Devorah had said she was once an actress. 'You go. I give my permission.'

He shook his head. He would not leave her in the rain with full shopping bags. He was a good boy really.

Just then they announced the next speaker, an Aldermaston marcher from the 1950s. Scattered applause.

'Let's go, Larry,' Edie said, 'I've heard him a hundred times. They always bring him in at the end.'

Devorah turned. 'He's wonderful. He's been in every anti-war demo.'

'Since the beginning of time,' Edie mumbled to Larry. 'Who wants to hear an old man?' Larry had never heard her like this before, actually sour. 'Always at the end. Because he's so old and isn't he just great? They don't even listen.'

'Byee.' She waved to the group. Larry waited for Devorah to say anything, but she stared at the two of them, then turned away.

Sometimes there is a defining moment in a relationship, Talia used to say: 'And you Larry are the last to know it.'

The others, the Martian, Ralph and Clark, did not turn. Only Gershom pushing the stroller with his now sleeping daughter back and forth looked at him. 'You lucked out.'

'Fuck you Gershom,' Larry whispered though he had never thought himself a warlike man.

'What's that? What? What? You being a sore loser?'

Larry turned his back and began to walk with Edie. She said: 'Don't worry. She'll come around and if she doesn't, there'll be someone else. You're so cute.' She squeezed his arm. 'I couldn't get you together. I tried. I tried everything. Putting it back to the eighteenth century. Making you a prince, her a peasant. I even tried you as a pirate and she was a Puritan. I had you meeting all right, but then something always goes wrong.'

'You mean I'm in your novel? Edie, you never said.'

'I just couldn't manage it. Something always happened. One of you would drown or fall off the edge of some castle. You think maybe I haven't got the gift?'

'You had the wrong characters.' Because Devorah was like some gorgeous fish he could grasp only in moments. She was never his. Never. He was her conquest and up till now happy to remain so.

If he only could take her away. She had said, 'Let's not run back home for Christmas like all the others. We'll pretend this is home, what d'you say?'

He had thought of days luxuriating in her apartment. But she would still be queen and he her half-witted fool. He had imagined her without her drapery in the heat and suggested Spain.

She shrugged. 'It's up to you Larry.'

His mother had said, 'It's not for me to say if you want to stay over there. I mean you're coming home sometime?' When he cancelled the flight he had booked, he lost only his deposit.

In the first year he had not run back to his mother for Christmas, though none of his English girlfriends thought to ask him home. It wasn't his holiday was it? He stayed and finished off a can of Campbell's tomato soup then wandered out into Wimbledon High Street, alone in the chill dark wind, not even the gangly figure of the anxious man on Christmas Day.

'Larry, you okay?' Edie asked. They'd reached the parting of ways, the Northern Line platform at Charing Cross. He was still holding her bags.

'Just let me put you on the train,' he said.

'Go. You're soaked. Go. I hear your train.'

The brush of her lips, the smell of her old lady powder and candy. 'Don't languish,' she called after him. 'It's not like you.'

By the time he reached his apartment in Wimbledon, he was shivering. He drank two whiskies in his grandfather's schnapps glass, then ran a bath. He drank a third whisky, got in and fell asleep. When he woke his mouth was full of water. Something far off was ringing. As far off as he had come to live on this slimy porpoise of an island. He rose like some sea

158

creature dripping his way to the phone. But there was no one there.

CHAPTER 19

He had Devorah at the end of his day. She had sounded funny over the phone, but friendly. Not a word about the demonstration and her hard-heartedness. When he said, 'You were shitty on Saturday', she didn't deny it, neither did she apologize. She said almost too lightly, 'Can't we forget about it? Can't we please?' Like some child, his child woman. Maybe they could go back to it, the meals in dives Devorah found, the return to her musk-scented bedroom. Maybe, but he was thinking he needed a fall-back position. His father always said, 'Don't go out without your spares.'

He thought of the glossy women in the pubs and wine bars of Wimbledon who listened with eager eyes to his spiel about being adrift in London. He took one home once. An estate agent. And then in the middle of the night took her back to Raynes Park. She had looked so bewildered wandering down the hallway of his railway flat. In bed the sight of her long white legs and arms made him shiver. 'I love Americans,' she had said.

Devorah was in her bathrobe when he arrived. 'You shouldn't have come. I told you I thought I was coming down with something. I'm fluish. My head is like.'

'You look pale.' He cupped her delicious chin.

'You'll catch it.'

'I already have.' He winked at her. He was in love with her new woebegone look as if she had finally given in to him after a long struggle.

He should have been the one sick after standing in rain-drenched clothes and her not caring. He said nothing about last Saturday. Peace had come between them. Who was he to meddle?

He kissed her forehead, what his mother always did to find out if he had fever. Kiss and tell.

'Ooh, you're hot.'

'I could've told you. You'll catch it for sure.' She lay down on the sofa and drew up her knees. 'I got chills.'

'Go to bed Devorah. C'mon.' He pulled her up, put an arm around her and led her to the darkened bedroom.

'You want anything?'

She was deep under the quilt and the heavy crimson bedspread. Almost small.

'No. Just leave me here to die.' This was followed by a series of chesty coughs. 'Oh God.'

'What about some soup? My mother believes in soup when you're sick.' Canned chicken noodle. 'Bathwater', his father called it.

'I'll puke.'

'You just call me if you need anything.'

He would stay and stand guard over her. He wandered back into her other room, her living-room-kitchen, pulled some papers out of his plastic case and sat down at the table. Late term papers from American boobies.

Not like Carla's barren land. He had to clear a space between jars of honey, a large black and red geometrically patterned bowl filled with oranges and several piles of books and magazines. Always there was fullness in Devorah's apartment, as if she could not bear to leave an empty space. Yet she could be so severe.

He would not snoop now that he could move freely. Would not. He tried to consolidate the books into one pile. Two volumes of *Living my Life*, by Emma Goldman, some high-sounding book about dance and a history of the British empire. She liked to dabble. Actually she didn't, she was specifically not a dabbler. We are all mysteries, his father said. You, me, even, turning to his mother, even her.

He worked at the small space he had cleared and listened for her. Once he went in to watch her sleeping face. It was how you learned what you needed to know about a person, watching when they were not thinking about being watched. In the courtroom the 'not at home' sign coming down over the judge's eyes. Talia like a lioness in pyjamas, almost cute.

161

The room smelled of sickness, her musk perfume and something else: a heavy sweetness he remembered from little ethnic stores in Boston and Cambridge, darkened emporiums of incense, candles and clay beads where an ethereal girl sat weaving and if you asked for something she never knew.

Did Carla ever sleep? He shook his head. The eyelids came down but she never went under. This was why he slept so badly with her next to him. It explained her crazy talk, the wing she gave him. All of it. She lived in the dream she never had.

He tiptoed out, made himself a mug of coffee and with a sigh began to read. He remembered Talia's flu, the violence of her coughing. Even in a fever she prowled through the house. But Devorah continued to sleep like a good girl.

He thought about dinner, inspected her refrigerator, but found only tuna salad, cheese, and fruit yoghurt. He tried to remember if there was an Indian restaurant nearby. He wanted the sharpness in his mouth, the consuming spiciness, the way it raced through him, clearing his gut. If he could not have Devorah tonight, he would taste her acrid sweetness, have his mouth assaulted, his fingers stained.

Suddenly he heard a jaunty little tune and located her phone in the bowl of oranges. Should he answer? It stopped. He looked into the bedroom but she hadn't stirred. It started again, the phone vibrating unpleasantly against his palm. He had to answer, didn't he, because it would wake her and anyway she would expect him to.

A male voice stumbling, asking with awkward formality if this was Devorah's phone. No he did not want to leave a message or a name: 'I am sorry to trouble.'

But you do trouble. Larry was not a jealous man. He had endured Talia's flirtations. He himself had his spares. There was Carla. He willed her face out of his mind. He knew that Devorah still heard from her boyfriend back in New York, a writer of political crime novels who drove a cab.

'He hangs on. I keep telling him, let's cut it, let's not have all these post mortems.'

'You're heartless.'

162

'Every time he calls, I'm set back again. He's just so needy.'
But the man on the phone did not sound American or needy.
He wandered around the flat after that. Did he really care if
she was seeing someone else, some continental with beautiful
manners and a leather handbag? She had not given this person
her weekends; he, Larry, had most of those. So he was at best
a weekday evening job if a job at all. He could be one of her
students. She had begun to teach jazz dance in the basement
of some arts centre out in east London; always she was below
ground level. Larry, Larry, this is not like you.

He was hungry, that was all. He wanted a curry, aftertaste
of burnt liquorice. He searched for her key and found it in a
basket of turquoise stones. There was nothing she did not touch
with color.

He wandered down her little side street past short pastel houses
like dwarves all in a line till he reached the main street, one of
these nothing London roads with herds of cars and vans baying
at traffic lights and smell of spent gasoline and dirt. Metal
gates were coming down as he walked along: a hardware, an
everything-a-bargain store, Woolworth's, a hole-in-the-wall
candy store. He passed the Loon Moon café, just a take-away
counter and from the smell he knew this was Carla's type of
Chinese, Carla, who rejected her mother's good food for the
poison of strangers. He thought of her thin arms and bony chest.
She had enchanted him, turned him into some winged creature
she could display in front of her other worldly friends. Was he
actually angry at her, the shadow girl? Not Larry, happy-go-
lucky kid from the sky. No. It was just that when he thought
of her he felt hungry. He wanted that sweet acrid taste in his
mouth, sharp enough to expunge the doubt creeping into his
clothes, gripping his sad heart on this god-forsaken road which
led from nowhere to nowhere he had ever been.

Just beyond a pub, he came upon a row of restaurants side
by side as if they needed each other. He stepped inside dark
fragrant warmth, brass filigree lamps above an empty room, a
man coming forward as if to welcome him east. Larry decided

163

to take the food away in case Devorah needed him. She might even be hungry. But more he wanted to be there if this caller called again, he wanted to say that he had got there first.

When he returned she was still asleep. He laid the food out on one of her large blue and yellow ceramic plates and drank from a thick blue glass goblet. Even the forks had cumbersome ceramic handles. Did she never long for the ordinary?

The tune started up again. He eyed her phone like it was taunting him. If it was her friend again, he could leave it to ring. He forked some lamb laden with green sauce into his mouth. It would not stop.

He answered with his mouth still full of meat, his hello like some disguised terrorist voice on the radio.

'Hello? Hello?' Then a pause. 'Is this Devorah Shatner's phone?'

'Yes, Devorah is here, but—'

'Who are you?' Loud American male.

'I'm just, I'm just a friend. She's sick.'

'Who are you? I want to speak to my daughter.'

'She's got flu. She's sleeping. You don't want to wake her.'

'What are you, her personal answering service or what?'

'My name's Larry in case you want to know.' Feeble Larry.

'Oh yeah. Where's my daughter anyway?' He sounded old and Brooklyn, and as if he thought 'Larry the impostor'.

'She's in bed and actually I'm not waking her. Unless it's an emergency. She's feverish.'

'Who are you anyway?' The voice was so loud now that he drew the phone away from his ear.

'Who is it?' Devorah leaning against the doorway, hand outstretched. Larry put his hand over the phone and in a whisper: 'Your father. He thinks I killed you.'

'Lemme speak to him.'

'But you're sick.'

She sat down at the table with the phone. 'Daddy? Yeah. I'm all right. He's just here. Okay? Yeah, he's a friend.'

Larry stood with arms folded.

'Dad. Dad. Dad listen. You listening? I'm staying here. I'm not moving. No. No.' A sigh. 'Very funny. Look dad, I'm really wiped out so. How's mom?'

Larry walked into the tiny living-room area and sat down on the sofa draped with reddish tapestries where brilliant birds flew between doe-eyed women dancers. He felt like a tourist.

A friend. So he was just like so many in her life. And her father sounded like one of these chunky guys who came on TV late at night to sell mattresses. Devorah should have one of these tall lean aristocrat fathers, a disdainful Jew.

She came to sit on the sofa. 'He drives me mad.'

He said nothing. He was sulking but could not even lean back without disturbing the layers of cloth. Why didn't she just have a sofa like everyone else where you could feel the arms and when you leaned back you knew there was something solid underneath?

'He just won't let up about this place. When am I getting out? Have the rats moved in yet? He's just so middle class.'

He looked at her feverish face and wondered who she was. 'So it's middle class not to like rats?'

'Larry, he took one look at this place and decided I lived in a slum. Because it's old. Old to him is any place built before 1950. I said to him "it's Victorian, don't you understand?" When I was at Columbia and decided to live off campus, he came to school and moved me back into the dorm. I felt so terrible. Okay so it was an old rundown building, and he saw a few cockroaches. Nobody else minded.'

'You went to Columbia?'

'I'm going back to bed.' She turned from him, then turned back. 'At least he can't come over here so often. But every time he phones it's "when you gonna move?" He calls this my "shtetl".'

'What about your mother? What does she think?'

He tried to remember what Devorah had told him about her parents. Somehow each of them had shed their family when they came to the old world, she like some goddess born from the sea. He knew only that she grew up in New York. He had

165

imagined her one of these children playing in the street in front of an old brownstone, until she told him she came from Long Island. There were no brownstones on the 'Island' as she called it, or children chasing their ball into the gutter. It was the only time he doubted the woman Devorah had become for him.

'She doesn't,' Devorah said, 'just doesn't think of anything but her drapes, her sofa, her new kitchen. Every year she's getting a room done. She discovered avocado green a couple of years ago and now everything looks like someone's bad shit. Sam and Gertie. The perfect couple. My brother doesn't even speak to them.'

'Maybe you should go back to bed,' he said. Very soon her rage would be turned on him.

'I've been in bed. I wanted to say about Christmas.'

This was it. She was going to drop him at Christmas all because of her mother's bad taste. Hadn't she told him how bourgeois he sounded? He wouldn't stay around again to eat out of a can like some tramp.

'I know we talked about going somewhere like Spain. But I've changed my mind. I just feel I need to be not far from here.'

'So what're you saying?'

'Just not far. We could go some place in the country.'

He was trying to understand. If she didn't want him, she could just say. She could say straight out and then he would know.

'If you're not sure. If you want to forget about Christmas.'

'We'll be together, Larry. Just around here. Or not far from here.'

'By the way you had another phone call. Some confused foreign guy.'

He watched her, but she knew he was watching.

'He wouldn't even say who he was. He just muddled around.'

'Maybe it's someone from school,' she said.

His father would say, 'Something's fishy, Larry'. Just then Devorah came over to the sofa and curled up inside his arms, as if such a body could curl.

'Let's just go somewhere cosy like Wales,' she said.

He thought of Gershom's wife whom he had never met and his ugly half-Welsh child. He put his hands under her nightgown, her flesh so hot.

She shivered. 'Larry, get off. Your hands are like death.'

'I'm warming them.'

He heard a curious sound like something was running beneath them, something small and furious.

'What was that?'

'Oh I don't know.'

He heard it again.

'It sounds like—'

'Okay, so I've got mice. Probably. What do you expect with a basement in an old house?'

'Your father's not so crazy.'

She sighed, then said: 'What about Christmas?'

'We'll stay here,' he said.

'Here?'

'Yeah. With the mice.'

'They might be rats actually. You don't want to spend Christmas with them, do you?'

'I'm not going to Wales.'

Later in bed beside her, he lay awake with his arms under his head. Could this be it? Talia had always said he didn't know from love. Was this the way he would feel beside a feverish animal woman? Almost dulled with pleasure. He knew now that she came from a family even more conventional than his own. Devorah Shatner. She had been ashamed to tell him that she grew up on Long Island. He heard the sound again, but the little feet could just as well have been the trembling of the radiators. She was fooling with him again, not telling him the joke.

CHAPTER 20

'He was like, weird. A zombie. I mean like I said, "when are you coming back to college?" He just like ignored me like I wasn't even on the same planet. He's whoo.' Bobby rolled his head around. 'Like a space cadet.'

He had never said anything to the Dean and now one of them had seen Joel body-snatched. *'In loco parentis,'* a chorus of mommies shrieked.

'What's the matter, Larry? You got water in your ears?' The boys at the back had quieted down since they were allowed back, but this was the last day of term. Even Chin reclined with a grin.

Larry had said they could have a party in the last half after he'd talked about what he called the 'right of silence' and handed back their term papers, pathetic attempts to understand one corner of the American constitution. In the whole class only Sarah had managed to get a clear A, an A not eaten into by plagiarism. When they got tired of their own incomprehensible sentences and non-sequiturs, they copied the textbook, or just paraded their ignorance. The boys at the back knew their rights were inalienable but where and what they were was lost somewhere between learning times tables and screwing their first girl. The others, Omar, Kalifa, saw these as gifts stolen from God.

Larry sipped his wine. Sarah had brought bits of meat like beef jerky which she deposited on everyone's desk. They were offerings from her grandfather's funeral back in Lagos. 'So everyone not there is there,' she said. Larry had spent the first ten minutes of the party trying to chew and swallow one of these pieces of gamey leather, while looking solemnly at her.

Chin had produced a large bag of potato chips and Kalifa had come with bottles of Pepsi. The boys had brought cans of beer, nuts and some round chocolate marshmallow things which he was biting into and regretting. Larry was the only one who brought wine. The bottles had stood there untouched till he urged them all to come and imbibe.

Kalifa and Omar were the first to leave. Kalifa shook Larry's hand and told him how much he had learned. Larry knew as he looked into his lean face that he, like all the others, had sat through his classes like a stone.

'Have you decided what you're going to do? I mean after.' He lowered his voice. 'Will you try to marry?'

'Maybe. Who knows? I meet a nice girl but she may not. You know. Goodbye Professor Greenberg. You are a fine teacher.'

'You mean you actually met someone?'

Kalifa smiled and seemed to wink. 'Who knows?'

Omar put his hand on Kalifa's shoulder. 'He wants to fall in love.'

'You wanna come? We're going down to the bar.' The whole class, Chin, Sarah, Bobby and boys, had bonded at last.

'Come Professor Greenberg,' Sarah called. Suddenly he was one of them.

He shook his head. He had decided to tell on Joel. Now that someone else had seen him there was no excuse. His back ached with the weight of it, heavy with the heaviness of all things.

Karen lounged in the doorway perfuming the air, hair drawn back like a little girl. Didn't she smell herself or was she so used to the stench? His father used to nose his own armpits before spraying on deodorant, 'So I know who I am'.

'He's not home,' she said.

'You mean. He's gone for the day?' His wings seemed to rise a little on a puff of unscented air.

She shrugged. 'I haven't seen him. No one has.'

If he left a message for the Dean, then he would have made the decision about Joel's fate here in front of this small smelly woman whose large breasts seem to point at him: 'You, you, you.'

'I guess I'll try him Monday.'

'Don't count on it.'

'Why? Is he sick?' Maybe very sick. The Dean had not shown any signs of mortality. Or ordinary life.

'Just don't.' Then she went back into the office.

Why did he care? One way or other the kid was gone. 'Just decide, Larry,' Talia would say, 'any decision is better than no decision.' Leave it, why don't you, leave him be for God's sake. He did not know who spoke those words, but he lifted his shoulders, shook out the torn gossamer of his wings.

CHAPTER 21

He'd never even heard of the place. So was he responsible for the rain which pursued them from London like some shapeless wraith? Pursued them all the way out to the flattest land he'd ever seen in person.

They'd sat around her apartment on Christmas Day eating lamb chops and creamed spinach. She bought him some weird wooden hand-painted thing which looked like a totem pole but was actually the other kind of Indian: Krishna playing the flute. She wanted to get him the monkey god because that was more Larry, but they'd run out.

He gave her a cream-colored silk scarf, long, luminous and fine, which he bought at Selfridges. It was very expensive. The cute salesgirl said: 'It's so chic.' But Devorah didn't know from chic. He tried to explain to the pert girl with a nose of freckles just what Devorah wore, but all he could remember was the old fur coat and her skin tawny and smooth. Devorah pulled the scarf out of the wrapping, turned it in her hand like some distant peddler relative, then wrapped it around her neck with some other scarf, rich and velvet and red. 'Thanks. You must have spent.' She hated it. It was someone else's gift, he knew as soon as he saw it against her face, someone pale and reed-like. A ghost maybe.

He had been touched as he stood there in Selfridges, his hands dripping with silk scarves. He turned to see a plump man in a hat smiling at him, even holding out his hand.

'Should I know you?' His father's words. He was always being greeted by strangers.

The plump man seemed not to see his perplexity. He asked, 'So how are you finding things? We've wondered about you.'

The voice stirred something in Larry which made him want to cover his face, maybe even cry.

'Larry, isn't it? And you teach law at James's College? Did I tell you our daughter's studying law? Right this minute she's in the middle of exams.'

'That's wonderful. And how is, how are both of you?' Still he could not remember their names.

'Julia's fine. She would send her regards if she knew. She kept saying why didn't we invite you over. But you left so quickly. She thought you must miss going home for Shabbat.'

It was only then that he remembered: avocado and shrimp, Clive and Julia. He felt a kind of nostalgia for who he had been all those months ago before Carla had begun to turn him from man to bird.

He tried to remember what Clive's connection with James Carrington had been. All he could recall was sitting between them at that dinner party, Julia with her shelf bosom and Clive's happy face.

Clive had to rush off to buy his challah in the Food Hall before sundown, but he took Larry's phone number. 'You'll come round some Friday night when you're not too busy.' No one had ever invited him for Shabbat.

Devorah said suddenly on the evening of Christmas Day that she needed to get out into the country, as if some wilderness lay beyond the city, not the neat little squares. They could not agree at first for she was fixed on Wales, some part of the southern coast Gershom had told her about where Dylan Thomas had scattered his words. He became stubborn after the mention of Gershom, imagining that the two of them had some secret plan to meet, though he knew that Gershom would be nowhere near. His wife had banished him from Wales. Not that Devorah even wanted him, but a dog can make friends just by wagging and slobbering, even an ugly dog. 'Women are different from us,' his father used to say. 'They never see what's in front of their face. Just look at your mother.' But she could see nothing else.

They settled on a place Devorah had glimpsed on her junior year abroad, a seaside resort in the eastern thumb of England, open, flat and furrowed. 'You actually can see sky,' she said. 'I feel so hemmed in here.'

He said nothing. Since when did a Jewish girl from New York long for open country? Then he remembered she came

172

from Long Island, the Jewish prairie and birthplace of Linda Lipschitz, his lover for one summer. Linda invited him home for the weekend to a nameless street of ranch houses stretching towards infinity. She had taken him for a ride past cemeteries out to The Hamptons where you could look for Gatsby's house. Sitting on the beach with this Linda Lipschitz girl, he had longed for something which could block his view.

Not even cosy, the town they landed in, but a straggly place with its back to the sea. Maybe it was the rain made him see it that way.

'You could just be happy,' she said. She unpacked in the narrow little room in the narrow little bed and breakfast.

'I'm so happy. I can't tell you. Just could you warn me when you're about to move.'

'Honestly Larry, you sound like my Dad. What do you expect?'

She had said, 'We'll bed and breakfast it. That's what I always do.'

He had given them up in his first year after he had been forced to eat grease in a bed and breakfast in York. 'You'll be wanting the full English,' the woman had said and he nodded. He had been innocent then. The woman brought baked beans and fried sausage, fried bread, fried tomato and eggs which looked as though they had been frying all night to him with a happy smile as if this was the highest achievement of her cooking. She even called him 'luv' and stood in the doorway chatting while he forked measures of beans, greasy egg and gristle into his hapless mouth. He might survive the beans and egg but not the sausage: rat droppings, dirty water, pig's ears and nitrates filling his innocent intestines. He had thought of telling her that his religion forbade him to eat sausages, but imagined her puzzled hurt look as if he had suddenly grown side curls and a beard. The toast in the rack was hard, white and thin, but it kept him from puking, so he ordered seconds. She said, 'You are hungry.' Next morning she doubled his portions and added something called 'black pudding'.

Before dinner they took a walk on the pebble beach, the rain now an old friend. 'They say you can find amber here.' She poked around the wet stones while he held the umbrella.

The beach felt lower than the sea, so flat and featureless that he felt like a larger-than-life figure.

'Imagine dancing here. It's so open. I bet Isadora came here.'

'Wouldn't you hurt your little feet on the pebbles?' He wrapped his arms around her and whispered that they should go back to their little room for a pre-dinner canoodle.

'How horrible. Nylon,' she said pushing her way under the tightness. 'I've never had this before.'

'I have. It's slippery, that's all.' When he pulled back the flowered bedspread, he knew there would be baked beans for breakfast, could taste the metallic grease, the sausages as smooth and shiny as the pink sheets.

'It's like a brothel,' he said, turning to her and putting his hands around her nakedness. 'Just imagine the two of us meeting in one.' He thought suddenly of Edie. She would make something of it. Poor Edie.

'Nylon makes me sweat. It's just so yucky.'

'You wanna leave?'

'Don't be a jerk.'

Her hair was still wet from rain, her thick short black curls, all of her a challenge to this room with its flowered and pink everything, its doilies and prints of cocker spaniels.

In the evening the landlady appeared with a plate of gingerbread and Larry forgave her tomorrow's breakfast.

'You're not lucky with the weather. But keeping fingers crossed.' Her accent was not as flat as these parts. They discovered she was Scottish and a widow.

Larry liked her frank, round face. She was one of these hen women with a full high bust, small bottom and thin legs. She noticed Larry's love of her gingerbread, his capacity to drink tea. He followed her back into the kitchen to get more and carry the huge teapot.

174

Devorah refused seconds. She was quiet while Larry told the woman where they had come from, then went upstairs while he remained with the gingerbread. How could he just leave when the woman clearly needed someone to talk to?

'What is it with you and older women?' Devorah said.

'She's not that old. You can't just eat her gingerbread and not talk to her.'

'You followed her around like I don't know.'

This was beginning to sound familiar, but why he could not say. 'I was just helping.'

But already she was under the pink sheets with her bedside light out. He'd get no second coming tonight.

In the morning the rain had stopped and he could actually see a corner of beach from the window. Devorah begged not to eat breakfast 'in that room again', so he went down by himself, sat in the little breakfast alcove waiting his fate.

'Looks like you've the sun today. Shall I wait for Mrs Greenberg?'

Larry started. He had forgotten what had been assumed and then accepted. His mistress wife lay upstairs languishing.

'She's not a breakfast eater.'

'I thought Americans like a big breakfast. Oh well. Then there's more for you.'

He saw sausages rolling towards him. He opened his mouth to say he was a vegetarian, what he had planned, but saw her eager face and said nothing.

He should have known and trusted her. By the time he rose from the table, he had eaten a bowl of porridge, scrambled eggs, fried mushrooms, two racks of toast and drunk the contents of a large brown teapot.

'You like your food,' she said.

When he smiled at her, he felt like one of these tousled-haired boys with a bridge of freckles on a snub nose.

Devorah had changed into her leotard and sat in the small portion of floor left by the bed and side chair doing stretching exercises, her legs bare. Her phone lay beside her. She looked up at him with a wary look in her half-asleep eyes.

175

'You took forever.'

'You don't know what you missed.'

'I could smell it. Fried everything. Right?'

The breakfast made him a happy man, which even her scowl could not change. 'I love you in that outfit.' And he did. Her solid bare legs, her massive bottom.

She sighed, slapped her thighs. 'Only you would say that. I've gained.'

She had never talked about her size, but he wondered how with a body like a priestess, like the mother of all mothers, she could be a dancer. He had never seen her perform, but in bed she was so graceful that he could scarcely feel her weight on him.

They walked the beach silently, she in her long skirt and racoon coat, stopping to pick among the pebbles for something golden, he staring as the big sky revealed itself. The gap between them grew as he walked towards the sea. He felt. What did he feel? Could he actually be lonely? There was the time he went to the Cape with Talia. She had spent the weekend in bed while he walked on the beach. The one restaurant open in November had gone cranberry mad; everything – the juice, the bread, the gravy, even the curtains – was made with cranberries. Talia had had her period bad and could not look at the place.

She came up to him. 'It's endless,' she said, shading her eyes from the sky.

'That's what you wanted.'

'Do we have to stay another night here?'

He shrugged. Not like him to shrug. Maybe it was post-breakfast blues. He felt like some existential hero standing bleakly against the winter blue sky.

'Another night of those sheets will kill me.'

He thought of tonight's gingerbread and wanted to weep.

'It's so depressing. The whole place. The sheets are just a symptom of, I don't know. Something I can't hack.'

'They're just sheets. Since when did you care so much? I'm the one who's bourgeois.'

176

'You are.'

'And what about you? You sound like your dad.'

'I just don't like sleeping under nylon sheets. Nothing to do with anything.'

He had wounded her, but his pleasure at finally getting back after months of taunts was spoiled by her sad face, a look which said he had not made her happy, could not, would never.

He put his arms around her. 'You're like a furry penguin.' He kissed her forehead and she did not pull away. 'Why not stay one more night? It's so cosy.' For some reason he dreaded going back to London; he wanted her here in this bleak town in their narrow bed in the narrow room.

Larry, Larry, you're not getting possessive?

'Greenie, you're so strange.' She hadn't called him that the whole weekend. His unhappy nickname, but it meant he was back with her.

He thought again of the landlady with her plate of gingerbread looking at the empty sofa and shaking her head. His heart hurt. 'What'll we tell her?'

'Larry please.'

'She'll be so disappointed.'

'The thing is I need to get back.'

'You never told me that. You never said.'

'Well I am now. So.'

He dropped his arms, walked away with his hands in his pockets.

'Greenie don't sulk.' She came up behind him and pinched his ass. Never purely affectionate her pinches.

'Hey that hurt. I'm real you know.'

'No you're not,' she said and pinched him again.

'We're all charlatans,' Gershom liked to say. Sometimes while lecturing to students he found himself outside his skin as if he had died up there and was compelled to watch the curious jerky movements of his arms and listen to echoes of his voice.

'You want I should show you how real I am?' He put his arm around her. 'Let's go back to the room.'

177

'I just feel I can't stay here anymore. I have issues in my life.'

'You never even tried the breakfast.'

'January's my worst month,' his father used to say. 'People don't buy life insurance in January. They figure "my life's empty, so why bother". Remember Larry, people are very selfish. They don't think how someone else might wanna live it up after they go.'

Life was not tasty, that was all. The wind from the river caught him in the face as he walked towards Eureka. It was one of those rare clear days in London when the heavens cast their cold blue eye upon him. He felt new-born, he always did at the beginning of the year, but now with Devorah elusive, his mother talking about moving to be near his sister in Maryland, he was like one of those babies left outside a supermarket.

'I wanna live near one of my kids,' his mother had said.

'But suppose I come back to Boston?'

'When?' his mother asked. 'D'you know when? You don't know.' She wasn't keeping the light burning for her lost boy.

He pulled open the heavy black door and smelled the fug of Eureka: young bodies, old radiators, living ghosts. Groups of students stood around the dark high-ceilinged hall. He heard the shouts of Christmas returners, the 'like' and 'you know what I mean' conversations.

'Hey Professor Greenberg, how you doing?' Billy actually looked glad to see him. 'You know I'm taking your class? Don't worry. I'm gonna be good this semester. There's just me. The others went home. Couldn't handle it anymore.'

'What about Joel?'

'He's like disappeared from the face of the earth. He was weird anyway.'

He hadn't thought about him for a while. He'd made his decision. Leave Joel happy and if his parents came looking, well then, well then what? What if Joel told them he met Larry and Larry had kept mum? He lifted his shoulders and shook Joel off, but he clung. Just leave me, kid.

179

A large pinstriped suit walked by. Girlish face, hair parted in the middle. Should I know you? I should. A long dark corridor opened in his mind, him at the end with empty hands. Larry blushed. He hadn't seen James Carrington since that dinner at his house last fall. He strode past Larry, jacket lifted by the wind of his movement, the walk of a man of importance.

Odd to see him here going into the Dean's office like the college was his business. He never came to Eureka. His name was in the school prospectus but it was the Dean who ran the place. The Dean, the Dean. What was James Carrington doing around here?

Larry walked by the Dean's office, peered in. Karen standing in the outer office eating a chocolate chip cookie shook her head at him.

'I know. He's not in,' Larry said.

Then he watched James Carrington emerge from the office and cast smiles all around, including one in Larry's direction. He shook some hands, then reached out to Larry, even asked him how everything was going, but his eyes seemed to look everywhere but in Larry's face. Larry realized that he did not remember him from that dinner last September; even his graceless exit had been forgotten.

Always he needed time to compose himself before he stood in front of them with a grin, their lovable boy-teacher, but underneath the sad man. He had two classes back to back: Business Law, and something he had concocted called 'Crime and Punishments' which he should have dropped after the first year. It meant so much explaining. Last year he had spent weeks on the ins and outs of murder sentencing, had drawn diagrams, given case studies, even had them enact a trial. At the end of that class one of the Saudis, a good-natured boy, had said, 'But I don't understand, Professor Greenberg, why you trouble yourselves. Why for murderers?'

One of the American boys had said, 'Yeah, right, like just not bother with all this bullshit. Like just exterminate them.'

180

He was standing in the staff room reading his mail: a lecturers' meeting, a student pleading for a change in grade.

'You see our visiting dignitary?' Gershom had done something to himself. Or something had been done to him. Whoever had cut his hair and trimmed his beard. He looked diminished, like one of those nasty nocturnal animals with shiny eyes in a small hungry face. Larry stared at the glossy lips which now dominated. A shorn Gershom looked older, maybe even forty.

Larry nodded, willing himself not to ask Gershom what was happening with the director and the Dean. He would know, he always did or claimed to. But Gershom saw the questioning look in Larry's eyes.

'You heard he's left?'

'You mean him?'

'The Dean. Who else?'

'Really?' It was too late to contain his surprise, to pretend that he too had known.

'Rumor has it a young 'un fell for him and he was not slow to return the favor. The parents found out he was pawing their girl. So he left. His decision, they say, but you know.'

'Just like that?'

'That's what they say. Check his office if you want. See if he left his sticky shadow. The man was a flasher from way back.'

Why did Larry always feel as if had just got off the boat?

'Did you ever think he might just be fed up with this place?'

'You're so trusting Larry. Everyone else knows about him and his greasy fingers. Who cares anyway? He was a grade A schmuck.'

It made things easy for Joel. In all the chaos no one would remember him. But it also meant that Larry had been left with the boy's life. If he went off and joined a mass suicide, Larry would have to atone for the rest of his days. He imagined himself bowing his head in the synagogue, Joel's name on his lips.

'What's the matter? You look worried. Dean your special friend? I thought you hated him.'

'I'm just wondering who'll replace him.' He wasn't but Gershom was fishing.

'Probably another schmuck. In the meantime it's the director and Karen. The hulk and the smell.'

Larry ignored Gershom's hyena laugh. 'What about Guy Stevenson? Isn't he deputy?'

'Guy's too busy shtupping his Saudi boys.'

'You're kidding.'

'You don't believe me? If you paid more attention to what was going on you'd know. You'd know about a lot of things.' He looked almost angry. Gershom with his fool's face.

'We'll see. See if you're right.'

'Did anyone ever tell you? Oh forget it.'

'Had a good Christmas Gershom?'

'Fuck that. My wife's shitted on me. She took off with my kid somewhere. Didn't even switch her phone on. We were suppose to share her over Christmas.'

'I'm sorry.'

'What about your Christmas? I heard you got rained out.'

'Who told you that?'

Gershom ignored this or maybe he did not hear.

'You coming to the next Un-Americans meeting? We've got fresh blood. Well not exactly. I put an ad in *The Yankee Doodle*, would you believe? Have you seen it? It's this crap newspaper for rich elderly Americans. You know, the ones tracing their Scottish clan. The thing's full of ads for tartans and used castles. Two women called, one comes from a Republican family. She had voted for Reagan, but Bush's different she said, "He's just a damn fool."' Gershom lapsed into a New Yorker's version of a southern accent.

'Sounds like you don't need me.'

'I won't push you. We're meeting for lunch at the Sprout. It's a vegan raw food joint run by some American Buddhist group. Susan's idea.'

'Susan?' Nobody in that group had such an ordinary name.

'You must remember Susan.' Gershom said. He put two fingers over his head and made his eyes big.

182

The Martian. The Martian with an earth name. 'She's still around?'

'Sure. Where would she go? Anyway, she's on this weird diet where she's got to balance her yang with her ying. If she eats one wrong thing she loses it. She tells me her shits are something to behold.'

He looked at Larry. 'Okay, so she's a mental case. What d'you want me to do, kick her out?'

'I said nothing.'

'Edie'll miss you. You're a real hit with her. She said to me, "Don't forget Larry. He gets lonely you know."'

'She's very sweet but I can't. Not this weekend.'

Not ever, not ever to be treated like some freak among freaks. For weren't they all people who could fit nowhere? Susan Martian, petulant Ralph with his grudge against a country which had never noticed him, slow Fred who would be mugged the minute he set foot in his native Kansas City. And Gershom the post-hippie hippie with his incontinent child and native woman. Even if Devorah came, he wouldn't go back, especially if she came, Gershom slobbering over her. But then he hadn't mentioned her. Not directly.

Larry talked for four hours straight, the kids still sullen from Christmas, hadn't asked one question or even laughed when he asked: 'Is there anyone out there?' Afterward he climbed the four flights to his cell, his cold vegetable smelling office. He switched on the heavy brown radiator, the only ornate thing in the room, curlicued with its maker, 'R. Peters' in fancy script. He had cleared his desk on the last day before Christmas break and the room itself had been cleaned, his bin emptied. It was as if someone had died in there leaving only musty BO. Larry was the new inmate.

He would work for an hour, then go to the National Film Theatre to see a Busby Berkeley movie. He had developed an addiction to them after he'd seen a clip of girls emerging from a cloverleaf kicking all together, all in time, their voices like some celestial harmony. Then he would try the NFT bar where

183

he'd been told by one of the lecturers at Eureka there were interesting women on their own. He hadn't tried his luck out in the world for a while. He always hooked someone even if he had to throw her back afterwards.

He had turned his chair around and was staring out the high little window, his square of the Thames, when he felt someone's presence, one of the live ghosts coughing their way to eternal death. But the smell was not of sulphur, but aftershave. He turned to see Kalifa by the door.

'I did not want to disturb. You looked thoughtful.'

For some reason he reached out to shake Kalifa's hand. 'I thought you were leaving. You had to leave didn't you?'

'So they gave me some time. But soon I will leave. Maybe two month I go to America if—'

'So you managed to find a way through immigration?'

Kalifa looked uncomfortable. 'Not really. Maybe I marry. The American woman I told you.'

'You mean you'll marry to get into the country?'

'It's not like that. She is very fine. I could even use the love word.'

Why tell me? Why come all the way up here? He looked guilty. Maybe he wanted Larry's blessing. He could see Kalifa struggling with the kind of ambivalence he knew well.

'Maybe we'll stay together. I hope. She is a strong woman. She says we don't have to stay together afterwards.'

He was paying her. Of course he was. Why hadn't Larry thought? 'But what about the greenbacks?' his father had asked when Larry described his first lawyer job.

What did it matter to Larry what Kalifa did with his life? Kalifa had been the honourable one and now he too was sullied.

'You understand. I can't go home and I can't stay here. You understand.'

'Sure. And I'm glad you've found a way. I was just surprised.'

The little window was navy blue now and the lights strung out along the Thames had come on. A cart rolled slowly down the corridor. Doors open and shut, open and shut. The body

184

hunt. Soon they would reach him and he would be wheeled down and nobody would know. He imagined Kalifa celebrating with his bride, his glossy, blonde American girl, eyes the shade of dollar bills. Hadn't he taught Kalifa about 'the pursuit of happiness'? What other country fought a war just so everyone could have fun? Larry, the pure, floated in the Thames.

'Ah, you still here. Sorry.' The round face of the Nigerian cleaner.

'Come in. I'm leaving. I'm just leaving.'

The man grinned at him. 'You're always last. Why?'

Because I'm a deadbeat. Larry pretended to write while the man worked around him, sweeping, inspecting his empty bin, dusting his empty shelves. He was rotund but moved fast.

'But you stay.'

'I'll leave soon.'

For some reason this made the man laugh. 'When will you leave?'

'Soon. Like I said.'

'You are all the time leaving.' At this the man laughed again, could not stop laughing.

Larry was beginning, just beginning to become annoyed with this smiling guy. 'What about you? When will you leave?' Larry asked.

'I too am all the time leaving. Until.' He knocked the contents of his pan into a large bin in his cart. 'Until I am finished here. And then I go home. You understand?'

There were plenty of women lounging in the NFT bar but they were with other women. Gaggles of them chit-chatting in their brittle little voices. If there was anything worse than one Englishwoman, it was several, smirking, casting and then averting their eyes. Could he be bothered to separate one of the brood from her sisters? With each drink he moved to a different part of the room but the giggles would not release a single for him.

By the fourth drink, desperate for conversation, he befriended a lanky elderly man with broken veins in his cheeks and a bare domed head who had come down from Birmingham to see a series of films about railways. He showed Larry a notebook with numbers all closely written, the pen pressed so hard the pages felt like parchment. Larry could make nothing of this.

'I've been at it since I was twelve, don't you know,' the man said.

Why did he always pick the mad ones?

When the man lumbered off to Waterloo station, 'to do his usual', Larry talked to another ancient, a woman dressed as an artist with a beret, Mexican shawl and black braid hanging over one shoulder which looked like it was made of yarn. What she really did he never discovered for they talked about Fred and Ginger. 'I'll never understand, never never, what he saw in her. She was so coarse,' she said.

By midnight he felt good. The woman beside him, an Australian with a bright friendly face, confided that she had been one of five wives of a Nigerian tribal chief. 'They like big women. Not like here.'

He should have said, 'You're not big.' But she was what his father would call 'ample', more than ample.

'I felt appreciated for once. Like my body was good as it was. But I couldn't do it anymore. It wasn't the other wives, everyone thinks that. We all had nights when he would come. It was exciting actually. I got on with them. One of the older ones, she was like my auntie. But I missed my life. Going to a pub. Getting pissed. I was just so restless. So I left.'

'What about your—' he hesitated to say husband. 'You mean that's it? You won't go back even though—' Larry stopped because he could see she was beginning to get emotional.

'You know what he said?'

Larry shook his head once, then again when she kept looking at him. He felt like a puppet.

'He said, "I'm keeping your house for you".' Her voice definitely shook, and Larry was obliged to put his arm around her. He felt so skimpy beside her like a badly made shirt.

They walked along the river. She had cried, had even been silent for a moment. 'You know what?'

He shook his head, then nodded, then decided just to maintain eye contact.

'I felt real there.'

He thought of Devorah, how she would have scolded this woman for participating in her own oppression. Yet it was possible to multiple-love. He had a sudden empathy for the African chieftain hedging his bets. There would always be a woman for him.

CHAPTER 23

It was a funny place to meet. She had said they could go from there and when he had said where, she said wherever. But Trafalgar Square was wherever, a place for greenhorns his grandma would say.

Devorah sat on the edge of the dried-up fountain talking to a guy with straggly hair. She had her earnest face, was nodding. He was bent over, smoking one of those self-rolled cigarettes.

She caught sight of him, waved, but continued talking. The guy turned and grinned at Larry. His teeth had another smile. His father shook his head over the failure of a younger colleague to sell: 'You can get away with anything. But bad teeth. People don't want to know you.'

'This is Malcolm,' she said and they both stood up.

Malcolm was small, gremlin-like, a shaggy head on a thin little body. He put his hand out. 'You got a good woman.'

How would you know, you, you tramp. But he took his hand and pressed the limpness.

'Malcolm's writing poetry.'

'It's all in here.' Malcolm tapped his head.

Larry imagined the words strung across his mind like old-fashioned washing lines.

'Well it was nice knowing you.'

He sloped off, a stuttering walk with back hunched and feet uncertain.

'Where d'you pick him up?'

'He just came over and began reciting poetry to me. He's sad.'

'He looks quite happy actually. I mean apart from the fact that he's probably just crawled out.'

'He had a philosophy. You're just—' She looked at him. 'I don't know.'

'I'm just what?'

'Forget it. We'll only be fighting again.'

'I like a good fight.' He put his hands up in mock boxer style. Anything to lighten her up.

'Larry, just cool it, will you?'

'So where do you want to go?'

'Can't you decide for once?'

'You never like where I say.'

'I'll do anything just to get out of the cold.'

'Where's your fur?' That was it. She looked diminished without it like some kind of skinned animal.

'Don't ask.'

'You felt sorry for the racoon.'

'Things were living in it, okay?'

'Things? What things? You mean your coat gave birth to baby racoons?'

'Moths, Larry. Nests of them. Like I was wearing decay.'

'Poor Devorah. You've had a shock. Why don't I take you home?' He indicated with his eyebrows that there would be more than solace there.

'Whose home? We don't have any home here.'

She was beginning to annoy him. 'What about Chinese?' he asked. 'We'll walk up to Soho.'

They had argued so long night had come down with empty pools of darkness everywhere.

'Let's go. This place gives me the creeps.'

He looked out at the swirl of traffic. 'But where?'

'Listen. Maybe I'll go home. I'm so down.'

'I could get mad about this.'

'You don't know what you want to do, do you?'

Larry was thinking she wasn't so cute without the fur. This saddened him. Like the discovery that his mother dyed her hair. He'd come home from school early and there she was combing what looked like loose turds through her hair.

'Let's eat something and then we'll decide.'

'All you think about is food.'

'Have you thought about Paris?' He saw them in one of these velvet rooms humid with desire.

189

They had begun to climb the steps leading up from the fountain. She paused, her shoulders drooping. 'That's just it. I can't.'

'Can't? Can't?'

She put her hand on his shoulder; he could see actual pity in those bedroomy eyes, the lids so low and heavy he wanted to prise them up. She could have dimpled smiles sometimes. The roundness of her, what had someone said about 'globed fruit'?

Behind her the National Gallery's lights came on. She was like some figure in a Greek tragedy, her long skirt dragging in the wet, her hair matted from rain. He wouldn't even be in her play except for the moment when he would be called up on the stage to be ridiculed and dismissed.

'Do we have to talk about this here?'

'You keep asking.'

He wished they were back in the darkness, not here in public, the lights of cars bearing down on them.

'I don't know what I'm doing that far ahead. It's so complicated that maybe you should go without me.'

'Look. Have you got someone else?'

'Maybe and maybe not.'

'That's not an answer.'

'I didn't think it mattered to you. You're not a serious person so I never thought, I mean I didn't need to say anything. You're Larry lawyer.' She gave him one of her gentle smiles which upset him more than her words.

'I'm serious. Really serious. That's what you don't know, how serious I am. I mean I can be so serious.'

'Larry, just forget it.'

'So who is he? That poet you just met?' Gershom's oily face appeared in his mind like some kind of miasma. If he asked and she said yes, he would throw up or kill him. If he asked. 'Anyone I know?'

'I don't want to talk about it. Not yet. Not before I've made up my mind. Maybe I need to meditate. I'm thinking I might even go back home for the vacation. I just need to be clear.'

'I thought you had no home.'

190

'You know what I mean. We're just passing through here.'

'But do I know him?'

She looked guilty and so she should. How could she want, well, anybody after him? Once she told him, 'You've got such a cute ass.' How could she let Gershom slobber all over her?

'Why don't you go home? You look bedraggled.'

'So Paris is off? After all that.'

He stared at her but she was giving nothing away, not to him anyway.

'You're not really going home. You're going with this guy.'

'Will you stop all this?'

'Just tell me the truth, I can bear it.'

'You sound so pathetic. Believe me. I really don't know. Which is why I'm thinking of going back. And I'd be home for Passover.'

'Suddenly you're Jewish.'

She stood on the top of the stairs and smiled down at him. Gave him her Italian greeting, the open and shut hand like a child's goodbye. 'Bye bye, Greenie.'

Larry wandered back towards the fountain. It could not be Gershom. The fool would've thrown it in Larry's face, but then why didn't she say 'no, no one you know', why didn't she put him out of his misery? He walked round and round the pools of darkness, head lowered, so he did not see Malcolm until the guy was standing in front of him.

'What happened? You had a fight?'

Larry shrugged and began to turn away.

'She's a fine woman, but maybe too good for us. You know what I mean?'

'Look I don't want—'

'She really listens. That's why I told her everything. I been through a bad patch, but I'm clean now. She said how poetry could be something outside me, something I could do which wasn't anything to do with me. That's what's important she said, not who we are, but what we give to the world. She's beautiful.'

191

Larry nodded. Her usual spiel and now she's giving it to drug addicts. He began walking towards the empty plinth. He could always ask someone else to Paris.

'Take care of yourself,' Malcolm called out like he meant it.

Larry felt almost like crying. 'You too,' he called back.

CHAPTER 24

He knew it was a mistake the minute he said it. The words just dropped out of his mouth in a fit of self-pity. 'I've got a vacation coming up. Why don't you come over here?'

For a week his mother was hemming and hawing about the flight. Somebody told her there was special turbulence over the Atlantic. She didn't want to miss her mah-jong group. He began hoping she'd say no, had stopped arguing with her; then she spoke to his sister who told her how hurt Larry would be, poor kid on his own.

The crowd at the gate thinned slowly as the plane from Boston emptied and he was left with a taxi driver holding a placard for 'Mr Charles'.

'Just said "Charles" so I thought it could be his first name. You know Americans, they're very informal. But I felt like a git holding up a sign for "Charles". Maybe I confused him. You think he saw "Mr Charles" and thought it was someone else?'

Larry was beginning to tense. Normally he would have involved himself in the probabilities of the taxi driver's situation, but now he just shook his head: 'He'd have to be pretty dumb.'

'Well they are, aren't they? Excepting yourself of course.'

He wasn't going to worry. His mother was a slow walker. Maybe her luggage had been last. He'd got excited with everyone else, watching the doors open, looking even sometimes behind people emerging as if she were so small he might not have seen. But no her.

'I'm off. If you see some geezer looking around tell him I left.'

Larry nodded. She was just taking her time. Maybe she was wandering somewhere between luggage and immigration. His mother in limbo.

'You lost your mum.' The woman at the British Airways counter winked at him and in the middle of his anguish he thought he had never had a real Irishwoman. If that's what she was. In Boston he took out descendants of descendants, but never someone actually smelling of clover like this one. She told him his mother would have been out by now, unless she was detained.

'She's an elderly American woman,' he said. 'They'd be crazy to stop her.'

He had a sudden vision of her small form wheeled out under a white sheet. Heart attack. She couldn't take the turbulence. 'Do you think, do you think maybe something happened?'

She never made it to the plane. Her heart gave way from the excitement and she was lying on the floor alone while everyone thought she was on the plane.

'Shall I check the passenger list?'

Lillian Greenberg. 'Little Lil,' his father called her.

Her name wasn't there. 'What does it mean? What could it mean?'

'You think your mum just forgot to get on the plane? They get confused don't they?'

He shook his head. His mother was not senile yet.

'Why don't you go home and phone her?'

He turned away. He remembered a thriller where a passenger got sucked out of the plane. A little old Jewish lady whirling around the earth.

She answered on the tenth ring, her voice thick with sleep. 'Hello? Hello?'

'Mom? Is that you?'

'Larry? What's wrong?'

'Why aren't you here? I went all the way to the airport.'

'You woke me. I just got back to sleep.'

'What're you doing there?'

'Larry, Larry, you're driving me crazy. It's five o'clock in the morning.'

'What're you doing there? You're supposed to be here.'

'I'm going tonight. I told you.'

Then it hit him. She had told him the date she was leaving and the time she would arrive. But somehow she had not realized that this would be the next day. A whole night would

194

pass with her in the air, five hours gobbled up before she would land in the old world. She couldn't imagine it.

He'd forgotten how small she was and beginning to bend as she walked, a bony little woman with stiff dyed hair and glasses too big for her. He wanted to cry. She struggled with two bags, one heavy with what turned to be wooden hangers.

'You brought them all the way here. It's crazy.'

'I didn't know what you would have. It's a different country.'

'You think they don't have hangers here? They probably invented them.'

'Larry you're so cute.'

He had planned so that each day was filled by some large gloomy monolith: the Houses of Parliament, The Tower of London, St Paul's, Westminster Abbey. By the fourth day his mother had a look he remembered from childhood when he brought her a succession of books to read aloud to him.

They arrived late in the day at Westminster Abbey after she had spent some time in a tourist shop picking out a canvas bag imprinted with the Houses of Parliament. 'Mom, you don't want that.' She did. She wanted it even after she had shaken her head as they stood on the bridge gazing at Parliament and Big Ben and said, 'They look wrinkled.'

They reached Westminster Abbey just in time for the last queue of people waiting to be let in by the guards. She was rummaging in her handbag as usual when she realized that she had left the canvas bag on a bench. He almost said 'does it matter?' but she looked like she might cry. The whole point of the day lost.

It had only been minutes but when he returned the great doors had shut behind her. Even the guards were inside and the little sign told him there would be no more visitors that day. He thought about finding another entrance but was so afraid she would suddenly come out and not see him that he waited. He tried knocking, but made no impression on those heavy doors. And people stared at him. He was reminded of the time when he was taken by his father on the Freedom Trail in Boston.

When he knocked on the door of Paul Revere's house, a passing policeman shouted, 'He's not home' and went off laughing.

He had never known what it was to worry about her, to imagine her crying in the gloom like an abandoned child. When she did emerge blinking in the sunlight she told him she had asked the guards to open the doors for her son, but they acted like they hadn't heard her.

'Maybe they didn't understand.'

'I said. I got my son out there. I told them I've come all the way from Boston to see him.'

'Maybe they hate Americans.' It was like in the old days when some kid beat him up, his father shaking his head and blaming anti-Semitism.

She had traipsed around the marble floors with another woman till the two of them got tired and sat down.

'You made a friend.'

His mother looked at him. 'She prayed.'

'Well that's natural. You're in a church after all.'

'She was on her knees.'

'That's what they do.'

'Larry. No more churches for me.'

He took her to Oxford Street. 'This was a mistake,' he said pulling her through the crowd in front of Selfridges.

Then in the quiet of some back street, she shook her head. 'It's not what I thought it would be. I thought it would all be old-fashioned little houses like you read about. Like Oliver Twist. Quaint. I haven't seen anything quaint since I got here.'

The next day she wanted to stay in Wimbledon. 'It reminds me of Brookline.'

'Brookline? It's nothing like.'

'It's homey.'

He stared at her. He had not understood the word 'ennui' until he'd spent Saturday shopping in Wimbledon.

She'd seen a McDonald's on the way home from the train station and wanted to have lunch there.

'I feel homesick.'

'Mom, you've only been away for a week.'

The place was so crowded they had to wait for seats.

'You see,' she said. 'Everyone has the same idea.'

He brought her French fries and a burger.

'Aren't you eating?'

'I won't.'

'C'mon. It's fun.'

'I won't eat at McDonald's while I'm over here. I'd feel like a fool.'

'Did anyone ever tell you how cute you are?'

Then she took a bite out of her burger and looked thoughtful. 'It tastes the same. Looks the same. But I know it's not the same. Something not there about it.'

His father called her dizzy, said she had a buzz where other people have brains. But she knew her mah-jong, sometimes even called out sets in her sleep.

After that lunch in McDonald's he had trouble persuading her to leave Wimbledon. 'Cosy,' she called it, the rest, the great beast of London she only half believed in. 'When I was there,' she would say, like it had been not two days ago, but years, a dream life away.

He would find quaint for her. He remembered during his first month in England he had gone to Stratford and taken a day trip into what the American guidebook had called the 'incomparable Cotswolds'. He'd seen his first thatched cottage there. Why he had never returned for a closer look, he could not say.

'I'm happy here,' she said.

'But this isn't the real England.' If he could have brought his mother down to Witherins to see Carla's mother, one glimpse of the covered pies, the jams with their little hats would have been enough.

'If you want.'

'Mom, you can't go home and tell everyone you spent three weeks in McDonald's.'

'If that's what you want.'

What happened to him? He had been her boy, eaten her bad meals, worn the clothes she never ironed, the darling

197

curly-headed little boy she waved goodbye to every morning. He knew that she would appear somewhere in the house when he returned, as if she was real only for him. 'What does she do all day?' His father said. Now he wanted to drag her out of the solid house and bring her to one of straw.

They were in fact made of stone. The little town was just one winding street of golden stone houses some with lattice windows and sinking dormers. 'It's nice,' his mother said.

'Nice? Just nice. What about charming and quaint and—'

'Will you look at that?' She stood before a window hung with rabbits and the bloody parts of deer.

'It's an old-fashioned butcher.'

'They should wrap it up. Why don't they?'

They wandered into a covered stone market place. His mother stumbled around the uneven floor. 'They should do something about this. You could fall.'

'It's historical, Mom. Seventeenth century.'

'So what? If people fall they fall.'

Curved doorways, gargoyles, a damp place where sun never reached, sinister and smelling faintly of pee. He imagined women put into stocks and strangers beheaded, the whole town gathering to watch. But there were only tourists in this little town: Americans and more Americans in the antique shops, the jeweller's, the embroidery store. They were the only buyers in 'Cotswold Curiosity', a store which sold little figures of Dickens characters. 'At last,' his mother said.

They stayed in an old inn with low ceilings, wood beams and bathtubs with feet. His mother took a shower every day of her life. Bathtubs she said were for babies. The restaurant had a real fireplace surrounded by hunting pictures and shelves of rose-infested china. A little plaque told them that beneath their feet had once been a dungeon.

His mother leaned forward and whispered, 'Where's everyone? You think maybe they have a problem?'

'We're early. Who eats at 5:30?'

They came and spread themselves out in the room. Even so he could hear them, all of them American: the two elderly

198

couples, the guy with slicked-back hair who complained that his steak was too rare. One of the dumpy husbands, who sounded New York, asked the waitress, 'You sure it's steak? You sure it's not pork? It tastes like pork. You sure?'

'No, it's steak.' She was sweet about it.

'It tastes like pork.' He shook his head.

After the waitress left, his wife said, 'How would you know? You've never even eaten pork.'

In the corner, a lone young man with a long ponytail with the kind of accent Larry heard at Eureka, slow and flat, told the waitress he needed more time to order. Larry wondered about this. The man had been there when they arrived.

Finally he said, 'I'll have the Yorkshire pudding, carrots and mushrooms.'

'You mean the roast beef?'

'Oh it comes with roast beef. Oh I see. I'll need more time.'

In the end he ordered a bowl of soup and a salad and asked for a jug of water without lemon or ice.

Larry heard the clink of ice cubes when the waitress brought him his food and water. He waited for the young man to protest, but he was quiet.

'It's cute, this place.' His mother had brightened when the others came in. 'Real English.'

The New York man heard this and asked Larry's mother in a voice which carried through the room: 'How long you here for?'

'My son lives here. He's a lawyer.'

'You must be having a ball,' the man said to Larry.

Larry had never been an unfriendly person, but he could not manage a smile for this pork eater.

When they returned to Wimbledon his mother seemed restless. He spent one morning preparing for his next term's class while she wandered about the house.

'Go out if you want. Go into London. You know how. You said you wanted to shop.'

'Without you?'

'Yeah. It would be good for you.'

199

'Well okay. If you're sure you have to work.'

'I've got a job, mom. I work here.'

She looked almost puzzled as if she could not imagine an everyday life here with breakfast and pay checks.

He found her later on in his little living room, her coat on, her handbag in her lap, staring out the window.

'You've been sitting there the whole time?'

'I just couldn't go out. I got downstairs but it felt so creepy. I thought I'd wait till you finished.'

He should not be so cruel to her. He knew what she felt, how she was not quite here, no longer there, as if the very atoms of her being no longer held together. During his first month in London Larry waited for someone to put his hand through him.

'I don't know anyone here. If only I had someone to talk to.'

'What about me?'

'You're Larry. You're my son.'

He sat down next to her and gave one of her narrow bony shoulders a squeeze. 'Let's do something ordinary. Like go to a supermarket.'

'You got a supermarket?'

'I'll introduce you to my dry cleaner.'

'Larry you're adorable.'

By the end of that week she went out on her own, but only in Wimbledon. She made friends with the woman who checked out books in the library and the old deaf man who sold fruit on a side street near the tube station. She went twice to McDonald's by herself and even shopped for him at Sainsbury's. He heard her on the phone to his sister: 'I'm having a ball. You may not recognize me when you pick me up. I got an accent and I'm different. I've been living in a foreign country so I'm different. Larry's got an accent. Yeah, yeah, I'm telling you.'

'I left the hangers with you. You never know.'

'Sure. They might decide to phase out hangers.'

They sat over tall coffees at the airport. She talked about her life back home with nostalgia. 'It's cosy. I wake up, have my breakfast by the TV. I go shopping in the morning.'

200

It was as if he and everything which had whirled around her in the damp air of that foreign place were to be extinguished once she stepped off the plane in Boston. She was going back to real life.

He was grateful she did not cry or plead with him to come home. But then she had never questioned anything he'd done. When one girlfriend changed to another she said, 'That was quick. Is the new one a nice girl?' Even in fourth grade when he told her he was leaving home to train for the Red Sox, she just said, 'If that's what you want, Larry.'

'I'll have to leave you here,' he said, kissing her cheek.

'Can't you come?' She looked around, noticed the kissing and hugging going on. 'They'd let you if you said something to one of the guards.'

'No mom. This is passport control. They're strict. You gotta go in without me.'

'Bye bye then.' But she would not let go of him.

He realized that he had never seen her off before. Always he was the one waving goodbye, while she, Lil, dizzy Lil, was the fixed point, home base. And somewhere beyond her was his father. Even now.

'I always tell everyone Larry's gone across the ocean to find himself, but they say why does he have to go so far?'

'It's not so far.'

Her lips started to tremble. 'It's not like you're getting married. If you were getting married—'

He felt shaken. She had never talked about marriage to him. 'Mom, you talk like I'm lost.'

She smiled, wiped at her wet eyes. 'So I'll see you sometime.'

She let go of him and walked to passport control, then gave him a flap of her hand and was gone.

I am the same Larry, he should have told her, just the same. He raised and lowered his shoulders. The wings shook themselves out, shiny as a newborn's, wet with his mother's tears.

201

He just wanted to know what was going on with her. For the past month he had dated a woman he'd met at the Wimbledon wishee washie. 'Those are my smalls,' she had shrieked when he had begun pulling out the wrong wash. She herself was statuesque, a blonde Gretchen type with corn-rolled hair who worked as a travel agent in Guildford and lived in the flatlands of Wimbledon. A generous spirit, she let him spend night after night in her little flat. For some reason he had still not invited her to his place.

But Devorah still rankled. When he phoned she sounded tired and answered his questions about how she was with single words. He knew not to leap in too soon with her. He had his laundry pick-up, yet he was dreading what Devorah would say.

'You make up your mind?'

'What do you mean?'

Of course she knew but was ashamed. Who wouldn't be to take up with Gershom?

'You went home to make up your mind.'

'I didn't. In the end I just stayed around.'

'Poor Devorah. So you haven't made up your mind which man.' He mocked but in truth felt relief. If he couldn't have her at least no one else could.

'It's not like that. It's nothing like that.'

'I mean, how can you not know about something like that? What is it, some beauty contest? Did you ever consider this guy's feelings?' Let her believe that he had stepped aside, unwilling to battle with lesser men.

'You can talk. Since when did you ever even think about what someone else was thinking.'

'Could you repeat that?'

'You're just so. You never delve deeper than your own ego.'

'My ego's quite deep actually.'

'Larry, stop it.'

'So I'll see you when I see you. In the hereafter.' He still had his Gretchen.

'You going to our meeting?'

'I haven't been. It's not exactly fun.'

'Why not come, Larry?'

This gave him some heart. If Gershom were the one, she would not want him there. Would she? He thought of Gershom's nose hairs on one of Devorah's velvet pillows.

'Just come. Don't be such a tight ass.' He said nothing to this; he had become good at phone silence. 'I'd like to see you, Larry.'

He went through his 'I don't knows. Not sures', even pretended to look in his diary, then found his mouth saying the word 'yes'.

The door was open as usual to a long unlit hall. Always in this country he was feeling his way through dark passages. The dog accompanied him licking his hand like some guide in hell.

'Where is everyone?'

Clark sitting alone on the couch did not hear this. He smiled up at Larry, who wondered where his partner was, the sour Ralph. The red-faced academic whose name he never remembered lay on the floor in front of the couch doing some kind of breathing exercise.

'We haven't seen you in a long time,' Clark said. 'Have you been away?'

'I am away,' Larry thought.

'Usually we meet somewhere. But I think Gershom has something to tell us.'

No Edie or Devorah. Not even the Martian. Maybe the group was ending. Maybe that's what Gershom had called them to say.

He walked around the sofa, past the table where the group had gathered for Thanksgiving dinner. He thought he heard Devorah's voice and walked into the kitchen.

It was what one of his girlfriends, an English major from Des Moines, called a 'Jamesian moment'. She'd done her PhD

203

on Henry James's scenes: 'Nobody has to say anything, you just know from looking at where everyone is standing, you just know what you've been avoiding knowing for so long.' The two of them were close, not hugging, but heads close. Before he could hear more than Devorah's 'I'm not sure, I'm just not', they saw him and moved apart fast. Devorah wiped her eyes, gave him one of her sleepy smiles. If he was having his Jamesian moment it was not the spiritual wash, the epiphany his girlfriend always talked about. He felt like a creep.

'I didn't think you were coming.'

'You asked me. Remember?'

Gershom walked away and Larry began to wonder if he had seen what he had seen.

'What are you doing with him anyway?' he said.

Devorah looked at him. 'What are you talking about?'

Now it was his turn to walk away. He headed for the passage, followed by the dog.

'Hey, wait.' Gershom stood before Clark and the red-faced man.

'Something's been happening I wanted to share.'

This was really too much. Larry continued to walk towards the hallway.

'Larry, will you wait.'

Larry turned. Gershom stood with not even a minyan around him.

'Somebody's been tapping my phone.' He looked around, nodded his head as if responding to someone's doubt, but no one had said a word. 'Yeah really. I keep hearing these sounds.'

Clark had not heard and wore the same smile. The red-faced academic man was picking at his toes.

'Don't laugh, but I think we have some kind of CIA plant. I say this because somehow they know our movements.'

Larry looked across at Devorah who grinned at him.

'I'm serious.'

'That's what worries us,' said Devorah.

'This guy turns up last Friday with some cock and bull story about how he's selling half-price kitchens and needs to look at mine. It was frightening.'

Gershom did not look scared. He did not even look as if he believed the words coming out of his mouth.

'The thing is everything started when Susan left. She just disappeared from the group. When I called her number she was no longer there.'

'You mean all the time she was getting signals through her antennae?' said Larry.

Devorah came forward. 'She went home, didn't you know? She had some kind of breakdown.'

'Why didn't you tell me? I thought—' Gershom said.

'You really are a fool,' Devorah said.

'Can I leave now?' Larry said.

'Why don't you?'

But when Larry got up, Gershom called out, 'Hey Larry, stay. I was joking. Larry.'

He heard someone running behind him on the street, thought it was Gershom and walked faster. 'Just leave me, you slanderous dog.'

But the running continued and he would have to run himself to escape. He turned and saw Devorah without her coat or her bike. Just herself, panting, running after him for once.

'Larry, I wanted to tell you something.'

'Maybe I don't want to hear.'

'Don't be a baby.'

'I'm a boy not a baby.'

'Will you stop, I've got a stitch.'

Even in the midst of this he reached out for her waist and rubbed.

'I wanted to let you know before. Even now I don't know for sure.'

They didn't usually tell him on the street standing in full sunlight. It was after nights in which he confessed his infidelities, his neverness, that they weeping would say that it

205

was over. He had learned not to upset himself at this point. The 'over' was always a prelude to another year of acrimony.

'The thing is I might get married.'

'Married? You're marrying him?'

She stared.

'I just can't believe. Anyway he's married.'

'What are you talking about?'

'Him. Gershom.'

'You mean you thought all this time... How could you?'

'That's what I thought. How could you?'

'He's not so bad.' She rubbed his arm. 'Don't get at him. He's sad because the group's breaking up. It's like his family.'

No, he wouldn't hate him anymore. Because Gershom was right about the alien presence. It had come and taken her even as they spoke, body snatched.

He almost asked her who the guy was. He never wanted to know who replaced him, even if it was someone he knew.

But of course it wasn't and what did he care? The relief he felt, even the kinship with Gershom was tempered by something else. What was it, he asked himself, as she turned back to Gershom's house? He had lost her.

Chapter 26

There was an odd sense of freedom at Eureka as if the Dean's flight had released everyone from some spell. Nobody was running the school. The director made brief appearances, waving and shaking hands like some portly pope. Karen lounged openly. Guy was seen in the canteen with his arm around one of his students. Only Larry felt the dour spirit of the place persisted beneath the party atmosphere. He avoided his students and Gershom by always taking the back stairs to his office, by moving swiftly from the front door to his classroom, by looking neither to the left nor the right nor even sometimes in front of himself. He imagined Gershom knew about Devorah all along and was laughing at him, but his grinning face never appeared in his office doorway.

When, despite his efforts, he did see Gershom across the crowded school hall, Gershom left before Larry could avoid him. Maybe he was taking it hard. After all he had wanted her. They'd both been shafted, but it was not like Gershom to cower.

He began to wonder. He saw Gershom staring at him a couple of times, but Larry had only to stare back and Gershom left. At a meeting in which the director announced the new Dean, Gershom said nothing. He came late, sat beyond everyone in a row of empty seats and left before Larry. It seemed that Larry had only to walk towards Gershom for him to shy away.

He was having what Talia would call an approach of the dreads. It was bad enough when Gershom pursued and mocked him. Now this. Something had happened and for once Gershom was too afraid to tell him. He barged into a conversation between Gershom and another lecturer, but when Larry appeared Gershom seemed to falter, his eyes everywhere but on Larry, and then he said, 'Well, I'll leave you two', as if he had been the intruder.

They were passing on the stairs, Larry coming down from his office, Gershom climbing. There was no way out for him.

'Edie asked for you,' Gershom said. 'She calls you her wounded spirit.'

'I thought she left the group. I thought the group left the group.'

'You're so cynical.'

Larry ignored this. There was something about Gershom's look, something familiar about the evasive eyes, the frightened smile. He remembered a criminal case he'd followed as a law student. The defendant, an undergraduate, murdered his roommate and left the body sitting in front of the television in the dorm lounge.

'Seen your Americans?'

Gershom seemed to shrug.

'You know Devorah's getting married?'

'Of course I know.' So that was what that scene in the kitchen was about. He knew before Larry and was trying to stop her. Why had she told him first? Why?

Gershom began to speak but seemed only to stutter. 'Larry I just wanted—'

He wouldn't ask him who it was. And what did it matter? Only that he knew what Larry didn't. He knew and always knew even though he was a fool. He, Larry, was a bigger fool.

'Look Larry, I've known since Christmas.'

'Known what? She didn't even know herself.'

'I mean—' He looked at Larry. 'Don't you know who it is?'

There was something he was not getting here. She told him first, what she hadn't even known herself? 'Larry, you're so innocent,' Talia saying even after she had called him 'prevaricator'.

'I was keeping mum because I didn't know what would happen in the end. Didn't want to upset you.'

There was an odd feeling in his head as if each of his hairs was standing at attention. 'Don't give me that. She wouldn've confided in you.'

'Oh yeah?'

'You don't know, do you? You're just full of it. You don't know her.'

208

Gershom stared at him with bloodshot eyes. Then he said, 'It's Kalifa she's marrying. Right under your nose.'

It was like that game when you tried to remember where cards were after they were turned up and turned over again. How could he have known? Did she give hints, had cards been turned so quickly that he had not seen?

'Kalifa. I don't understand how she could. She didn't know him.'

'It's a happy ending. Kalifa gets to live in the States.'

'I can't believe it. You mean after all that she's marrying so he can get a Green Card.' He remembered how he, Larry, had been her hero at Thanksgiving.

'Maybe it's not so simple, Larry.'

'How did she even meet him?'

'When I told her about him, that he was almost a political refugee, she got interested. One thing led to another.'

Larry could feel his hair alive again. He stared at Gershom's lips.

'Okay. So I introduced them.'

Larry hadn't hit anyone since he was little, but he felt his hand curl into a fist, his arm rise. Gershom pulled back, but Larry got him under the chin, his blow cushioned by beard.

Gershom staggered, his hands to his face. Larry wiped his eyes. Even in that moment, he thought Gershom moved in an exaggerated way.

'You stupid schmuck. I got a glass jaw. You stupid, stupid.' He cowered against the wall, his hands over his eyes.

Larry's face was burning. He pulled his fist down.

'Just get a hold. I don't wanna fight.' He wiped his eyes. 'My wife's just shacked up with a Welsh nationalist. Now this.'

'Why d'you do it anyway? You don't care about Kalifa.'

'I do actually. I wasn't just trying to fuck you over, though really you need fucking over.'

Then it dawned on Larry. 'Just because you couldn't have her, you made sure I couldn't either.'

209

'You can say what you want. I was trying to help the guy. He was desperate and I couldn't think of anyone else. You think I'd ask Susan mental case?'

'She's going to be happy with him? You really think?'

'You were just fooling around. You're never serious. She didn't think you'd care. You and her weren't really a number anyway. Not even a decimal.'

'Shut up Gershom.'

'Okay, okay.' He put his hands up. 'Truce. I got my wife speaking only in Welsh. You know what that's like? Imagine Hebrew without vowels. Anyway I need all the friends I can get.'

Larry began walking up the stairs. His mother always said, if you see a fight, just walk away, but what if you were one of the fighters?

'Larry,' Gershom called, 'don't just go away like that. We gotta talk. Larry.'

But he was mounting those metal stairs towards the sick rooms, the shut doors of those who would never emerge, the air thick with nurses' whispers. He unlocked his office door. The close air choked him and he pushed open the high square window. In the past year he had learned to fly close but never to land; he knew he could live in flight. As he stared into the night above the Thames, he tried to shake out his wings, the long gossamer wet with birth, but he had lost them.

CHAPTER 27

'I was going to tell you in person. I wanted to be the one. I was just waiting till I was sure. He shouldn've. What a jerk.'

Larry hadn't expected to hear from her. He held the phone slightly away from his ear and said nothing.

'I know you think he's using me. I knew you'd say it. But it's more than that. I'm helping him, okay, but I'm also helping his cause. He's trying to liberate his people. I'm doing something larger than just me. We don't matter, Larry.'

'We're just two little people. Is that how it goes?'

She sighed: 'You can make fun of me if you want.'

'I'm trying to remember what Ingrid says.'

'Could you just stop?'

'Actually I don't think she says anything. She just stares at Bogart with tears in her eyes.'

'Will you just shut up, Larry, and listen to me?'

His mind wouldn't let him listen. Kalifa is good-looking but so thin she'll crush him. His legs must be rods compared with my shapely ones, full and firm around her. How could she resist me?

'Try to understand. I wanted to do it for him. Maybe I love him, I don't know.'

But you don't love me, Larry.

'Are you there?'

'I just want to know one thing. How long did you know him when we had that argument with Gershom at Thanksgiving? I thought we really told him off. Did you know him then? Were you just bullshitting?' He had this funny feeling in his throat like something was stuck there and yet there was no space for anything.

'Don't get mad. We wouldn've lasted. You're still a boy.'

'What's wrong with that? What do you want, an old man? I'll be a boy forever, a boy without pimples. What more could you want?'

'Even now you're not serious.'

211

'I'm serious. I'm so serious.'

'Kalifa thinks you're wonderful. He doesn't know anything about us. He thinks you're just the most decent man he's ever met. And from him that's quite something.'

He moved the phone still further from his ear, could just hear her ask: 'You all right?'

He stared at the phone then moved it close again. 'I was just looking for the best place to throw up.'

'You really are a shithead, you know that?'

His dull heart was gladdened by actual anger from her but he said nothing to this. She asked, 'Are you still there?'

And then there was silence. He was not sure who had hung up first. He went to the refrigerator and pulled out a bottle of Pepsi, a remnant of his mother's visit. 'There's something comfortable about drinking it,' she had said. Beneath the sugar he tasted bitterness.

He went out after that, walking fast up the hill till he reached the pond with its flat grassland, round once, then again, watched by a seagull and two women holding babies. Then he went down, down till he reached the windy main street. He walked to the station, then turned and began walking back again. He could not stop.

Kalifa had done this. His supplicant. And now when he and Devorah would talk of Larry, those rare times when his woebegone face surfaced in their daily communion, they would shake their heads over him. They might even have a gentle laugh. He made one hand into a fist which he punched into the other like it was a baseball glove.

'Kalifa doesn't know from nothing. She took you for a ride, make no mistake about it. Why'd you let her?'

You know why. He sighed, remembering how his father told him to beware of the goody goodies. 'They have badness like everyone else but with them you don't know where.'

She was making a mistake. The guy had charm but who knows where he came from? He could be linked to some crazy group. Why warn her? She'd say he would say that. She'd make him the bad one. Would, should, could.

212

He was staring at the ground while he walked still punching his hand; otherwise he would have seen him coming, the road runner, the man in torment walking even faster than Larry, overtaking only to turn around again. Somehow they had collided. Larry felt the man's bony body against him and for a moment he seemed to notice Larry, his fearful eyes roving around Larry's face, then he was off again. He reached the station and turned. How many times in a day, how many miles had he travelled in just two blocks?

'You never really see anyone else,' Devorah once said, 'except in relation to yourself.'

He wanted to tap the guy on the shoulder, yell, 'Stop, stop right there.' A woman stared at him, not at the road runner, but at Larry punching his own hand. There was actual fear in her face.

He went home. He thought of calling Gemma, the laundry pickup. But her smooth Gretchen face saddened him. So young. The last time they met she confessed she had never heard of Bruce Springsteen. John Lennon's songs had been nursery rhymes for her.

He wanted to talk. Had the desperate man stopped he might have asked him to the pub. Who knows what wisdom he had gained on his journeys?

There was Talia. Warm, big-mouthed Talia, her legs around him, her musk smell. She had been nice to him last time.

He had forgotten her hello, the tone which seemed to ask 'why are you calling me now or ever?'

'It's me. Larry.'

There was a long pause.

This was not friendly, not like the honey of their last conversation.

'Just wanted to see how you're doing. It's been months and—'

'Don't bullshit me. You got a problem?'

'What's the matter Talia? Last time we talked you were delicious.'

213

'You know how that set me back? I kept thinking, did I do the right thing throwing you out? You were like a stone in my gut.'

'I'm sorry.' He felt a smile break out of his sad man face. She loved him still.

'I removed it. Did my own surgery. I didn't even see my shrink. Just snip. No blood. You're out.'

'Good for you.'

'I should tell you I'm getting married.'

'But you just met the guy.' Not you too, no, no, not. I am marrying, she is marrying, we got the marrying. Like an infection.

'We've been together nearly a year. Okay so we're both in with shrinks, but that's a requirement nowadays.'

'A year? But—'

'I wanna have babies, Larry. I've grown up.'

Was everyone was doing it? Growing up?

'Well mazel tov in advance. I guess I better let you go.'

'What is it Larry?' She sounded softer now that she'd hit him with it.

'Nothing. Nothing that you could do anything about.'

'Get the shaft again?'

'In a manner of speaking. She chose a Muslim over me. A Jewish girl.'

'Larry, what's happened to your self-esteem? You should be making up stories of conquests to me.'

'The thing is, he's one of my students. And she. Well.'

'At least he's not your best friend.'

But he was. Who else but Kalifa was his best friend in the class?

'You'll meet someone else. You always do.'

He was shaking his head.

'You're such a charmer Larry. You got that curly black hair women die for. I'm telling you.'

'Something's happened to me here.'

'You got bald?'

'I'm serious. I'm not who I thought I was.'

214

'You don't sound like yourself.'

'I'm not, I tell you.'

'Poor Larry. Don't you have any friends out there?'

He saw all the island women lying on beds with their backs to him. He shook his head.

'You must know someone.'

He thought of Carla and could feel a sob coming.

'Nobody,' he whispered and felt as if he had flung himself into her lap.

'So come home. Come home for home.'

His voice trembled as he asked: 'Do you think that all the time it was really you and me?'

For some reason he waited for a time with the phone beside his ear even though there was no more voice coming out. Just to make sure.

CHAPTER 28

Men were turning the earth in St James's Park and the air had begun to taste of something more than city damp, a raw zing which made him feel horny all the time, even when he was eating. Not lust really. The sad hunger of a stray dog. Everyone else had the food he wanted. Everyone.

Maybe Talia was right, maybe he was hungry for home. He hadn't signed his contract for next year yet. He should grow up like everyone else, and growing up meant rooting himself back there. He could survive for a while doing oddball cases. He once tried to help a college girl sue her dorm because she found a fly in the tuna fish. Then there was the old guy who'd been picketing in front of city hall since he'd been evicted in 1960. Rosen, White and Abbott might have him back again: his shiny black shoes mounting the stairs, the brass door knob where he had once glimpsed his mournful face.

He noticed him first before the kid had lifted his eyes. He was flopped down on a bench near the duck pond, skinny legs splayed out, arms folded, forelock of hair grown again. But alone. Larry paused, decided to make a zigzag around the kid, because he wasn't his problem anymore, was he? Joel had dropped out. Officially. Signed his name to a form which cut him loose from the mommies and daddies.

Then he raised his head and seemed to see Larry, but when Larry stood before him, Joel looked surprised.

'Professor Greenberg. What're you doing here?'

'What about you? You just disappeared.'

'I thought I'd never see you again. How you doing?' He actually shook Larry's hand. 'You're gonna sit down?'

He didn't want to. But he did because the kid really wanted him down on the bench with him. Because hadn't he abandoned him?

'People worried about you. The Dean.'

'But you didn't tell them. You were cool.'

Larry squirmed.

'I live around here. But not much longer.' The kid was a kid again, slumped down, hair over face.

'I'm leaving. Leaving this whole place. I'm going home.'

'But what about your—' Larry tried to remember what Joel's movement had been called. Something like 'the oneness of one'. 'Your group.'

'Oh that.'

'And your girlfriend.'

'We split. A couple of weeks ago.'

'I'm sorry,' Larry said. 'Well this happens.' He felt old for the first time in his young life.

'If you wanna know the truth, she was the one who wanted out. I would've stayed with her.' He opened up his arms, the most expansive gesture Larry had ever seen him make. 'Forever maybe.' He looked at Larry then down at his creased lap. All the signs were there: wobbly chin, eyes beginning to waterfall.

Please don't cry on me, Larry thought.

Joel wiped his eyes. 'She let me stay at her place for a while, but it was like—' He choked on his words.

You want me to say it for you kid.

'Like painful.'

Larry nodded. 'Sure. I know what you mean. It would be wouldn't it?' Shut up Larry, will you for once?

'So I moved into a student hostel. Which is like so grungy. So I called my parents who didn't even sound mad. They sent me a plane ticket. So that's it. Friday.' He was sulking Joel again, as if the past months had never happened to him.

'You're really going home?' Why should he, Larry, feel sad about it or even the beginnings of something like anger, a low-grade irritation, not even proper rash? As if the kid had let him down.

'What's the point of staying? I dropped out of college. I have nothing here anymore. I thought you'd think it was a good idea.'

'Just wondering. Are you sure you want to go home?' With your tail between your legs kid, and don't you forget it.

217

Joel didn't say anything. He pulled a bag of potato chips out of his knapsack, offered them to Larry who declined, then threw some to a passing Canada goose. There was a rush of webbed feet; the goose's friends and relatives and even some outsiders, a couple of demented-looking tufted ducks, approached.

Joel kicked his leg at them. 'We've got a love-hate relationship.'

'Who we talking about, Joel?'

But Joel didn't even smile.

'So you come here a lot?'

'Every day.' He emptied the bag on them, the potato chips landing on the backs of geese who did not care so long as they ate.

'What's the point of staying?'

You haven't been here long enough, Larry thought. But what was long enough? Enough for what? When was it time to click your heels and wish for home?

'These guys at the hostel asked me what I was doing here. Like, was I studying or working? When I said I was just hanging out, they looked at me like "weird guy". I don't ever want to be weird.'

Not like me Larry thought. I am beyond weird, kid.

'I don't know anyone anymore. All the guys at school will be going back the end of term. I'd feel, I dunno, like I was just being left. Like I'm not even sure who I am here.'

Was it Carla who said, 'You should stay till you know what it's like not to be you?' Or was Joel better off home? Maybe they were both. Could he spend another year wandering the streets with nobody to remember him from one day to the next as if he were always being born?

Why did he want to shake Joel, make his cowlick flop? The kid was running out on him.

'Something the matter, Professor Greenberg?'

'Nothing.' Larry stood up. 'Good luck with it all.'

'I don't have any more,' Joel spoke to the crowd of geese. 'No more.'

Then he looked up at Larry with an actual smile. 'Take care of yourself.'

Larry walked away and turned. The kid was watching him and waved as if his boat was just departing, and Larry had thrown the last streamer.

Maybe I'll join you, kid. His mouth moved as he turned. I'm talking to myself already. He turned again but the kid had settled back on the bench, head forward before the retreating geese.

What he had planned before meeting Joel was a stroll through the park, a cake and coffee before taking the tube down to Waterloo and Eureka. He needed treats every day now, rewards for not giving into despair.

In the afternoon he had a class of nodders for Business Law. Everything he said was greeted by dog-like agreement: yes Mr Greenberg, yes, yes, yes. We don't know from nothing, but yes, yes. Sometimes he longed for his bad boys. He had seen Bobby in the canteen, big Bob joking in the middle of his nation state. He avoided him as he did all students now. His office hour was for drinking coffee and staring out the window, for taking out and putting away the contract for next year. What was keeping him here?

He reached the edge of the park but was stopped from crossing by a policeman. A bunch of Guards on horses trotted by. In the old days he would have grinned to himself and whispered: 'Now that wouldn't happen on Coolidge Corner.' But today he wore a bored look. Just the Queen's men again.

A man asked him something in a foreign language. Larry shook his head. The man repeated himself and Larry realized that he was speaking English. In fact he was English but from a place where syllables were crushed together and sung: 'Is that the way to Buckingham Palace?' The man pointed.

I live here, I a Brookline Jew, whose grandma spits in the air every time she kisses me. Secretly. He would only admit this to the person within his person within, secretly he was thrilled. He felt his shoulders tremble as his wings like live creatures shook themselves free of his shoulder blades.

219

After he crossed the Mall he decided to walk to Eureka going the long way around: down Whitehall, past the Houses of Parliament, back over Westminster Bridge.

Who could resist the yellowing filigree buildings? 'They remind me of ancient teeth,' Devorah had said. But if she had stood with him on the bridge over the mud river, she would feel the delicacy of them.

'Larry.' Talia pulling his name out syllable by syllable. 'You're a time waster. You don't want to be a man, do you?'

He turned his back to the river and joined the people heading over down towards Waterloo. There's nothing that can't be solved by running away. He was moving his lips again. What would be running? Would staying be running? Could you stay and run at the same time? He reached Eureka with a mouth down-turned. As he walked up the back stairs, he smelled the sulphur again. Did no one else smell it; did no one else choke when they entered? Why don't they fumigate the place?

His room always surprised him, as if he had wandered into someone else's office. Because there was nothing of him on the high white walls. He could gather his papers and evacuate in ten minutes if he wanted. He pulled out the contract with the letter from the acting Dean, a gangly youngish Englishman with red hair and the high voice of a schoolboy, a voice which could slip from giggly to a sneer in an instant. He had come from some university up in Essex, so he told everyone, but Larry imagined him tormenting the fat boy in *Lord of the Flies*. His letter talked about syllabi and sets of aims and objectives and good teaching practice. In place of pipe smoke, there was an odd smell in the Dean's office like burnt candy.

The contract had been in his desk for a week and had begun to look used. It never committed him for more than a year. He reckoned that Eureka might close down at any time. He had heard that one year they offered students free video games to join up.

'Eureka has no endowment,' the old Dean had said. 'You get it? It's like a raft in a sea of ships. That's why they need us over here in London, us and our refugees. We bring in the cash.'

Poor kids. Not kids even. They looked at him with such openness. Prof Greenberg, will we be lawyers soon in the land of lands? Will we stride down the burnished streets of New York, pockets full of our promise? More like the shuffle he heard from the corridor. Shuffle, then a sniff and a cough, a tap on the door. The shy smile of Chin.

'You're busy. I'm sorry. I'm really—'

Why did he say that when Larry was sitting before an empty desk, his chair braced against the wall, his eyes turned upward? Larry beckoned and Chin shuffled forward, but did not sit down.

'I wanted you first to know. I go to America next year to study. They said yes. Connecticut University. I didn't think, well, I was surprised because I know how difficult it is.'

'I'm not surprised Chin. You worked hard.' But he was. He had thought Chin never saw the glittering surface of law, its permutations, how there was nothing which could not be twisted into its opposite. It was all surface and Chin looked deep.

'I want to thank you for helping me. Without your class I could not do it.'

Larry waved his hand. Chin felt guilty about complaining to the Dean about him; now he brought his achievement like a burnt offering.

'It's true Professor Greenberg. I had to write an essay, so I picked the Bill of Rights. I remembered so well what you taught us. So well. What you said about divining rods.'

'You did it yourself.' Larry was feeling nauseous. He imagined Chin's disquisition on freedom, his misuse of all of Larry's fun examples, the legal bagel Chin could never digest. But they took him, they took him.

Chin reached forward and extended his hand. Larry had to shake the soft paw. Years later when he was befuddling everyone in some court of law, Chin might still remember Larry. His teaching had sown a hundred mutant seeds.

After Chin left, Larry sat for a long time not moving, his chin braced against the palm which had touched the palm of Chin. Nobody's special, not even you Larry. With that he opened his plastic briefcase, took out first his notes and then a copy of *Time Out*. He did not want to go home straight after class. He would find some darkened room where he could watch other people make fools of themselves or love each other to destruction. Larry, Larry, where's your fun? You're a charmed boy aren't you? Everyone loves your dimpled face.

He continued to turn the pages from film to fringe theatre to dance where he imagined Devorah's slow turning and then, as he was moving past visual arts, he noticed almost without taking it in, a picture of a man with a wing instead of one arm. It took some time for his mind to gather. Him. It was him. His face was shadowed so no one would know but he knew. Carla had made an exhibition of him. She had a show all to herself in a gallery somewhere in east London called 'The Changeling'. The caption under his picture said: 'One more week to see Carla Sanderson's eerie manifestations of nudity.'

He could just turn up, but why? There was no guarantee she would be there. Anyway he didn't want to see her. He didn't need her weirdness. He still had Gemma of the blonde corn-rolled hair, young Gemma. But wasn't he dropping her; hadn't he decided that celibacy was better than sleeping with a girl whose secret, told only to him and countless others, was that she fancied her sixth form geography teacher? At the thought of Carla he felt the touch of his wings. He couldn't understand it, how he could smile again.

CHAPTER 29

It was not easy to find, but then that was Carla's way. Pick some street not even featured in his *A to Z* or so it seemed. He looked hard in the grey mishmash which was East London. Off he walked down what looked like a highway of shut warehouses and stores devoted to the parts of toilets, a road thundering with trucks. He turned down a quieter street where people seemed to live, then turned again and entered what looked like an alleyway but was a very narrow street, a cul-de-sac with the backside of some factory, a boarded-up window of a store with a faded sign for J. Isaac's Upholstery. At the end of this dismal passage the white door of the Changeling Gallery gleamed.

It was the last day of her exhibition but no Carla. Only a skinny woman in a black shiny coat huddled at the back smoking. Did she nod? Maybe it was the emptiness of the long low room which made him shiver, so quiet that he could hear the sigh of the black-jacketed woman. He once had a girlfriend who talked about house vibes. This must be what was making the goose bumps on his arms. The room spoke to him, told him it had once been something else, a whirling, droning, clicking place where sepia women with hair in buns bent all day pushing cloth into sewing machines.

Poor Carla. The last day and no one. Who would come out here? He looked towards the woman to see if it was okay him being there, but she was deep in herself. He placed his hands behind his back, tried to pretend that this was a museum. He saw his portrait from a distance, turned away with a blush and decided he would see everything before looking at himself: lovers with blindfolds, a naked man poised like the thinker but with one hand fondling his penis, a large pen and ink drawing of a woman who could be Carla, her naked back and ass filled with a fine web as if every capillary in her body were exposed. The room was full of her eccentricities. But no her.

'Are they for sale?' He drew close to the black-jacketed woman, picked up her sour perfume of used clothes and loneliness. She seemed to glare at him, but perhaps it was just her face, lean and older than he had thought, with black hair drawn close as if it had been painted onto the sides of her skull. She nodded with what looked like a sneer. But why would she sneer at him, at Larry? He had done nothing to her. She didn't know him from Adam. 'She doesn't like men,' father whispered. Even he was afraid of her.

'Did you have one in mind?'

He pointed to the one of himself. Would he have the vanity to actually buy it? He blushed again. He would hate for her to know it was him.

But the woman was looking down her list, her bony finger stopped. 'If you mean "Winged Victory", that's not available.' Her voice was surprisingly deep for such a skinny string of a woman.

'Someone bought it already?' He saw himself pinned to the wall of some weirdo's living room, forever peering down on naked lovers with their poor asses stuck to a leather sofa.

'No, she's keeping that one. That the only one you want?'

He smiled not at her but just because he felt a sudden joy and to his astonishment she smiled back, or something like a smile, a cracking of her tight little face. 'You've got a shitload of charm,' Talia always said.

'I'll buy another one.' Poor Carla. Nobody came out there. Maybe he should take them all, like the sick prince in the fairy tale who bought a whole tray of little carved lambs from the poor shepherd because just the sight of their woolly little heads had made him feel better. He'd buy her up.

The woman made no comment. She watched him glide around the room. He knew which one. The thin woman with the naked back was her, wasn't it? It was called 'The Inner City'.

'It's a self-portrait, isn't it?' he asked as she once more looked down her list.

'It all is, isn't it?' she said. 'And that one's been bought. Sorry. You're not having much luck. You should've come last week. A lot of these have gone, actually.'

But I didn't know that she would be taken. Whoever took her self-portrait would own some portion of her.

'Who bought it, by the way?'

She shrugged. 'It wasn't a dealer. I think some friend.'

She stood up and her jacket opened. She was wearing a black leotard and tights and nothing else, her body like some Victorian worker's child. Larry shivered again. She watched him look at her and now had only disdain for him.

'Does it have to be that one? If you like her work, you'll take anything, won't you?'

When he left she would dance down the gallery mocking him before Carla's blindfolded lovers. He felt a kind of panic and walked out without even thinking where he was going.

CHAPTER 30

He turned on the phone, paused, put it down, decided he needed a pretzel and walked down the hall to the kitchen. He poured himself a glass of wine and emptied the bag of pretzels into his cereal bowl, then sat staring out over the rooftops while he ate and drank slowly. He thought, 'Why d'you want to get mixed up with her again?' He continued to munch till he'd finished the last of the American pretzels he had asked his mother to bring over.

He wandered back to the phone. 'Why, why why? She's only half a woman.' 'But I'm only half a man.' He was scrolling to her number, hand reaching for her, when the phone came alive. He'd changed from 'Waltzing Matilda' to a chirping ring which startled him. He expected to hear Carla's voice. Hadn't she always known what he never said?

But the woman who said, 'Larry? Is that you?' was Julia Berman, calling down to him like the angel in Jacob's dream, come up the ladder to Finchley for Shabbat dinner.

He hadn't said his prayers since his voice had broken, how could he go? And what would happen to Carla? He felt superstitious about her, as if her exhibition was a sign he must heed. If he did not see her immediately she would disappear once again like a spirit he had called up, and he would be left scrounging in the beds of moist and callow Englishwomen.

He heard his father: 'She's an anytime girl. But them, you'll make them happy.' He pictured Clive and Julia week after week at their laden table saying prayers to each other, trying to finish a meal made for the multitudes, for the stranger Jews. He heard in Julia Berman's voice the hunger of a mother for a son.

They lived beyond where the Northern line climbed out of its cocoon, down a hilly street of what novelists might call 'well-manicured houses', so well-manicured that Larry examined his nails for dirt as he walked. In the little walled front gardens, bushes grew out of paving, and white stucco surrounded bay windows. He thought of his mother's house in Brookline and warmed to the half-glass front doors with their fisted knockers and lantern lights. He felt almost nostalgic as he waded through the soapsuds of a man washing his car and saw a kid shrieking while his mother tried to blow his nose.

He could not help himself thinking of Julia's generous frontage when he saw the double bay windows of the Bermans' large mock Tudor house. He wondered if they were watching for him, Julia darting between the upstairs windows.

He should have known by the four cars in the driveway that he was not to be the only child. A young woman in a dress of swirling stripes opened the door to a room lit with four bright globes. No dark passages here. He handed her his daffodils and learned that she was a daughter. He knew he was late but thought they would have preludes just like James Carrington, only more cosy. Larry saw himself on their sofa with a glass of sweet red wine, telling them about Devorah and her Egyptian; they would take his side. About Carla he would keep mum, hoping they would not remember the skeleton who had taken him away. But he was led immediately to a long table where the others waited. The sun was going down fast; God couldn't wait for chitchat.

He was cast into someone else's family: the bearded jokey uncle, the older daughter with her husband of the jumpy eyes and kid under the table, Clive's white-suited brother with his blonde wife from a Clairol ad. And even what looked like a grandmother, a neat woman with white upswept hair and a gargoyle for a face. He thought of his own flimsy family: no more dad, a mother who drifted through the house, a sister who never visited.

Julia stood before the candles, her hands raised. Larry had a memory of Friday nights at his grandma's in the days when she kept Shabbat. This was before she began asking strangers if it was true she looked like Jack Benny. His mother said Shabbat was old fashioned: 'They don't do it nowadays.' He remembered the smell of chicken soup with little islands of fat, soup chicken and roasted chicken just in case you liked one not the other and the chicken's neck stuffed with something called 'kishkas',

227

which sounded like the side ache he got from running. This his grandma presented to his father who always said, 'You telling me something?'

He had been smelling fish since he arrived. Fish on a Friday night. Even he knew this was wrong. He tore at the piece of challah bread Julia had handed him. Beside him the bearded uncle adjusted the clip of his yarmulke and seemed to chant rhymes.

'Excuse me,' he could say, 'but I think I've got the wrong day, or the wrong home.' Wrong was what he was here. But could he say that to Naomi of the swirling shapes who sat beside him, his assignment, a woman made for a Jew boy? Small, round, luscious with a smell like warm chicken fat clinging to her clingy dress, Naomi smiled even while she ate.

Julia put a piece of deep fried something which may have once been fish on his plate. It was so oily he had to wipe his lips after each bite. On the other side of him the old uncle's rhymes had become a little tune which he sang as he cut his fish up into tiny pieces.

Larry was happy to eat in silence and let them speak, but Clive would not let him alone. Everyone had to know that Larry had once been a lawyer with a partnership in Boston. I was just a junior, one of the ones who did for the partners even if it meant collecting dust from their bellybuttons.

'And not just any partnership. They are one of the best,' Clive said, looking at Naomi, then around at the gathered eaters. Naomi nodded politely and smiled at Larry, her mouth shiny from fish. He knew she had been briefed about him.

Clive's brother, a silent grinning presence up till now, said: 'I could use a lawyer.'

The old uncle stopped his tune, and there were glances around the table. The blonde wife smiled at Larry. She looked like one of those done-over Jewish women: nose job, breast job, maybe even ass job and hair golden as the golden calf. And yet there was something real about her perky nose.

Clive ignored his brother's words. He turned to Larry again. 'How're your classes going?' Before Larry could answer, Clive told them: 'Larry's a professor of law at James's college.'

Larry winced at 'professor'. Even his own mother had not done this to him. She often forgot where he worked.

'Actually, well, actually I'm not really.' He looked over at Naomi who raised her eyes and seemed to shake her head in sympathy with him.

'I mean I'm just there for now. Who knows what I'll do next.'

Julia had emerged once again from the kitchen. 'You're not thinking of leaving us? Larry, you just got here.'

Naomi winked at him as if to say: 'It's all right. I don't want you anyway.'

Julia put a large hunk of roast beef in front of Clive and he began to carve while his skinny son-in-law of the jumpy eyes passed down the plates.

Clive's brother, whose name Larry never heard, leaned back in his chair. He asked Larry: 'You take cases here?'

Larry was chewing on a piece of meat and could only shake his head.

'Too bad. You could recommend somebody?'

Gershom's hangdog face appeared. Then he shook his head again. He did not know who he was trying to save from whom.

Naomi gave him two of the best roast potatoes he had ever seen. Since you cannot have me I will console you.

The jumpy-eyed son-in-law stared at Larry or seemed to. He had his son on his lap and was all the time putting bits of food in his mouth or trying to; the kid wanted to be back on the floor again. His wife, the silken sister of Naomi, was up and down with Julia, bringing more potatoes, a tureen of gravy. But Naomi stayed by Larry's side like his handmaiden.

The brother continued to recline as if the meal had ended. He took off his white jacket. His shirt was also white and his tie which gleamed down his front.

'Why do you need a lawyer?' Larry asked.

The brother shrugged. 'When you're in business—'

229

'Some business,' the uncle said.

'What's that?'

'I said some business you're in,' the old uncle said and started to sing again some tune with yips in it. Across the table the gargoyle grandmother made a 'tsk' sound and shook her head at the uncle. Larry realized that they might be a couple and she not anybody's grandmother but a 'tante', a great and terrible aunt.

The jumpy-eyed guy looked from one to the other as if he could no longer control his eyeballs. The blonde wife kept up her grin and offered to help Julia who was taking yet another trip to the kitchen. But Julia said no, she had her daughter, she had two daughters and this child of Christ was not one of hers.

The wife looked at Larry, willing him to talk to her. Larry tried to think of some topic which would cause no trouble, some word which would calm the son-in-law's eyes and solace the uncle. He tried to remember what they had talked about at James Carrington's dinner.

The brother sat up and seemed to smile at the uncle. A stream of gravy now ran down his white frontage. Larry's father spoke in his ear: 'White is the colour of guilt. White is a person telling you they haven't done what they've done.'

His wife continued to look across at Larry with such pleading eyes that he must do something. He remembered the talk of window boxes and summer 'hols' as they called it. The window boxes had got him into trouble so he asked her: 'Are you going anywhere interesting this summer?'

The brother grinned at him: 'You're sure you're not a hairdresser?'

I hit a man once, he wanted to say.

'Just joking. So what do you do for fun anyway? You got a girlfriend?'

Naomi looked modestly down at her swirling dress.

Larry shut one ear against the yipping sound from the uncle and said, 'Well who knows?'

'You should know from girls,' the uncle said to the brother, then whispered to Larry: 'You know he owns dirty magazines. He's treft and so's his wife.'

'What's treft?' Larry wanted to ask his father, but he'd gone. There was so much he didn't understand here.

If the brother heard the uncle, he said nothing. His wife across the table had heard and tried and failed to keep up her smile.

'I know what it's like,' Larry wanted to say to her. As if no one looks under your skin.

You could have too much family, he thought. After he kissed Naomi, a chaste moistening of her lips, Clive and Julia walked with him to the door. Julia hugged him so hard he almost cried out. They had made him their son for the evening and now he was leaving them.

CHAPTER 31

Carla hesitated and he thought she would say no. He was prepared just this once to prostrate himself in front of her. But the hesitation was only a prelude to a description of her tangled life. Could she fit him in between tai chi and shiatsu or maybe after teaching her vegetable drawing class? He imagined bell peppers and eggplants seated in old-fashioned desks, a cucumber in a dunce cap. She'd quit her job so she could be more crazy.

'Can't do next week or the week after or the week after that. What about June?'

'But that's a month from now. I could be someone else by then.'

She ignored this. Wilfully, he thought. 'I could pencil you in for lunch on the twentieth.'

He wasn't anyone you could pencil in and erase, some smudged personality. And since when did she keep a diary?

'If you're too busy just forget it. We'll meet in this heaven you people are always talking about.'

'I didn't say that.'

'You sound,' he thought how to describe her prevaricating, 'you don't sound like yourself.'

'It's just a matter of slotting you in,' she said. Then as if she could not contain herself: 'Who do I sound like?'

He remembered a Yiddish proverb his uncle Lennie wrote on his graduation card: 'If you would be someone else, who will be you?' Poor uncle Lennie. He was a dapper little man who took malpractice cases and lived alone in some Beacon Hill pigeonhole till he died.

'He never married,' Larry's mother used to say in a mournful voice.

Was he gay or just a man who could not commit?

'Carla. This is me, Larry, the man with a wing instead of an arm, not one of your faceless ten-a-penny guys. In a month I might not be here. You just have to decide.'

'You're leaving?'

'In a manner of speaking. Who knows?' He would torment her.

'All right. Tomorrow then. You pick me up in Tavistock Square, near Gandhi.'

The sun had not reached him. He looked cold and forlorn sitting there with just a few dried-up flowers at his feet. What was he doing here anyway, a half-naked supplicant longing for the heat of his land?

At the far end of the little square on a patch of shining grass, he saw her circling the air with her cupped hand, then turning with one arm raised like some slow-motion agitator.

Larry was not early but he knew not to disturb her. He went right up to Gandhi and was surprised at his muscular arms and chest, at his hands, large and powerful, at the deep furrows of his face, his Jew ears. He was no weakling. As he stood close and looked up at his face, Gandhi's eyes seem to look down into Larry as if he could see every foolish thought he had ever had.

He sat on a bench and watched, then thought maybe he shouldn't. Her eyes were shut. He could move behind a tree without her ever knowing that he had seen. Because she knew that no one could see her. She was like those gods who make themselves invisible when they come down to earth.

But when he stood up, she called to him. Could she see through eyelids? She held out her arms and even as he hugged her, he wondered if this was just another part of her dance.

They drew apart. He noted that she was glad to see him. She looked different, almost human with flesh on her cheeks, not just bone structure. Carla had turned into a woman.

He squeezed her upper arm, which was no longer frightening to look at. 'You're zaftig.'

'I gained a stone. Maybe more. Over Christmas I was down at my mother's and ate and ate. I went into a decline after I broke up with—' she paused, perhaps realizing the delicacy of

233

the situation. She'd thrown over yet another man and here she was crying on Larry's shoulder.

'You look—' He wanted to say 'normal'. 'You look great.'

'Maybe it wasn't him.' She stared at him. Larry looked with wonder as her eyes began to fill with actual tears. He patted her back like the old uncle he'd become.

'Don't talk to me about him. Who was he? That black shirt at the ICA? I could've told you about him. He looked like a starved vampire.' Actually Larry never saw the guy's face, just his shirt and the outline of his ghoul head. He was too busy at the time wondering who would recognize her drawing of him, how many of his students. And would they comment on the size of his schlong?

Carla continued to speak as if he hadn't spoken. Maybe he hadn't. With her there was no difference between his thoughts and what came out of his mouth.

'I was crackers for a while, I know I was. But now I've gone celibate, I'm okay. It's brilliant actually. You please yourself.'

'From one extreme. Carla, when are you going to stop being weird?'

She ignored this and began touching her breasts.

'What are you doing?'

'It's so amazing. I never had anything before. I just can't get used to it.'

'Do you tie yourself down as well? Or just pretend?'

She began doing her exercises again, swinging her arms in an arc. He had to move quickly to escape being smacked in the face. Then she stopped and turned to him: 'I thought we finished. After you just walked out on me.'

'I thought you— you were the one. Carla, you distort.'

She stared at him as if she was just now noticing him. Suddenly she reached up and yanked out one of his hairs.

'Hey. Stop it.'

'You're getting grey. I thought you were one of those people who never age.'

'I was. Something's happened to me here.'

234

'You're still dishy.'

He hated when they said that as if he were some pot roast.

'My mum asks after you all the time. So does Margaret. You were an event down there.'

He couldn't stop the smile spreading over him like a blush. He wanted to be mad at Carla but he pulled her over for a kiss. She allowed this, then broke away with an odd expression on her face. He could not get over how real she looked.

'You think you could go down there again?' she asked.

'There's nothing I'd like more.'

'You don't have to say yes yet. You've time. I mean we're not even together.' She actually looked him in the face.

'You mean "really" together. But we can make up and be friends again.' He squeezed her waist, still like a dressmaker's dummy.

'I'm serious. Margaret's turning seventy in June. Mum's giving her a little party. All her cronies. I have to go because I'm her only godchild. My brother lucked out. His godmother died.'

How his sad heart quickened. He saw again the long refectory table with Rowena waiting for him.

CHAPTER 32

He walked through the whole train, peering in at the first class and stopping on the way at the buffet for a mouth-twisting tea. He couldn't keep still.

Larry came down alone on Saturday morning. He couldn't leave with Carla on Friday because his summer term remedial students were having their finals. There was no real difference between the ordinary American students and these rejects. After they passed their pre-course courses, they would appear in September grinning at him: 'Hello again.'

He had thought carefully about what to wear to an English garden party and settled for the short-sleeved open-neck checked shirt, linen pants and pale jacket he wore on summer evenings back in Boston when Talia wanted to go to Chez Pierrot to eat soft shell crab. She had laughed at his best clothes. 'You're Jay without the Gatsby. He changed himself, but you'll always be you.'

He left his suitcase in the little entrance where Rowena kept her onions and potatoes, 'her festering room' Carla called it. No one answered his 'hello'. The wind from the door blew through the kitchen, but there were no white covers to lift. Had Carla put an end to her mother's pies? Then he saw it on the table, a large, iced chocolate cake sweating under a glass bowl. Rowena had written 'Happy Birthday Margaret' in green and red and thoughtfully placed a yellow frog in one corner, or what looked like a frog. She'd tied a red ribbon around the cake. 'Bad taste,' his father said, 'we all have it, just some of us won't say.'

He walked through the house: darkened living room, the sun lounge filled with cacti and succulents, and wicker chairs with soft, old cushions. Then he saw them out on the grass between the tiny pond with its willow and the stunted pear tree. 'All these years it's never fruited,' Rowena had said, 'but I can't bring myself to get rid of it.' He had thought she was talking about Carla.

They sat beyond a table set with a white tablecloth, the brown teapot and plates of what looked like potatoes but when he got closer turned out to be dark or possibly burnt scones. Could he step into this, this scene like a postcard with a ruffled edge?

They didn't notice him at first, but then Rowena turned and would have got up if the soft net chair hadn't hampered her. 'Larry, I'm so glad you could come.' She held out her hand.

'You think you're the queen?' Carla said.

But the queen had never smiled up at Larry as if she had been waiting just for him.

Carla grasped her teacup with both hands like it was a workman's cracked mug, not some fluted confection of flowers and gold. She looked different again, every time he saw her now she changed a little, as if she were going through the stages of childhood fast.

Margaret stood up, such a little woman. She reached on tiptoes to kiss him. 'Carla was missing you.'

'Let me introduce everyone,' Rowena said.

'Oh please. He'll only forget. Just calm down,' Carla said.

Rowena gave Carla a little reproving nod then turned to the group. 'Larry's come down from London.'

He poured himself a cup of tea and sat down next to Carla. It was not a large party. He endured the emotionless stare from a long-headed salamander with a cane and the smiling nods of a snow woman in a pleated skirt. The florid man in a blue double-breasted suit with brass buttons turned out to be Margaret's son. Larry wanted to ask him if he had grown up with the frogs. He looked unfroglike, he and his perky wife who darted around the table serving tea like some itinerant squirrel.

Next to Rowena, an old man with a nose from a Nazi cartoon of Jews tipped the tea from the saucer into his cup and drank it at one go. He caught Larry gazing at him. 'Who are you?' he asked suddenly in a loud voice.

Everyone stared at Larry. He was holding his teacup daintily by the handle. He even had one finger raised. What am I doing here?

'That's Larry. Carla's Larry. You remember? He's from America,' Rowena said. What happened to 'Greenberg'? Was she afraid to dangle him fully in front everyone?

She turned to Larry. 'This is my father.'

For such a short heavy guy he dressed dapper in a grey waistcoat and jacket. He gave Carla a sly look as if he knew just what went on with her and the futon. Then he asked Larry, 'You staying awhile?'

Rowena leaned forward suddenly and whispered: 'Could you bring in the cake?'

Larry looked at Carla but she wasn't budging. She grinned at her grandpa.

He walked back into the house but instead of the kitchen, found himself deep in Rowena's dinosaur sofa in the dusky light of a tasselled lamp. He hadn't remembered how brown and heavy everything was: the nest of tables Rowena pulled out when they had tea in there, the curved oak sideboard like a portly matron with short ugly legs, the mantel over the gas fire where ancient relatives looked gravely at Larry. Beyond the room, the sun lounge with its doors open to the garden was like some day he could never reach.

If he disappeared now, Carla might miss him for a time and Rowena worry that she had somehow upset him, but in the end they would forget him or if they remembered, he would be that American who couldn't settle. The grandfather was right to question his existence.

'What's with you? The old guy's just joshing you.'

'It's not him really.'

'What does he know? You're a boy dropped from the sky.'

Even before he heard father move around the room, Larry smelled frying and hot salty meat.

'This furniture's from hunger. Don't they ever throw anything out?'

Latkes and pastrami, that's what it was. 'My heart attack food,' his father used to say of his favourites, and it had happened finally.

Larry felt a hand on his shoulder. He opened his mouth to call 'Dad', but nothing came out, though he could not hold back the tears.

'What happened to you?' Carla rubbed at his neck. When he didn't speak, she came round the sofa and looked at him. 'You're not upset? Mum thought you were.'

She was still growing up and hadn't reached the age of empathy.

'I told her, of course he's bored shitless sitting around with you lot.'

He was trying to find his voice, but she was never one to care if he kept silent.

'Grandpa's asking where you went. He thinks he scared you.'

'You didn't tell me about him.'

'I guess my mother was going to break it to you gently about Grandpa. Not that you'd care.'

Madness. Some genetic trait which skipped a generation and appeared in full bloom in Carla. Only the grandfather was the sanest English person he had ever met.

'He was a pork butcher. Really. In his time a master sausage maker. And so dirty-minded with it. When a woman came into his shop he fancied, he'd say, "you want a real sausage?" I love Grandpa.'

She sat down next to him, her head on his shoulder. He squeezed her. 'You're so, so there now. Do you think we could just go upstairs for a minute?'

'They'll be wanting the cake,' she said.

Since when did that ever stop her, the expectations of others?

He held on to her.

'Can't you save it for later?'

'Who knows?'

'I'm feeling god-daughterish.'

He remembered the sister who left her youngest brother to cope with a swan wing. 'Just don't forget about me,' he warned.

They arranged seven candles on the cake, one for each decade of Margaret's life. Then Larry walked slowly with it from the kitchen through the living room into the sun lounge. He placed it on the little table where he had played Scrabble and Cluedo with Rowena. Carla used a long white taper to light the candles.

'Are you ready?' she asked.

He lifted up the cake.

The sun had gone to someone else's garden. Rowena was standing over her father pouring him some tea. Margaret sat with her little head inclined, better to hear what her rosy son said.

Nobody saw them coming.

THE AUTHOR

Wendy Brandmark is a fiction writer, reviewer and lecturer. She writes both novels and short stories. Her first novel, The Angry Gods, was published by Dewi Lewis in 2003, and the US edition in 2005.

Wendy's short stories have been widely published in British and American magazines and anthologies, including *The Massachusetts Review, Riptide Journal, Stand Magazine, Lilith Magazine* and *The Warwick Review.*

In 2013 she was a fellow at the Virginia Centre for the Creative Arts and she has been awarded a writing residency for 2014 at the Tyrone Guthrie Centre in Ireland.

Her reviews have appeared in *The Financial Times, New Statesman, The Literary Review, The Independent* and *The Times Literary Supplement.*

Wendy has taught creative writing in London for over fifteen years and at present she supervises second year students in the Oxford University Master of Studies (MSt) in Creative Writing, and she teaches fiction writing at The City Lit.

Wendy is currently working on a short story collection and two novels. She grew up in the Bronx and went to university in Boston. London is now her home.

More details are available from

www.wendybrandmark.com
and
www.hollandparkpress.co.uk/brandmark

Holland Park Press is a unique publishing initiative. It gives contemporary Dutch writers the opportunity to be published in Dutch and English. We also publish new works written in English and translations of classic Dutch novels.

To

- Find out more
- Learn more about Wendy Brandmark
- Discover other interesting books
- Read our unique Anglo-Dutch magazine
- Practice your writing skills
- Take part in discussions

Visit www.hollandparkpress.co.uk

Bookshop: http://www.hollandparkpress.co.uk/books.php

Holland Park Press in the social media:

http://www.twitter.com/HollandParkPres
http://www.facebook.com/HollandParkPress
http://www.youtube.com/user/HollandParkPress